Fritz Reuter Leiber Jr.

Time Travel & Apocalyptic War Stories

OK Publishing 2021

Fritz Reuter Leiber Jr.
Time Travel & Apocalyptic War Stories

Published by
MUSAICUM
Books

- Advanced Digital Solutions & High-Quality book Formatting -

musaicumbooks@okpublishing.info

2021 OK Publishing

ISBN 978-80-272-7917-3

Contents

The Big Time

Chapter 1
Enter Three Hussars

When shall we three meet again
In thunder, lightning, or in rain?

When the hurlyburly's done.
When the battle's lost and won.

—Macbeth

My name is Greta Forzane. Twenty-nine and a party girl would describe me. I was born in Chicago, of Scandinavian parents, but now I operate chiefly outside space and time-not in Heaven or Hell, if there are such places, but not in the cosmos or universe you know either.

I am not as romantically entrancing as the immortal film star who also bears my first name, but I have a rough-and-ready charm of my own. I need it, for my job is to nurse back to health and kid back to sanity Soldiers badly roughed up in the biggest war going. This war is the Change War, a war of time travelers-in fact, our private name for being in this war is being on the Big Time. Our Soldiers fight by going back to change the past, or even ahead to change the future, in ways to help our side win the final victory a billion or more years from now. A long killing business, believe me.

You don't know about the Change War, but it's influencing your lives all the time and maybe you've had hints of it without realizing.

Have you ever worried about your memory, because it doesn't seem to be bringing you exactly the same picture of the past from one day to the next? Have you ever been afraid that your personality was changing because of forces beyond your knowledge or control? Have you ever felt sure that sudden death was about to jump you from nowhere? Have you ever been scared of Ghosts-not the story-book kind, but the billions of beings who were once so real and strong it's hard to believe they'll just sleep harmlessly forever? Have you ever wondered about those things you may call devils or Demons-spirits able to range through all time and space, through the hot hearts of stars and the cold skeleton of space between the galaxies? Have you ever thought that the whole universe might be a crazy, mixed-up dream? If you have, you've had hints of the Change War.

How I got recruited into the Change War, how it's conducted, what the two sides are, why you don't consciously know about it, what I really think about it-you'll learn in due course.

The place outside the cosmos where I and my pals do our nursing job I simply call the Place. A lot of my nursing consists of amusing and humanizing Soldiers fresh back from raids into time. In fact, my formal title is Entertainer and I've got my silly side, as you'll find out.

My pals are two other gals and three guys from quite an assortment of times and places. We're a pretty good team, and with Sid bossing, we run a pretty good Recuperation Station, though we have our family troubles. But most of our troubles come slamming into the Place with the beat-up Soldiers, who've generally just been going through hell and want to raise some of their own. As a matter of fact, it was three newly arrived Soldiers who started this thing I'm going to tell you about, this thing that showed me so much about myself and everything.

When it started, I had been on the Big Time for a thousand sleeps and two thousand night-mares, and working in the Place for five hundred-one thousand. This two-nightmares routine every time you lay down your dizzy little head is rough, but you pretend to get used to it because being on the Big Time is supposed to be worth it.

The Place is midway in size and atmosphere between a large nightclub where the Entertainers sleep in and a small Zeppelin hangar decorated for a party, though a Zeppelin is one thing we haven't had yet. You go out of the Place, but not often if you have any sense and if you are an Entertainer like me, into the cold light of a morning filled with anything from the earlier dinosaurs to the later spacemen, who look strangely similar except for size.

Solely on doctor's orders, I have been on cosmic leave six times since coming to work at the Place, meaning I have had six brief vacations, if you care to call them that, for believe me they are busman's holidays, considering what goes on in the Place all the time. The last one I spent in Renaissance Rome, where I got a crush on Cesare Borgia, but I got over it. Vacations are for the birds, anyway, because they have to be fitted by the Spiders into serious operations of the Change War, and you can imagine how restful that makes them.

"See those Soldiers changing the past? You stick along with them. Don't go too far up front, though, but don't wander off either. Relax and enjoy yourself."

Ha! Now the kind of recuperation Soldiers get when they come to the Place is a horse of a far brighter color, simply dazzling by comparison. Entertainment is our business and we give them a bang-up time and send them staggering happily back into action, though once in a great while something may happen to throw a wee shadow on the party.

I am dead in some ways, but don't let that bother you —I am lively enough in others. If you met me in the cosmos, you would be more apt to yak with me or try to pick me up than to ask a cop to do same or a father to douse me with holy water, unless you are one of those hard-boiled reformer types. But you are not likely to meet me in the cosmos, because (bar Basin Street and the Prater) 15th Century Italy and Augustan Rome-until they spoiled it-are my favorite (Ha!) vacation spots and, as I have said, I stick as close to the Place as I can. It is really the nicest Place in the whole Change World. (Crisis! I even *think* of it capitalized!)

Anyhoo, when this thing started, I was twiddling my thumbs on the couch nearest the piano and thinking it was too late to do my fingernails and whoever came in probably wouldn't notice them anyway.

The Place was jumpy like it always is on an approach and the gray velvet of the Void around us was curdled with the uneasy lights you see when you close your eyes in the dark.

Sid was tuning the Maintainers for the pick-up and the right shoulder of his gold-worked gray doublet was streaked where he'd been wiping his face on it with quick ducks of his head.

Beauregard was leaning as close as he could over Sid's other shoulder, one white-trousered knee neatly indenting the rose plush of the control divan, and he wasn't missing a single flicker of Sid's old fingers on the dials; Beau's co-pilot besides piano player. Beau's face had that dead blank look it must have had when every double eagle he owned and more he didn't were riding on the next card to be turned in the gambling saloon on one of those wedding-cake Mississippi steamboats.

Doc was soused as usual, sitting at the bar with his top hat pushed back and his knitted shawl pulled around him, his wide eyes seeing whatever horrors a life in Nazi-occupied Czarist Russia can add to being a drunk Demon in the Change World.

Maud, who is the Old Girl, and Lili-the New Girl, of course-were telling the big beads of their identical pearl necklaces.

You might say that all us Entertainers were a bit edgy; being Demons doesn't automatically make us brave.

Then the red telltale on the Major Maintainer went out and the Door began to darken in the Void facing Sid and Beau, and I felt Change Winds blowing hard and my heart missed a couple of beats, and the next thing three Soldiers had stepped out of the cosmos and into the Place, their first three steps hitting the floor hard as they changed times and weights.

They were dressed as officers of hussars, as we'd been advised, and-praise the Bonny Dew! —I saw that the first of them was Erich, my own dear little commandant, the pride of the von Hohenwalds and the Terror of the Snakes. Behind him was some hard-faced Roman or other, and beside Erich and shouldering into him as they stamped forward was a new boy, blond, with a face like a Greek god who's just been touring a Christian hell.

They were uniformed exactly alike in black-shakos, fur-edged pelisses, boots, and so forth-with white skull emblems on the shakos. The only difference between them was that Erich had a Caller on his wrist and the New Boy had a black-gauntleted glove on his left hand and was clenching the mate in it, his right hand being bare like both of Erich's and the Roman's.

"You've made it, lads, hearts of gold," Sid boomed at them, and Beau twitched a smile and murmured something courtly and Maud began to chant, "Shut the Door!" and the New Girl copied her and I joined in because the Change Winds do blow like crazy when the Door is open, even though it can't ever be shut tight enough to keep them from leaking through.

"Shut it before it blows wrinkles in our faces," Maud called in her gamin voice to break the ice, looking like a skinny teen-ager in the tight, knee-length frock she'd copied from the New Girl.

But the three Soldiers weren't paying attention. The Roman —I remembered his name was Mark-was blundering forward stiffly as if there were something wrong with his eyes, while Erich and the New Boy were yelling at each other about a kid and Einstein and a summer palace and a bloody glove and the Snakes having booby-trapped Saint Petersburg. Erich had that taut sadistic smile he gets when he wants to hit me.

The New Boy was in a tearing rage. "Why'd you pull us out so bloody fast? We fair chewed the Nevsky Prospekt to pieces galloping away."

"Didn't you feel their stun guns, *Dummkopf*, when they sprung the trap-too soon, *Gott sei Dank*?" Erich demanded.

"I did," the New Boy told him. "Not enough to numb a cat. Why didn't you show us action?"

"Shut up. I'm your leader. I'll show you action enough."

"You won't. You're a filthy Nazi coward."

"*Weibischer Engländer!*"

"Bloody Hun!"

"*Schlange!*"

The blond lad knew enough German to understand that last crack. He threw back his sable-edged pelisse to clear his sword arm and he swung away from Erich, which bumped him into Beau. At the first sign of the quarrel, Beau had raised himself from the divan as quickly and silently as a —no, I won't use that word-and slithered over to them.

"Sirs, you forget yourselves," he said sharply, off balance, supporting himself on the New Boy's upraised arm. "This is Sidney Lessingham's Place of Entertainment and Recuperation. There are ladies —"

With a contemptuous snarl, the New Boy shoved him off and snatched with his bare hand for his saber. Beau reeled against the divan, it caught him in the shins and he fell toward the Maintainers. Sid whisked them out of the way as if they were a couple of beach radios-simply nothing in the Place is nailed down-and had them back on the coffee table before Beau hit the floor. Meanwhile, Erich had his saber out and had parried the New Boy's first wild slash and lunged in return, and I heard the scream of steel and the rutch of his boot on the diamond-studded pavement.

Beau rolled over and came up pulling from the ruffles of his shirt bosom a derringer I knew was some other weapon in disguise —a stun gun or even an Atropos. Besides scaring me damp for Erich and everybody, that brought me up short: us Entertainers' nerves must be getting as naked as the Soldiers', probably starting when the Spiders canceled all cosmic leaves twenty sleeps back.

Sid shot Beau his look of command, rapped out, "I'll handle this, you whoreson firebrand," and turned to the Minor Maintainer. I noticed that the telltale on the Major was glowing a reassuring red again, and I found a moment to thank Mamma Devi that the Door was shut.

Maud was jumping up and down, cheering I don't know which-nor did she, I bet-and the New Girl was white and I saw that the sabers were working more businesslike. Erich's flicked, flicked, flicked again and came away from the blond lad's cheek spilling a couple of red drops. The blond lad lunged fiercely, Erich jumped back, and the next moment they were both floating helplessly in the air, twisting like they had cramps.

I realized quick enough that Sid had shut off gravity in the Door and Stores sectors of the Place, leaving the rest of us firm on our feet in the Refresher and Surgery sectors. The Place has sectional gravity to suit our Extraterrestrial buddies-those crazy ETs sometimes come whooping in for recuperation in very mixed batches.

From his central position, Sid called out, kindly enough but taking no nonsense, "All right, lads, you've had your fun. Now sheathe those swords."

For a second or so, the two black hussars drifted and contorted. Erich laughed harshly and neatly obeyed-the commandant is used to free fall. The blond lad stopped writhing, hesitated while he glared upside down at Erich and managed to get his saber into its scabbard, although he turned a slow somersault doing it. Then Sid switched on their gravity, slow enough so they wouldn't get sprained landing.

Erich laughed, lightly this time, and stepped out briskly toward us. He stopped to clap the New Boy firmly on the shoulder and look him in the face.

"So, now you get a good scar," he said.

The other didn't pull away, but he didn't look up and Erich came on. Sid was hurrying toward the New Boy, and as he passed Erich, he wagged a finger at him and gayly said, "You rogue." Next thing I was giving Erich my "Man, you're home" hug and he was kissing me and cracking my ribs and saying, "*Liebchen! Doppchen!*" —which was fine with me because I do love him and I'm a good lover and as much a Doubleganger as he is.

We had just pulled back from each other to get a breath-his blue eyes looked so sweet in his worn face-when there was a thud behind us. With the snapping of the tension, Doc had fallen off his bar stool and his top hat was over his eyes. As we turned to chuckle at him, Maud squeaked and we saw that the Roman had walked straight up against the Void and was marching along there steadily without gaining a foot, like it does happen, his black uniform melting into that inside-your-head gray.

Maud and Beau rushed over to fish him back, which can be tricky. The thin gambler was all courtly efficiency again. Sid supervised from a distance.

"What's wrong with him?" I asked Erich.

He shrugged. "Overdue for Change Shock. And he was nearest the stun guns. His horse almost threw him. *Mein Gott*, you should have seen Saint Petersburg, *Liebchen*: the Nevsky Prospekt, the canals flying by like reception carpets of blue sky, a cavalry troop in blue and gold that blundered across our escape, fine women in furs and ostrich plumes, a monk with a big tripod and his head under a hood-it gave me the horrors seeing all those Zombies flashing past and staring at me in that sick unawakened way they have, and knowing that some of them, say the photographer, might be Snakes."

Our side in the Change War is the Spiders, the other side is the Snakes, though all of us-Spiders and Snakes alike-are Doublegangers and Demons too, because we're cut out of our lifelines in the cosmos. Your lifeline is all of you from birth to death. We're Doublegangers because we can operate both in the cosmos and outside of it, and Demons because we act reasonably alive while doing so-which the Ghosts don't. Entertainers and Soldiers are all Demon-Doublegangers, whichever side they're on-though they say the Snake Places are simply ghastly. Zombies are dead people whose lifelines lie in the so-called past.

"What were you doing in Saint Petersburg before the ambush?" I asked Erich. "That is, if you can talk about it."

"Why not? We were kidnapping the infant Einstein back from the Snakes in 1883. Yes, the Snakes got him, *Liebchen*, only a few sleeps back, endangering the West's whole victory over Russia —"

" —which gave your dear little Hitler the world on a platter for fifty years and got me loved to death by your sterling troops in the Liberation of Chicago —"

" —but which leads to the ultimate victory of the Spiders and the West over the Snakes and Communism, *Liebchen*, remember that. Anyway, our counter-snatch didn't work. The Snakes had guards posted-most unusual and we weren't warned. The whole thing was a great mess. No wonder Bruce lost his head-not that it excuses him."

"The New Boy?" I asked. Sid hadn't got to him and he was still standing with hooded eyes where Erich had left him, a dark pillar of shame and rage.

"*Ja*, a lieutenant from World War One. An Englishman."

"I gathered that," I told Erich. "Is he really effeminate?"

"*Weibischer?*" He smiled. "I had to call him something when he said I was a coward. He'll make a fine Soldier-only needs a little more shaping."

"You men are so original when you spat." I lowered my voice. "But you shouldn't have gone on and called him a Snake, Erich mine."

"*Schlange?*" The smile got crooked. "Who knows-about any of us? As Saint Petersburg showed me, the Snakes' spies are getting cleverer than ours." The blue eyes didn't look sweet now. "Are you, *Liebchen*, really nothing more than a good loyal Spider?"

"Erich!"

"All right, I went too far-with Bruce and with you too. We're all hacked these days, riding with one leg over the breaking edge."

Maud and Beau were supporting the Roman to a couch, Maud taking most of his weight, with Sid still supervising and the New Boy still sulking by himself. The New Girl should have been with him, of course, but I couldn't see her anywhere and I decided she was probably having a nervous breakdown in the Refresher, the little jerk.

"The Roman looks pretty bad, Erich," I said.

"Ah, Mark's tough. Got virtue, as his people say. And our little starship girl will bring him back to life if anybody can and if..."

"...you call this living," I filled in dutifully.

He was right. Maud had fifty-odd years of psychomedical experience, 23rd Century at that. It should have been Doc's job, but that was fifty drunks back.

"Maud and Mark, that will be an interesting experiment," Erich said. "Reminiscent of Goering's with the frozen men and the naked gypsy girls."

"You are a filthy Nazi. She'll be using electrophoresis and deep suggestion, if I know anything."

"How will you be able to know anything, *Liebchen*, if she switches on the couch curtains, as I perceive she is preparing to do?"

"Filthy Nazi I said and meant."

"Precisely." He clicked his heels and bowed a millimeter. "Erich Friederich von Hohenwald, *Oberleutnant* in the army of the Third Reich. Fell at Narvik, where he was Recruited by the Spiders. Lifeline lengthened by a Big Change after his first death and at latest report Commandant of Toronto, where he maintains extensive baby farms to provide him with breakfast meat, if you believe the handbills of the *voyageurs* underground. At your service."

"Oh, Erich, it's all so lousy," I said, touching his hand, reminded that he was one of the unfortunates Resurrected from a point in their lifelines well before their deaths-in his case, because the date of his death had been shifted forward by a Big Change after his Resurrection. And as every Demon finds out, if he can't imagine it beforehand, it is pure hell to remember your future, and the shorter the time between your Resurrection and your death back in the cosmos, the better. Mine, bless Bab-ed-Din, was only an action-packed ten minutes on North Clark Street.

Erich put his other hand lightly over mine. "Fortunes of the Change War, *Liebchen*. At least I'm a Soldier and sometimes assigned to future operations-though why we should have this monomania about our future personalities back there, I don't know. Mine is a stupid *Oberst*, thin as paper-and frightfully indignant at the *voyageurs*! But it helps me a little if I see him in perspective and at least I get back to the cosmos pretty regularly, *Gott sei Dank*, so I'm better off than you Entertainers."

I didn't say aloud that a Changing cosmos is worse than none, but I found myself sending a prayer to the Bonny Dew for my father's repose, that the Change Winds would blow lightly across the lifeline of Anton A. Forzane, professor of physiology, born in Norway and buried in Chicago. Woodlawn Cemetery is a nice gray spot.

"That's all right, Erich," I said. "We Entertainers Got Mittens too."

He scowled around at me suspiciously, as if he were wondering whether I had all my buttons on.

"Mittens?" he said. "What do you mean? I'm not wearing any. Are you trying to say something about Bruce's gloves-which incidentally seem to annoy him for some reason. No, seriously, Greta, why do you Entertainers need mittens?"

"Because we get cold feet sometimes. At least I do. Got Mittens, as I say."

A sickly light dawned in his Prussian puss. He muttered, "Got mittens ... *Gott mit uns* ... God with us," and roared softly, "Greta, I don't know how I put up with you, the way you murder a great language for cheap laughs."

"You've got to take me as I am," I told him, "mittens and all, thank the Bonny Dew —" and hastily explained, "That's French —*le bon Dieu* —the good God-don't hit me. I'm not going to tell you any more of my secrets."

He laughed feebly, like he was dying.

"Cheer up," I said. "I won't be here forever, and there are worse places than the Place."

He nodded grudgingly, looking around. "You know what, Greta, if you'll promise not to make some dreadful joke out of it: on operations, I pretend I'll soon be going backstage to court the world-famous ballerina Greta Forzane."

He was right about the backstage part. The Place is a regular theater-in-the-round with the Void for an audience, the Void's gray hardly disturbed by the screens masking Surgery (Ugh!), Refresher and Stores. Between the last two are the bar and kitchen and Beau's piano. Between Surgery and the sector where the Door usually appears are the shelves and taborets of the Art Gallery. The control divan is stage center. Spaced around at a fair distance are six big low couches-one with its curtains now shooting up into the gray-and a few small tables. It is like a ballet set and the crazy costumes and characters that turn up don't ruin the illusion. By no means. Diaghilev would have hired most of them for the Ballet Russe on first sight, without even asking them whether they could keep time to music.

Chapter 2
A Right-Hand Glove

> Last week in Babylon,
> Last night in Rome,

> —Hodgson

Beau had gone behind the bar and was talking quietly at Doc, but with his eyes elsewhere, looking very sallow and professional in his white, and I thought-Damballa! —I'm in the French Quarter. I couldn't see the New Girl. Sid was at last getting to the New Boy after the fuss about Mark. He threw me a sign and I started over with Erich in tow.

"Welcome, sweet lad. Sidney Lessingham's your host, and a fellow Englishman. Born in King's Lynn, 1564, schooled at Cambridge, but London was the life and death of me, though I outlasted Bessie, Jimmie, Charlie, and Ollie almost. And what a life! By turns a clerk, a spy, a bawd-the two trades are hand in glove —a poet of no account, a beggar, and a peddler of resurrection tracts. Beau Lassiter, our throats are tinder!"

At the word "poet," the New Boy looked up, but resentfully, as if he had been tricked into it.

"And to spare your throat for drinking, sweet gallant, I'll be so bold as to guess and answer one of your questions," Sid rattled on. "Yes, I knew Will Shakespeare-we were of an age-and he was such a modest, mind-your-business rogue that we all wondered whether he really did write those plays. Your pardon, 'faith, but that scratch might be looked to."

Then I saw that the New Girl hadn't lost her head, but gone to Surgery (Ugh!) for a first-aid tray. She reached a swab toward the New Boy's sticky cheek, saying rather shrilly, "If I might..."

Her timing was bad. Sid's last words and Erich's approach had darkened the look in the young Soldier's face and he angrily swept her arm aside without even glancing at her. Erich squeezed my arm. The tray clattered to the floor-and one of the drinks that Beau was bringing almost followed it. Ever since the New Girl's arrival, Beau had been figuring that she was his responsibility, though I don't think the two of them had reached an agreement yet. Beau was especially set on it because I was thick with Sid at the time and Maud with Doc, she loving tough cases.

"Easy now, lad, and you love me!" Sid thundered, again shooting Beau the "Hold it" look. "She's just a poor pagan trying to comfort you. Swallow your bile, you black villain, and perchance it will turn to poetry. Ah, did I touch you there? Confess, you are a poet."

There isn't much gets by Sid, though for a second I forgot my psychology and wondered if he knew what he was doing with his insights.

"Yes, I'm a poet, all right," the New Boy roared. "I'm Bruce Marchant, you bloody Zombies. I'm a poet in a world where even the lines of the King James and your precious Will whom you use for laughs aren't safe from Snakes' slime and the Spiders' dirty legs. Changing our history, stealing our certainties, claiming to be so blasted all-knowing and best intentioned and efficient, and what does it lead to? This bloody SI glove!"

He held up his black-gloved left hand which still held the mate and he shook it.

"What's wrong with the Spider Issue gauntlet, heart of gold?" Sid demanded. "And you love us, tell us." While Erich laughed, "Consider yourself lucky, *Kamerad*. Mark and I didn't draw any gloves at all."

"What's wrong with it?" Bruce yelled. "The bloody things are both lefts!" He slammed it down on the floor.

We all howled, we couldn't help it. He turned his back on us and stamped off, though I guessed he would keep out of the Void. Erich squeezed my arm and said between gasps, *"Mein Gott, Liebchen,* what have I always told you about Soldiers? The bigger the gripe, the smaller the cause! It is infallible!"

One of us didn't laugh. Ever since the New Girl heard the name Bruce Marchant, she'd had a look in her eyes like she'd been given the sacrament. I was glad she'd got interested in something, because she'd been pretty much of a snoot and a wet blanket up until now, although she'd come to the Place with the recommendation of having been a real whoopee girl in London and New York in the Twenties. She looked disapprovingly at us as she gathered up the tray and stuff, not forgetting the glove, which she placed on the center of the tray like a holy relic.

Beau cut over and tried to talk to her, but she ghosted past him and once again he couldn't do anything because of the tray in his hands. He came over and got rid of the drinks quick. I took a big gulp right away because I saw the New Girl stepping through the screen into Surgery and I hate to be reminded we have it and I'm glad Doc is too drunk to use it, some of the Arachnoid surgical techniques being very sickening as I know only too well from a personal experience that is number one on my list of things to be forgotten.

By that time, Bruce had come back to us, saying in a carefully hard voice, "Look here, it's not the dashed glove itself, as you very well know, you howling Demons."

"What is it then, noble heart?" Sid asked, his grizzled gold beard heightening the effect of innocent receptivity.

"It's the principle of the thing," Bruce said, looking around sharply, but none of us cracked a smile. "It's this mucking inefficiency and death of the cosmos-and don't tell me that isn't in the cards! —masquerading as benign omniscient authority. The Spiders-and we don't know who they are ultimately; it's just a name; we see only agents like ourselves-the Spiders pluck us from the quiet graves of our lifelines —"

"Is that bad, lad?" Sid murmured, innocently straight-faced.

" —and Resurrect us if they can and then tell us we must fight another time-traveling power called the Snakes-just a name, too-which is bent on perverting and enslaving the whole cosmos, past, present and future."

"And isn't it, lad?"

"Before we're properly awake, we're Recruited into the Big Time and hustled into tunnels and burrows outside our space-time, these miserable closets, gray sacks, puss pockets-no offense to this Place-that the Spiders have created, maybe by gigantic implosions, but no one knows for certain, and then we're sent off on all sorts of missions into the past and future to change history in ways that are supposed to thwart the Snakes."

"True, lad."

"And from then on, the pace is so flaming hot and heavy, the shocks come so fast, our emotions are wrenched in so many directions, our public and private metaphysics distorted so insanely, the deepest thread of reality we cling to tied in such bloody knots, that we never can get things straight."

"We've all felt that way, lad," Sid said soberly; Beau nodded his sleek death's head; "You should have seen me, *Kamerad,* my first fifty sleeps," Erich put in; while I added, "Us girls, too, Bruce."

"Oh, I know I'll get hardened to it, and don't think I can't. It's not that," Bruce said harshly. "And I wouldn't mind the personal confusion, the mess it's made of my spirit, I wouldn't even mind remaking history and destroying priceless, once-called imperishable beauties of the past, if I felt it were for the best. The Spiders assure us that, to thwart the Snakes, it is all-important that the West ultimately defeat the East. But what have they done to achieve this? I'll give you some beautiful examples. To stabilize power in the early Mediterranean world, they have built up Crete at the expense of Greece, making Athens a ghost city, Plato a trivial fabulist, and putting all Greek culture in a minor key."

"You got time for culture?" I heard myself say and I clapped my hand over my mouth in gentle reproof.

"But *you* remember the dialogues, lad," Sid observed. "And rail not at Crete —I have a sweet Keftian friend."

"For how long will I remember Plato's dialogues? And who after me?" Bruce challenged. "Here's another. The Spiders want Rome powerful and, to date, they've helped Rome so much that she collapses in a blaze of German and Parthian invasions a few years after the death of Julius Caesar."

This time it was Beau who butted in. Most everybody in the Place loves these bull sessions. "You omit to mention, sir, that Rome's newest downfall is directly due to the Unholy Triple Alliance the Snakes have fomented between the Eastern Classical World, Mohammedanized Christianity, and Marxist Communism, trying to pass the torch of power futurewards by way of Byzantium and the Eastern Church, without ever letting it pass into the hands of the Spider West. That, sir, is the Snakes' Three-Thousand-Year Plan which we are fighting against, striving to revive Rome's glories."

"Striving is the word for it," Bruce snapped. "Here's yet another example. To beat Russia, the Spiders kept England and America out of World War Two, thereby ensuring a German invasion of the New World and creating a Nazi empire stretching from the salt mines of Siberia to the plantations of Iowa, from Nizhni Novgorod to Kansas City!"

He stopped and my short hairs prickled. Behind me, someone was chanting in a weird spiritless voice, like footsteps in hard snow.

"*Salz, Salz, bringe Salz. Kein' Peitsch', gnädige Herren. Salz, Salz, Salz.*"

I turned and there was Doc waltzing toward us with little tiny steps, bent over so low that the ends of his shawl touched the floor, his head crooked up sideways and looking through us.

I knew then, but Erich translated softly. "'Salt, salt, I bring salt. No whip, merciful sirs.' He is speaking to my countrymen in their language." Doc had spent his last months in a Nazi-operated salt mine.

He saw us and got up, straightening his top hat very carefully. He frowned hard while my heart thumped half a dozen times. Then his face slackened, he shrugged his shoulders and muttered, "*Nichevo.*"

"And it does not matter, sir," Beau translated, but directing his remark at Bruce. "True, great civilizations have been dwarfed or broken by the Change War. But others, once crushed in the bud, have bloomed. In the 1870s, I traveled a Mississippi that had never known Grant's gunboats. I studied piano, languages, and the laws of chance under the greatest European masters at the University of Vicksburg."

"And you think your pipsqueak steamboat culture is compensation for —" Bruce began but, "Prithee none of that, lad," Sid interrupted smartly. "Nations are as equal as so many madmen or drunkards, and I'll drink dead drunk the man who disputes me. Hear reason: nations are not so puny as to shrivel and vanish at the first tampering with their past, no, nor with the tenth. Nations are monsters, boy, with guts of iron and nerves of brass. Waste not your pity on them."

"True indeed, sir," Beau pressed, cooler and keener for the attack on his Greater South. "Most of us enter the Change World with the false metaphysic that the slightest change in the past —a grain of dust misplaced-will transform the whole future. It is a long while before we accept with our minds as well as our intellects the law of the Conservation of Reality: that when the past is changed, the future changes barely enough to adjust, barely enough to admit the new data. The Change Winds meet maximum resistance always. Otherwise the first operation in Babylonia would have wiped out New Orleans, Sheffield, Stuttgart, and Maud Davies' birthplace on Ganymede!

"Note how the gap left by Rome's collapse was filled by the imperialistic and Christianized Germans. Only an expert Demon historian can tell the difference in most ages between the former Latin and the present Gothic Catholic Church. As you yourself, sir, said of Greece, it is as if an old melody were shifted into a slightly different key. In the wake of a Big Change, cultures and individuals are transposed, it's true, yet in the main they continue much as they were, except for the usual scattering of unfortunate but statistically meaningless accidents."

"All right, you bloody savants-maybe I pushed my point too far," Bruce growled. "But if you want variety, give a thought to the rotten methods we use in our wonderful Change War. Poisoning Churchill and Cleopatra. Kidnapping Einstein when he's a baby."

"The Snakes did it first," I reminded him.

"Yes, and we copied them. How resourceful does that make us?" he retorted, arguing like a woman. "If we need Einstein, why don't we Resurrect him, deal with him as a man?"

Beau said, serving his culture in slightly thicker slices, *"Pardonnez-moi,* but when you have enjoyed your status as Doubleganger a *soupcon* longer, you will understand that great men can rarely be Resurrected. Their beings are too crystallized, sir, their lifelines too tough."

"Pardon me, but I think that's rot. I believe that most great men refuse to make the bargain with the Snakes, or with us Spiders either. They scorn Resurrection at the price demanded."

"Brother, they ain't that great," I whispered, while Beau glided on with, "However that may be, you have accepted Resurrection, sir, and so incurred an obligation which you as a gentleman must honor."

"I accepted Resurrection all right," Bruce said, a glare coming into his eyes. "When they pulled me out of my line at Passchendaele in '17 ten minutes before I died, I grabbed at the offer of life like a drunkard grabs at a drink the morning after. But even then I thought I was also seizing a chance to undo historic wrongs, work for peace." His voice was getting wilder all the time. Just beyond our circle, I noticed the New Girl watching him worshipfully. "But what did I find the Spiders wanted me for? Only to fight more wars, over and over again, make them crueler and stinkinger, cut the swath of death a little wider with each Big Change, work our way a little closer to the death of the cosmos."

Sid touched my wrist and, as Bruce raved on, he whispered to me, "What kind of ball, think you, will please and so quench this fire-brained rogue? And you love me, discover it."

I whispered back without taking my eyes off Bruce either, "I know somebody who'll be happy to put on any kind of ball he wants, if he'll just notice her."

"The New Girl, sweetling? 'Tis well. This rogue speaks like an angry angel. It touches my heart and I like it not."

Bruce was saying hoarsely but loudly, "And so we're sent on operations in the past and from each of those operations the Change Winds blow futurewards, swiftly or slowly according to the opposition they breast, sometimes rippling into each other, and any one of those Winds may shift the date of our own death ahead of the date of our Resurrection, so that in an instant-even here, outside the cosmos-we may molder and rot or crumble to dust and vanish away. The wind with our name in it may leak through the Door."

Faces hardened at that, because it's bad form to mention Change Death, and Erich flared out with, *"Halt's Maul, Kamerad!* There's always another Resurrection."

But Bruce didn't keep his mouth shut. He said, "Is there? I know the Spiders promise it, but even if they do go back and cut another Doubleganger from my lifeline, is he me?" He slapped his chest with his bare hand. "I don't think so. And even if he is me, with unbroken consciousness, why's he been Resurrected again? Just to refight more wars and face more Change Death for the sake of an almighty power —" his voice was rising to a climax —"an almighty power so bloody ineffectual, it can't furnish one poor Soldier pulled out of the mud of Passchendaele, one miserable Change Commando, one Godforsaken Recuperee a proper issue of equipment!"

And he held out his bare right hand toward us, fingers spread a little, as if it were the most amazing object and most deserving of outraged sympathy in the whole world.

The New Girl's timing was perfect. She whisked through us, and before he could so much as wiggle the fingers, she whipped a black gauntleted glove on it and anyone could see that it fitted his hand perfectly.

This time our laughing beat the other. We collapsed and slopped our drinks and pounded each other on the back and then started all over.

"Ach, der Handschuh, Liebchen! Where'd she get it?" Erich gasped in my ear.

"Probably just turned the other one inside out-that turns a left into a right —I've done it myself," I wheezed, collapsing again at the idea.

"That would put the lining outside," he objected.

"Then I don't know," I said. "We got all sorts of junk in Stores."

"It doesn't matter, Liebchen," he assured me. "Ach, der Handschuh!"

All through it, Bruce just stood there admiring the glove, moving the fingers a little now and then, and the New Girl stood watching him as if he were eating a cake she'd baked.

When the hysteria quieted down, he looked up at her with a big smile. "What did you say your name was?"

"Lili," she said, and believe you me, she was Lili to me even in my thoughts from then on, for the way she'd handled that lunatic.

"Lilian Foster," she explained. "I'm English also. Mr. Marchant, I've read A Young Man's Fancy I don't know how many times."

"You have? It's wretched stuff. From the Dark Ages —I mean my Cambridge days. In the trenches, I was working up some poems that were rather better."

"I won't hear you say that. But I'd be terribly thrilled to hear the new ones. Oh, Mr. Marchant, it was so strange to hear you call it Passiondale."

"Why, if I may ask?"

"Because that's the way I pronounce it to myself. But I looked it up and it's more like Pas-ken-DA-luh."

"Bless you! All the Tommies called it Passiondale, just as they called Ypres Wipers."

"How interesting. You know, Mr. Marchant, I'll wager we were Recruited in the same operation, summer of 1917. I'd got to France as a Red Cross nurse, but they found out my age and were going to send me back."

"How old were you-are you? Same thing, I mean to say."

"Seventeen."

"Seventeen in '17," Bruce murmured, his blue eyes glassy.

It was real corny dialogue and I couldn't resent the humorous leer Erich gave me as we listened to them, as if to say, "Ain't it nice, Liebchen, Bruce has a silly little English schoolgirl to occupy him between operations?"

Just the same, as I watched Lili in her dark bangs and pearl necklace and tight little gray dress that reached barely to her knees, and Bruce hulking over her tenderly in his snazzy hussar's rig, I knew that I was seeing the start of something that hadn't been part of me since Dave died fighting Franco years before I got on the Big Time, the sort of thing that almost made me wish there could be children in the Change World. I wondered why I'd never thought of trying to work things so that Dave got Resurrected and I told myself: no, it's all changed, I've changed, better the Change Winds don't disturb Dave or I know about it.

"No, I didn't die in 1917—I was merely Recruited then," Lili was telling Bruce. "I lived all through the Twenties, as you can see from the way I dress. But let's not talk about that, shall we? Oh, Mr. Marchant, do you think you can possibly remember any of those poems you started in the trenches? I can't fancy them bettering your sonnet that concludes with, 'The bough swings in the wind, the night is deep; Look at the stars, poor little ape, and sleep.'"

That one almost made me whoop-what monkeys we are, I thought-though I'd be the first to admit that the best line to use on a poet is one of his own-in fact, as many as possible. I decided I could safely forget our little Britons and devote myself to Erich or whatever needed me.

Chapter 3
Nine for a Party

Hell is the place for me. For to Hell go the fine churchmen, and the fine knights, killed in the tourney or in some grand war, the brave soldiers and the gallant gentlemen. With them will I go. There go also the fair gracious ladies who have lovers two or three beside their lord. There go the gold and the silver, the sables and ermine. There go the harpers and the minstrels and the kings of the earth.

—Aucassin

I exchanged my drink for a new one from another tray Beau was bringing around. The gray of the Void was beginning to look real pleasant, like warm thick mist with millions of tiny diamonds floating in it. Doc was sitting grandly at the bar with a steaming tumbler of tea —a chaser, I guess, since he was just putting down a shot glass. Sid was talking to Erich and laughing at the same time and I said to myself it begins to feel like a party, but something's lacking.

It wasn't anything to do with the Major Maintainer; its telltale was glowing a steady red like a nice little home fire amid the tight cluster of dials that included all the controls except the lonely and frightening Introversion switch that was never touched. Then Maud's couch curtains winked out and there were she and the Roman sitting quietly side by side.

He looked down at his shiny boots and the rest of his black duds like he was just waking up and couldn't believe it all, and he said, "*Omnia mutantur, nos et mutamur in illis*," and I raised my eyebrows at Beau, who was taking the tray back, and he did proud by old Vicksburg by translating: "All things change and we change with them."

Then Mark slowly looked around at us, and I can testify that a Roman smile is just as warm as any other nationality, and he finally said, "We are nine, the proper number for a party. The couches, too. It is good."

Maud chuckled proudly and Erich shouted, "Welcome back from the Void, *Kamerad*," and then, because he's German and thinks all parties have to be noisy and satirically pompous, he jumped on a couch and announced, "*Herren und Damen*, permit me to introduce the noblest Roman of them all, Marcus Vipsaius Niger, legate to Nero Claudius (called Germanicus in a former time stream) and who in 763 A.U.C. (Correct, Mark? It means 10 A.D., you meatheads!) died bravely fighting the Parthians and the Snakes in the Battle of Alexandria. *Hoch, hoch, hoch!*"

We all swung our glasses and cheered with him and Sid yelled at Erich, "Keep your feet off the furniture, you unschooled rogue," and grinned and boomed at all three hussars, "Take your ease, Recuperees," and Maud and Mark got their drinks, the Roman paining Beau by refusing Falernian wine in favor of scotch and soda, and right away everyone was talking a mile a minute.

We had a lot to catch up on. There was the usual yak about the war —"The Snakes are laying mine fields in the Void," "I don't believe it, how can you mine nothing?" —and the shortages-bourbon, bobby pins, and the stabilitin that would have brought Mark out of it faster-and what had become of people —"Marcia? Oh, she's not around any more," (She'd been caught in a Change Gale and green and stinking in five seconds, but I wasn't going to say that) —and Mark had to be told about Bruce's glove, which convulsed us all over again, and the Roman remembered a legionary who had carried a gripe all the way to Octavius because he'd accidentally been issued the unbelievable luxury item sugar instead of the usual salt, and Erich asked Sid if he had any new Ghostgirls in stock and Sid sucked his beard like the old goat he is. "Dost thou ask me, lusty Allemand? Nay, there are several great beauties, amongst them an Austrian countess from Strauss's Vienna, and if it were not for sweetling here ...Mnnnn."

I poked a finger in Erich's chest between two of the bright buttons with their tiny death's heads. "You, my little von Hohenwald, are a menace to us real girls. You have too much of a thing about the unawakened, ghost kind."

He called me his little Demon and hugged me a bit too hard to prove it wasn't so, and then he suggested we show Bruce the Art Gallery. I thought this was a real brilliant idea, but when I tried to argue him out of it, he got stubborn. Bruce and Lili were willing to do anything anyone wanted them to, though not so willing to pay any attention while doing it. The saber cut was just a thin red line on his cheek; she'd washed away all the dried blood.

The Gallery gets you, though. It's a bunch of paintings and sculptures and especially odd knick-knacks, all made by Soldiers recuperating here, and a lot of them telling about the Change War from the stuff they're made of-brass cartridges, flaked flint, bits of ancient pottery glued into futuristic shapes, mashed-up Incan gold rebeaten by a Martian, whorls of beady Lunan wire, a picture in tempera on a crinkle-cracked thick round of quartz that had filled a starship porthole, a Sumerian inscription chiseled into a brick from an atomic oven.

There are a lot of things in the Gallery and I can always find some I haven't ever seen before. It gets you, as I say, thinking about the guys that made them and their thoughts and the far times and places they came from, and sometimes, when I'm feeling low, I'll come and look at them so I'll feel still lower and get inspired to kick myself back into a good temper. It's the only history of the Place there is and it doesn't change a great deal, because the things in it and the feelings that went into them resist the Change Winds better than anything else.

Right now, Erich's witty lecture was bouncing off the big ears I hide under my pageboy bob and I was thinking how awful it is that for us that there's not only change but Change. You don't know from one minute to the next whether a mood or idea you've got is really new or just welling up into you because the past has been altered by the Spiders or Snakes.

Change Winds can blow not only death but anything short of it, down to the featheriest fancy. They blow thousands of times faster than time moves, but no one can say how much faster or how far one of them will travel or what damage it'll do or how soon it'll damp out. The Big Time isn't the little time.

And then, for the Demons, there's the fear that our personality will just fade and someone else climb into the driver's seat and us not even know. Of course, we Demons are supposed to be able to remember through Change and in spite of it; that's why we are Demons and not Ghosts like the other Doublegangers, or merely Zombies or Unborn and nothing more, and as Beau truly said, there aren't any great men among us-and blamed few of the masses, either-we're a rare sort of people and that's why the Spiders have to Recruit us where they find us without caring about our previous knowledge and background, a Foreign Legion of time, a strange kind of folk, bright but always in the background, with built-in nostalgia and cynicism, as adaptable as Centaurian shape-changers but with memories as long as a Lunan's six arms, a kind of Change People, you might say, the cream of the damned.

But sometimes I wonder if our memories are as good as we think they are and if the whole past wasn't once entirely different from anything we remember, and we've forgotten that we forgot.

As I say, the Gallery gets you feeling real low, and so now I said to myself, "Back to your lousy little commandant, kid," and gave myself a stiff boot.

Erich was holding up a green bowl with gold dolphins or spaceships on it and saying, "And, to my mind, this proves that Etruscan art is derived from Egyptian. Don't you agree, Bruce?"

Bruce looked up, all smiles from Lili, and said, "What was that, dear chap?"

Erich's forehead got dark as the Door and I was glad the hussars had parked their sabers along with their shakos, but before he could even get out a Jerry cussword, Doc breezed up in that plateau-state of drunkenness so like hypnotized sobriety, moving as if he were on a dolly, ghosted the bowl out of Erich's hand, said, "A beautiful specimen of Middle Systemic Venusian. When Eightaitch finished it, he told me you couldn't look at it and not feel the waves of the Northern Venusian Shallows rippling around your hoofs. But it might look better inverted. I wonder. Who are you, young officer? *Nichevo*," and he carefully put the bowl back on its shelf and rolled on.

It's a fact that Doc knows the Art Gallery better than any of us, really by heart, he being the oldest inhabitant, though he maybe picked a bad time to show off his knowledge. Erich was going to take out after him, but I said, "Nix, *Kamerad*, remember gloves and sugar," and he contented himself with complaining, "That *nichevo* —it's so gloomy and hopeless, *ungeheuerlich*. I tell you, *Liebchen*, they shouldn't have Russians working for the Spiders, not even as Entertainers."

I grinned at him and squeezed his hand. "Not much entertainment in Doc these days, is there?" I agreed.

He grinned back at me a shade sheepishly and his face smoothed and his blue eyes looked sweet again for a second and he said, "I shouldn't want to claw out at people that way, Greta, but at times I am just a jealous old man," which is not entirely true, as he isn't a day over thirty-three, although his hair is nearly white.

Our lovers had drifted on a few steps until they were almost fading into the Surgery screen. It was the last spot I would have picked for the formal preliminaries to a little British smooching, but Lili probably didn't share my prejudices, though I remembered she'd told me she'd served a brief hitch in an Arachnoid Field Hospital before being transferred to the Place.

But she couldn't have had anything like the experience I'd had during my short and sour career as a Spider nurse, when I'd acquired my best-hated nightmare and flopped completely (jobwise, but on the floor, too) at seeing a doctor flick a switch and a being, badly injured but human, turn into a long cluster of glistening strange fruit-ugh, it always makes me want to toss my cookies and my buttons. And to think that dear old Daddy Anton wanted his Greta chile to be a doctor.

Well, I could see this wasn't getting me anywhere I wanted to go, and after all there was a party going on.

Doc was babbling something at a great rate to Sid —I just hoped Doc wouldn't get inspired to go into his animal imitations, which sound pretty fierce and once seriously offended some recuperating ETs.

Maud was demonstrating to Mark a 23rd Century two-step and Beau sat down at the piano and improvised softly on her rhythm.

As the deep-thrumming relaxing notes hit us, Erich's face brightened and he dragged me over. Pleasantly soon I had my feet off the diamond-rough floor, which we don't carpet because most of the ETs, the dear boys, like it hard, and I was shouldering back deep into the couch nearest the piano, with cushions all around me and a fresh drink in my hand, while my Nazi boy friend was getting ready to discharge his *Weltschmerz* as song, which didn't alarm me too much, as his baritone is passable.

Things felt real good, like the Maintainer was just idling to keep the Place in existence and moored to the cosmos, not exerting itself at all or at most taking an occasional lazy paddle stroke. At times the Place's loneliness can be happy and comfortable.

Then Beau raised an eyebrow at Erich, who nodded, and next thing they were launched into a song we all know, though I've never found out where it originally came from. This time it made me think of Lili, and I wondered why-and why it's a tradition at Recuperation Stations to call the new girl Lili, though in this case it happened to be her real name.

Standing in the Doorway just outside of space,
Winds of Change blow 'round you but don't touch your face;
You smile as you whisper tenderly,
"Please cross to me, Recuperee;
The operation's over, come in and close the Door."

Chapter 4
Sos from Nowhere

De Bailhache, Fresca, Mrs. Cammel, whirled
Beyond the circuit of the shuddering Bear
In fractured atoms.

—Eliot

I realized the piano had deserted Erich and I cranked my head up and saw Beau, Maud and Sid streaking for the control divan. The Major Maintainer was blinking emergency-green and fast, but the code was plain enough for even me to recognize the Spider distress call and for a second I felt just sick. Then Erich blew out his reserve breath in the middle of "Door" and I gave myself another of those helpful mental boots at the base of the spine and we hurried after them toward the center of the Place along with Mark.

The blinks faded as we got there and Sid told us not to move because we were making shadows. He glued an eye to the telltale and we held still as statues as he caressed the dials like he was making love.

One sensitive hand flicked out past the Introversion switch over to the Minor Maintainer and right away the Place was dark as your soul and there was nothing for me but Erich's arm and the knowledge that Sid was nursing a green light I couldn't even see, although my eyes had plenty time to accommodate.

Then the green light finally came back very slowly and I could see the dear reliable old face—the green-gold beard making him look like a merman—and then the telltale flared bright and Sid flicked on the Place lights and I leaned back.

"That nails them, lads, whoever and whenever they may be. Get ready for a pick-up."

Beau, who was closest of course, looked at him sharply. Sid shrugged uneasily. "Meseemed at first it was from our own globe a thousand years before our Lord, but that indication flickered and faded like witchfire. As it is, the call comes from something smaller than the Place and certes adrift from the cosmos. Meseemed too at one point I knew the fist of the caller-an antipodean atomicist named Benson-Carter —but that likewise changed."

Beau said, "We're not in the right phase of the cosmos-Places rhythm for a pick-up, are we, sir?"

Sid answered, "Ordinarily not, boy."

Beau continued, "I didn't think we had any pick-ups scheduled. Or stand-by orders."

Sid said, "We haven't."

Mark's eyes glowed. He tapped Erich on the shoulder. "An octavian denarius against ten Reichsmarks it is a Snake trap."

Erich's grin showed his teeth. "Make it first through the Door next operation and I'm on."

It didn't take that to tell me things were serious, or the thought that there's always a first time for bumping into something from really outside the cosmos. The Snakes have broken our code more than once. Maud was quietly serving out weapons and Doc was helping her. Only Bruce and Lili stood off. But they were watching.

The telltale brightened. Sid reached toward the Maintainer, saying, "All right, my hearties. Remember, through this Doorway pass the fishiest finaglers in and out of the cosmos."

The Door appeared to the left and above where it should be and darkened much too fast. There was a gust of stale salt seawind, if that makes sense, but no stepped-up Change Winds

I could tell-and I had been bracing myself against them. The Door got inky and there was a flicker of gray fur whips and a flash of copper flesh and gilt and something dark and a clump of hoofs and Erich was sighting a stun gun across his left forearm, and then the Door had vanished like that and a tentacled silvery Lunan and a Venusian satyr were coming straight toward us.

The Lunan was hugging a pile of clothes and weapons. The satyr was helping a wasp-waisted woman carry a heavy-looking bronze chest. The woman was wearing a short skirt and high-collared bolero jacket of leather so dark brown it was almost black. She had a two-horned *petsofa* hairdress and she was boldly gilded here and there and wore sandals and copper anklets and wristlets-one of them a copper-plated Caller-and from her wide copper belt hung a short-handled double-headed ax. She was dark-complexioned and her forehead and chin receded, but the effect was anything but weak; she had a face like a beautiful arrowhead-and a familiar one, by golly!

But before I could say, "Kabysia Labrys," Maud shrilly beat me to it with, "It's Kaby with two friends. Break out a couple of Ghostgirls."

And then I saw it really was old-home week because I recognized my Lunan boy friend Ilhilihis, and in the midst of all the confusion I got a nice kick out of knowing I was getting so I could tell the personality of one silver-furred muzzle from another.

They reached the control divan and Illy dumped his load and the others let down the chest, and Kaby staggered but shook off the two ETs when they started to support her, and she looked daggers at Sid when he tried to do the same, although she's his "sweet Keftian friend" he'd mentioned to Bruce.

She leaned straight-armed on the divan and took two gasping breaths so deep that the ridges of her spine showed through her brown-skinned waist, and then she threw up her head and commanded, "Wine!"

While Beau was rushing it, Sid tried to take her hand again, saying, "Sweetling, I'd never heard you call before and knew not this pretty little fist," but she ripped out, "Save your comfort for the Lunan," and I looked and saw-Hey, Zeus! —that one of Ilhilihis' six tentacles was lopped off halfway.

That was for me, and, going to him, I fast briefed myself: "Remember, he only weighs fifty pounds for all he's seven feet high; he doesn't like low sounds or to be grabbed; the two legs aren't tentacles and don't act the same; uses them for long walks, tentacles for leaps; uses tentacles for close vision too and for manipulation, of course; extended, they mean he's at ease; retracted, on guard or nervous; sharply retracted, disgusted; greeting —"

Just then, one of them swept across my face like a sweet-smelling feather duster and I said, "Illy, man, it's been a lot of sleeps," and brushed my fingers across his muzzle. It still took a little self-control not to hug him, and I did reach a little cluckingly for his lopped tentacle, but he wafted it away from me and the little voice-box belted to his side squeaked, "Naughty, naughty. Papa will fix his little old self. Greta girl, ever bandaged even a Terra octopus?"

I had, an intelligent one from around a quarter billion A.D., but I didn't tell him so. I stood and let him talk to the palm of my hand with one of his tentacles —I don't savvy feather-talk but it feels good, though I've often wondered who taught him English-and watched him use a couple others to whisk a sort of Lunan band-aid out of his pouch and cap his wound with it.

Meanwhile, the satyr knelt over the bronze chest, which was decorated with little death's heads and crosses with hoops at the top and swastikas, but looking much older than Nazi, and the satyr said to Sid, "Quick thinkin, Gov, when ya saw the Door comin in high n soffened up gravty unner it, but cud I hav sum hep now?"

Sid touched the Minor Maintainer and we all got very light and my stomach did a flip-flop while the satyr piled on the chest the clothes and weapons that Illy had been carrying and pranced off with it all and carefully put it down at the end of the bar. I decided the satyr's English instructor must have been quite a character, too. Wish I'd met him-her-it.

Sid thought to ask Illy if he wanted Moon-normal gravity in one sector, but my boy likes to mix, and being such a lightweight, Earth-normal gravity doesn't bother him. As he said to me once, "Would Jovian gravity bother a beetle, Greta girl?"

I asked Illy about the satyr and he squeaked that his name was Sevensee and that he'd never met him before this operation. I knew the satyrs were from a billion years in the future, just as the Loonies were from a billion in the past, and I thought-Kreesed us! —but it must have been a real big or emergency-like operation to have the Spiders using those two for it, with two billion years between them —a time-difference that gives you a feeling of awe for a second, you know.

I started to ask Illy about it, but just then Beau came scampering back from the bar with a big red-and-black earthenware goblet of wine-we try to keep a variety of drinking tools in stock so folks will feel more at home. Kaby grabbed it from him and drained most of it in one swallow and then smashed it on the floor. She does things like that, though Sid's tried to teach her better. Then she stared at what she was thinking about until the whites showed all around her eyes and her lips pulled way back from her teeth and she looked a lot less human than the two ETs, just like a fury. Only a time traveler knows how like the wild murals and engravings of them some of the ancients can look.

My hair stood up at the screech she let out. She smashed a fist into the divan and cried, "Goddess! Must I see Crete destroyed, revived, and now destroyed again? It is too much for your servant."

Personally, I thought she could stand anything.

There was a rush of questions at what she said about Crete —I asked one of them, for the news certainly frightened me-but she shot up her arm straight for silence and took a deep breath and began.

"In the balance hung the battle. Rowing like black centipedes, the Dorian hulls bore down on our outnumbered ships. On the bright beach, masked by rocks, Sevensee and I stood by the needle gun, ready to give the black hulls silent wounds. Beside us was Ilhilihis, suited as a sea monster. But then … then…"

Then I saw she wasn't altogether the iron babe, for her voice broke and she started to shake and to sob rackingly, although her face was still a mask of rage, and she threw up the wine. Sid stepped in and made her stop, which I think he'd been wanting to do all along.

Chapter 5
Sid Insists on Ghostgirls

> Whenever I take up a newspaper and read it, I fancy I see ghosts creeping between the lines. There must be ghosts all over the world. They must be as countless as the grains of the sands, it seems to me.

—Ibsen

My Elizabethan boy friend put his fists on his hips and laid down the law to us as if we were a lot of nervous children who'd been playing too hard.

"Look you, masters, this is a Recuperation Station and I am running it as such. A plague of all operations! I care not if the frame of things disjoints and the whole Change World goes to ruin, but you, warrior maid, are going to rest and drink more wine slowly before you tell your tale and your colleagues are going to be properly companioned. No questions, anyone. Beau, and you love us, give us a lively tune."

Kaby relaxed a little and let him put his hand carefully against her back in token of support and she said grudgingly, "All right, Fat Belly."

Then, so help me, to the tune of the Muskrat Ramble, which I'd taught Beau, we got girls for those two ETs and everybody properly paired up.

Right here I want to point out that a lot of the things they say in the Change World about Recuperation Stations simply aren't so-and anyway they always leave out nine-tenths of it. The Soldiers that come through the Door are looking for a good time, sure, but they're hurt real bad too, every one of them, deep down in their minds and hearts, if not always in their bodies or so you can see it right away.

Believe me, a temporal operation is no joke, and to start with, there isn't one person in a hundred who can endure to be cut from his lifeline and become a really wide-awake Doubleganger —a Demon, that is-let alone a Soldier. What does a badly hurt and mixed-up creature need who's been fighting hard? *One individual* to look out for him and feel for him and patch him up, and it helps if the one is of the opposite sex-that's something that goes beyond species.

There's your basis for the Place and the wild way it goes about its work, and also for most other Recuperation Stations or Entertainment Spots. The name Entertainer can be misleading, but I like it. She's got to be a lot more than a good party girl-or boy-though she's got to be that too. She's got to be a nurse and a psychologist and an actress and a mother and a practical ethnologist and a lot of things with longer names-and a reliable friend.

None of us are all those things perfectly or even near it. We just try. But when the call comes, Entertainers have to forget grudges and gripes and envies and jealousies-and remember, they're lively people with sharp emotions-because there isn't any time then for anything but *help and don't ask who!*

And, deep inside her, a good Entertainer doesn't care who. Take the way it shaped up this time. It was pretty clear to me I ought to shift to Illy, although I wasn't quite easy in my mind about leaving Erich, because the Lunan was a long time from home and, after all, Erich was among anthropoids. Ilhilihis needed someone who was *simpatico.*

I like Illy and not just because he is a sort of tall cross between a spider monkey and a persian cat-though that is a handsome combo when you come to think of it. I like him for himself. So when he came in all lopped and shaky after a mean operation, I was the right person to look out for him. Now I've made my little speech and know-nothings in the Change World can go on making their bum jokes. But I ask you, how could an arrangement between Illy and me be anything but Platonic?

We might have had some octopoid girls and nymphs in stock-Sid couldn't be sure until he checked-but Ilhilihis and Sevensee voted for real people and I knew Sid saw it their way. Maud squeezed Mark's hand and tripped over to Sevensee ("Those are sharp hoofs you got, man" —she's picked up some of my language, like she has everything else), though Beau did frown over his shoulder at Lili from the piano, maybe to argue that she ought to take on the ET, as Mark had been a real casualty and could use live nursing. But it was plain as day to anybody but Beau that Bruce and Lili were a big thing and the last to be disturbed.

Erich acted stiffly hurt at losing me, but I knew he wasn't. He thinks he has a great technique with Ghostgirls and he likes to show it off, and he really is pretty slick at it, if you go for that sort of thing and-yang my yin! —who doesn't at times?

And when Sid formally wafted the Countess out of Stores —a real blonde stunner in a white satin hobble skirt with a white egret swaying up from her tiny hat, way ahead of Maud and Lili and me when it came to looks, though transparent as cigarette smoke-and when Erich clicked his heels and bowed over her hand and proudly conducted her to a couch, black Svengali to her Trilby, and started to German-talk some life into her with much head cocking and toothy smiling and a flow of witty flattery, and when she began to flirt back and the dream look in her eyes sharpened hungrily and focused on him-well, then I knew that Erich was happy and felt he was doing proud by the *Reichswehr*. No, my little commandant wasn't worrying me on that score.

Mark had drawn a Greek hetaera, name of Phryne; I suppose not the one who maybe still does the famous courtroom striptease back in Athens, and he was waking her up with little sips of his scotch and soda, though, from some looks he'd flashed, I got the idea Kaby was the kid he really went for. Sid was coaxing the fighting gal to take some high-energy bread and olives along with the wine, and, for a wonder, Doc seemed to be carrying on an animated and rational conversation with Sevensee and Maud, maybe comparing notes on the Northern Venusian Shallows, and Beau had got on to Panther Rag, and Bruce and Lili were leaning on the piano, smiling very appreciatively, but talking to each other a mile a minute.

Illy turned back from inspecting them all and squeaked, "Animals with clothes are so refreshing, dahling! Like you're all carrying banners!"

Maybe he had something there, though my banners were kind of Ash Wednesday, a charcoal gray sweater and skirt. He looked at my mouth with a tentacle to see how I was smiling and he squeaked softly, "Do I seem dull and commonplace to you, Greta girl, because I haven't got banners? Just another Zombie from a billion years in your past, as gray and lifeless as Luna is today, not as when she was a real dreamy sister planet simply bursting with air and water and feather forests. Or am I as strangely interesting to you as you are to me, girl from a billion years in my future?"

"Illy, you're sweet," I told him, giving him a little pat. I noticed his fur was still vibrating nervously and I decided the heck with Sid's orders, I'm going to pump him about what he was doing with Kaby and the satyr. Couldn't have him a billion years from home and bottled up, too. Besides, I was curious.

Chapter 6
Crete Circa 1300 B.C.

> Maiden, Nymph, and Mother are the eternal royal Trinity of the island, and the Goddess, who is worshipped there in each of these aspects, as New Moon, Full Moon, and Old Moon, is the sovereign Deity.

—Graves

Kaby pushed back at Sid some seconds of bread and olives, and, when he raised his bushy eyebrows, gave him a curt nod that meant she knew what she was doing. She stood up and sort of took a position. All the talk quieted down fast, even Bruce's and Lili's. Kaby's face and voice weren't strained now, but they weren't relaxed either.

"Woe to Spider! Woe to Cretan! Heavy is the news I bring you. Bear it bravely, like strong women. When we got the gun unlimbered, I heard seaweed fry and crackle. We three leaped behind the rock wall, saw our gun grow white as sunlight in a heat-ray of the Serpents! Natch, we feared we were outnumbered and I called upon my Caller."

I don't know how she does it, but she does-in English too. That is, when she figures she's got something important to report, and maybe she needs a little time to get ready.

Beau claims that all the ancients fit their thoughts into measured lines as naturally as we pick a word that will do, but I'm not sure how good the Vicksburg language department is. Though why I should wonder about things like that when I've got Kaby spouting the stuff right in front of me, I don't know.

"But I didn't die there, kiddos. I still hoped to hurt the Greek ships, maybe with the Snake's own heat gun. So I quick tried to outflank them. My two comrades crawled beside me-they are males, but they have courage. Soon we spied the ambush-setters. They were Snakes and they were many, filthily disguised as Cretans."

There was an indignant murmur at this, for our cutthroat Change War has its code, the Soldiers tell me. Being an Entertainer, I don't have to say what I think.

"They had seen us when we saw them," Kaby swept on, "and they loosed a killing volley. Heat- and knife-rays struck about us in a storm of wind and fire, and the Lunan lost a feeler, fighting for Crete's Triple Goddess. So we dodged behind a sand hill, steered our flight back toward the water. It was awful, what we saw there: Crete's brave ships all sunk or sinking, blue sky sullied by their death-smoke. Once again the Greeks had licked us! —aided by the filthy Serpents.

"Round our wrecks, their black ships scurried, like black beetles, filth their diet, yet this day they dine on heroes. On the quiet sunlit beach there, I could feel a Change Gale blowing, working changes deep inside me, aches and pains that were a stranger's. Half my memories were doubled, half my lifeline crooked and twisted, three new moles upon my sword-hand. Goddess, Goddess, Triple Goddess —"

Her voice wavered and Sid reached out a hand, but she straightened her back.

"Triple Goddess, give me courage to tell everything that happened. We ran down into the water, hoping to escape by diving. We had hardly gotten under when the heat-rays hit above us, turning all the cool green surface to a roaring white inferno. But as I believe I told you, I was calling on my Caller, and a Door now opened to us, deep below the deadly steam-clouds. We dived in like frightened minnows and a lot of water with us."

Off Chicago's Gold Coast, Dave once gave me a lesson in skin-diving and, remembering it, I got a flash of Kaby's Door in the dark depths.

"For a moment, all was chaos. Then the Door slammed shut behind us. We'd been picked up in time's nick by-an Express Room of our Spiders! —sloshing two feet deep in water, much more cramped for space than this Place. It was manned by a magician, an old coot named Benson-Carter. He dispelled the water quickly and reported on his Caller. We'd got dry, were feeling human, Illy here had shed his swimsuit, when we looked at the Maintainer. It was glowing, changing, melting! And when Benson-Carter touched it, he fell backward-death was in him. Then the Void began to darken, narrow, shrink and close around us, so I called upon my Caller-without wasting time, let me tell you!

"We can't say for sure what was it slowly squeezed that sweet Express Room, but we fear the dirty Snakes have found a way to find our Places and attack outside the cosmos! —found the Spiderweb that links us in the Void's gray less-than-nothing."

No murmur this time. This reaction was genuine; we'd been hit where we lived and I could see everybody was scared as sick as I was. Except maybe Bruce and Lili, who were still holding hands and beaming gently. I decided they were the kind that love makes brave, which it doesn't do to me. It just gives me two people to worry about.

"I can see you dig our feelings," Kaby continued. "This thing scared the pants off of us. If we could have, we'd have even Introverted the Maintainer, broken all the ties that bind us, chanced it incommunicado. But the little old Maintainer was a seething red-hot puddle filled with bubbles big as handballs. We sat tight and watched the Void close. I kept calling on my Caller."

I squeezed my eyes shut, but that made it easier to see the three of them with the Void shutting down on them. (Was ours still behaving? Yes, Bibi Miriam.) Poetry or no poetry, it got me.

"Benson-Carter, lying dying, also thought the Snakes had done it. And he knew that death was in him, so he whispered me his mission, giving me precise instructions: how to press the seven death's hands, starting lockside counterclockwise, one, three, five, six, two, four, seven, then you have a half an hour; after you have pressed the seven, do not monkey with the buttons-get out fast and don't stop moving."

I wasn't getting this part and I couldn't see that anyone else was, though Bruce was whispering to Lili. I remembered seeing skulls engraved on the bronze chest. I looked at Illy and he nodded a tentacle and spread two to say, I guessed, that yes, Benson-Carter had said something like that, but no, Illy didn't know much about it.

"All these things and more he whispered," Kaby went on, "with the last gasps of his life-force, telling all his secret orders-for he'd not been sent to get us, he was on a separate mission, when he heard my SOSs. Sid, it's you he was to contact, as the first leg of his mission, pick up from you three black hussars, death's-head Demons, daring Soldiers, then to wait until the Places next match rhythm with the cosmos-matter of two mealtimes, barely-and to tune in northern Egypt in the age of the last Caesar, in the year of Rome's swift downfall, there to start an operation in a battle near a city named for Thrace's Alexander, there to change the course of battle, blow sky-high the stinking Serpents, all their agents, all their Zombies!

"Goddess, pardon, now I savvy how you've guided my least footstep, when I thought you'd gone and left me-for I flubbed your three-mole signal. We've found Sid's Place, that's the first leg, and I see the three black hussars, and we've brought with us the weapon and the Parthian disguises, salvaged from the doomed Express Room when your Door appeared in time's nick, and the Room around us closing spewed us through before it vanished with the corpse of Benson-Carter. Triple Goddess, draw the milk now from the womanhood I flaunt here and inject the blackest hatred! Vengeance now upon the Serpents, vengeance sweet in northern Egypt, for your island, Crete, Goddess! —and a victory for the Spiders! Goddess, Goddess, we can swing it!"

The roar that made me try to stop my ears with my shoulders didn't come from Kaby-she'd spoken her piece-but from Sid. The dear boy was purple enough to make me want to remind him you can die of high blood pressure just as easy in the Change World.

"Dump me with ops! 'Sblood, I'll not endure it! Is this a battle post? They'll be mounting operations from field hospitals next. Kabysia Labrys, thou art mad to suggest it. And what's this prattle of locks, clocks, and death's heads, buttons and monkeys? This brabble, this farrago, this hocus-pocus! And where's the weapon you prate of? In that whoreson bronze casket, I suppose."

She nodded, looking blank and almost a little shy as poetic possession faded from her. Her answer came like its faltering last echo.

"It is nothing but a tiny tactical atomic bomb."

Chapter 7
Time to Think

After about 0.1 millisecond (one ten-thousandth part of a second) has elapsed, the radius of the ball of fire is some 45 feet, and the temperature is then in the vicinity of 300,000 degrees Centigrade. At this instant, the luminosity, as observed at a distance of 100,000 yards (5.7 miles), is approximately 100 times that of the sun as seen at the earth's surface ... the ball of fire expands very rapidly to its maximum radius of 450 feet within less than a second from the explosion.

—Los Alamos

Brother, that was all we needed to make everybody but Kaby and the two ETs start yelping at once, me included. It may seem strange that Change People, able to whiz through time and space and roust around outside the cosmos and knowing at least by hearsay of weapons a billion years in the future, like the Mindbomb, should panic at being shut in with a little primitive mid-20th Century gadget. Well, they feel the same as atomic scientists would feel if a Bengal tiger were brought into their laboratory, neither more nor less scared.

I'm a moron at physics, but I do know the Fireball is bigger than the Place. Remember that, besides the bomb, we'd recently been presented with a lot of other fears we hadn't had time to cope with, especially the business of the Snakes having learned how to get at our Places and melt the Maintainers and collapse them. Not to mention the general impression-first Saint Petersburg, then Crete-that the whole Change War was going against the Spiders.

Yet, in a free corner of my mind, I was shocked at how badly we were all panicking. It made me admit what I didn't like to: that we were all in pretty much the same state as Doc, except that the bottle didn't happen to be our out.

And had the rest of us been controlling our drinking so well lately?

Maud yelled, "Jettison it!" and pulled away from the satyr and ran from the bronze chest. Beau, harking back to what they'd thought of doing in the Express Room when it was too late, hissed, "Sirs, we must Introvert," and vaulted over the piano bench and legged it for the control divan. Erich seconded him with a white-faced *"Gott in Himmel, ja!"* from beside the surly, forgotten Countess, holding, by its slim stem, an empty, rose-stained wine glass.

I felt my mind flinch, because Introverting a Place is several degrees worse than foxholing. It's supposed not only to keep the Door tight shut, but also to lock it so even the Change Winds can't get through-cut the Place loose from the cosmos altogether.

I'd never talked with anyone from a Place that had been Introverted.

Mark dumped Phryne off his lap and ran after Maud. The Greek Ghostgirl, quite solid now, looked around with sleepy fear and fumbled her apple-green chiton together at the throat. She wrenched my attention away from everyone else for a moment, and I couldn't help wondering whether the person or Zombie back in the cosmos, from whose lifeline the Ghost has been taken, doesn't at least have strange dreams or thoughts when something like this happens.

Sid stopped Beau, though he almost got bowled over doing it, and he held the gambler away from the Maintainer in a bear hug and bellowed over his shoulders, "Masters, are you mad? Have you lost your wits? Maud! Mark! Marcus! Magdalene! On your lives, unhand that casket!"

Maud had swept the clothes and bows and quivers and stuff off it and was dragging it out from the bar toward the Door sector, so as to dump it through fast when we got one, I guess, while Mark acted as if he were trying to help her and wrestle it away from her at the same time.

They kept on as if they hadn't heard a word Sid said, with Mark yelling, "Let go, *meretrix!* This holds Rome's answer to Parthia on the Nile."

Kaby watched them as if she wanted to help Mark but scorned to scuffle with a mere-well, Mark had said it in Latin, I guess-call girl.

Then, on the top of the bronze chest, I saw those seven lousy skulls starting at the lock as plain as if they'd been under a magnifying glass, though ordinarily they'd have been a vague circle to my eyes at the distance, and I lost my mind and started to run in the opposite direction, but Illy whipped three tentacles around me, gentle-like, and squeaked, "Easy now, Greta girl, don't you be doing it, too. Hold still or Papa spank. My, my, but you two-leggers can whirl about when you have a mind to."

My stampede had carried his featherweight body a couple of yards, but it stopped me and I got my mind back, partly.

"Unhand it, I say!" Sid repeated without accomplishing anything, and he released Beau, though he kept a hand near the gambler's shoulder.

Then my fat friend from Lynn Regis looked real distraught at the Void and blustered at no one in particular, "'Sdeath, think you I'd mutiny against my masters, desert the Spiders, go to ground like a spent fox and pull my hole in after me? A plague of such cowardice! Who suggests it? Introversion's no mere last-ditch device. Unless ordered, supervised and sanctioned, it means the end. And what if I'd Introverted ere we got Kaby's call for succor, hey?"

His warrior maid nodded with harsh approval and he noticed it and shook his free hand at her and scolded her, "Not that I say yea to your mad plan for that Devil's casket, you half-clad lackwit. And yet to jettison.... Oh, ye gods, ye gods —" he wiped his hand across his face — "grant me a minute in which I may think!"

Thinking time wasn't an item even on the strictly limited list at the moment, although Sevensee, squatting dourly on his hairy haunches where Maud had left him, threw in a dead-pan "Thas tellin em, Gov."

Then Doc at the bar stood up tall as Abe Lincoln in his top hat and shawl and 19th Century duds and raised an unwavering arm for silence and said something that sounded like: "Introversh, inversh, glovsh," and then his enunciation switched to better than perfect as he continued, "I know to an absolute certainty what we must do."

It showed me how rabbity we were that the Place got quiet as a church while we all stopped whatever we were doing and waited breathless for a poor drunk to tell us how to save ourselves.

He said something like, "Inversh ... bosh ..." and held our eyes for a moment longer. Then the light went out of his and he slobbered out a *"Nichevo"* and slid an arm far along the bar for a bottle and started to pour it down his throat without stopping sliding.

Before he completed his collapse to the floor, in the split second while our attention was still focused on the bar, Bruce vaulted up on top of it, so fast it was almost like he'd popped up from nowhere, though I'd seen him start from behind the piano.

"I've a question. Has anyone here triggered that bomb?" he said in a voice that was very clear and just loud enough. "So it can't go off," he went on after just the right pause, his easy grin and brisk manner putting more heart into me all the time. "What's more, if it were to be triggered, we'd still have half an hour. I believe you said it had that long a fuse?"

He stabbed a finger at Kaby. She nodded.

"Right," he said. "It'd have to be that long for whoever plants it in the Parthian camp to get away. There's another safety margin.

"Second question. Is there a locksmith in the house?"

For all Bruce's easiness, he was watching us like a golden eagle and he caught Beau's and Maud's affirmatives before they had a chance to explain or hedge them and said, "That's very good. Under certain circumstances, you two'd be the ones to go to work on the chest. But before we consider that, there's Question Three: Is anyone here an atomics technician?"

That one took a little conversation to straighten out, Illy having to explain that, yes, the Early Lunans had atomic power-hadn't they blasted the life off their planet with it and made all those ghastly craters? —but no, he wasn't a technician exactly, he was a "thinger" (I thought at first his squeakbox was lisping); what was a thinger? —well, a thinger was someone who manipulated things in a way that was truly impossible to describe, but no, you couldn't possibly thing atomics; the idea was quite ridiculous, so he couldn't be an atomics thinger; the term was worse than a contradiction, well, really! —while Sevensee, from his two-thousand-millennia advantage of the Lunan, grunted to the effect that his culture didn't rightly use any kind of power, but just sort of moved satyrs and stuff by wrestling space-time around, "or think em roun ef we hafta. Can't think em in the Void, tho, wus luck. Hafta have —I dunno wut. Dun havvit anyhow."

"So we don't have an A-tech," Bruce summed up, "which makes it worse than useless, down-right dangerous, to tamper with the chest. We wouldn't know what to do if we did get inside safely. One more question." He directed it toward Sid. "How long before we can jettison anything?"

Sid, looking a shade jealous, yet mostly grateful for the way Bruce had calmed his chickens, started to explain, but Bruce didn't seem to be taking any chance of losing his audience, and as soon as Sid got to the word "rhythm," he pulled the answer away from him.

"In brief, not until we can effectively tune in on the cosmos again. Thank you, Master Less-ingham. That's at least five hours-two mealtimes, as the Cretan officer put it," and he threw Kaby a quick soldierly smile. "So, whether the bomb goes to Egypt or elsewhere, there's not a thing we can do about it for five hours. All right then!"

His smile blinked out like a light and he took a couple of steps up and down the bar, as if measuring the space he had. Two or three cocktail glasses sailed off and popped, but he didn't seem to notice them and we hardly did either. It was creepy the way he kept staring from one to another of us. We had to look up. Behind his face, with the straight golden hair flirting around it, was only the Void.

"All right then," he repeated suddenly. "We're twelve Spiders and two Ghosts, and we've time for a bit of a talk, and we're all in the same bloody boat, fighting the same bloody war, so we'll all know what we're talking about. I raised the subject a while back, but I was steamed up about a glove, and it was a big jest. All right! But now the gloves are off!"

Bruce ripped them out of his belt where they'd been tucked and slammed them down on the bar, to be kicked off the next time he paced back and forth, and it wasn't funny.

"Because," he went right on, "I've been getting a completely new picture of what this Spiders' war has been doing to each one of us. Oh, it's jolly good sport to slam around in space and time and then have a rugged little party outside both of them when the operation's over. It's sweet to know there's no cranny of reality so narrow, no privacy so intimate or sacred, no wall of was or will be strong enough, that we can't shoulder in. Knowledge is a glamorous thing, sweeter than lust or gluttony or the passion of fighting and including all three, the ultimate insatiable hunger, and it's great to be Faust, even in a pack of other Fausts.

"It's sweet to jigger reality, to twist the whole course of a man's life or a culture's, to ink out his or its past and scribble in a new one, and be the only one to know and gloat over the changes-hah! killing men or carrying off women isn't in it for glutting the sense of power. It's sweet to feel the Change Winds blowing through you and know the pasts that were and the past that is and the pasts that may be. It's sweet to wield the Atropos and cut a Zombie or Unborn out of his lifeline and look the Doubleganger in the face and see the Resurrection-glow in it and Recruit a brother, welcome a newborn fellow Demon into our ranks and decide whether he'll best fit as Soldier, Entertainer, or what.

"Or he can't stand Resurrection, it fries or freezes him, and you've got to decide whether to return him to his lifeline and his Zombie dreams, only they'll be a little grayer and horrider than they were before, or whether, if she's got that tantalizing something, to bring her shell along for a Ghostgirl-that's sweet, too. It's even sweet to have Change Death poised over your neck, to know that the past isn't the precious indestructible thing you've been taught it was, to know that there's no certainty about the future either, whether there'll even be one, to know that no part of reality is holy, that the cosmos itself may wink out like a flicked switch and God be not and nothing left but nothing!"

He threw out his arms against the Void. "And knowing all that, it's doubly sweet to come through the Door into the Place and be out of the worst of the Change Winds and enjoy a well-earned Recuperation and share the memories of all these sweetnesses I've been talking about, and work out all the fascinating feelings you've been accumulating back in the cosmos, layer by black layer, in the company of and with the help of the best bloody little band of fellow Fausts and Faustines going!

"Oh, it's a sweet life, all right, but I'm asking you —" and here his eyes stabbed us again, one by one, fast —"I'm asking you what it's done to us. I've been getting a completely new picture, as I said, of what my life was and what it could have been if there'd been changes of the sort that even we Demons can't make, and what my life is. I've been watching how we've all been responding to things just now, to the news of Saint Petersburg and to what the Cretan officer told beautifully-only it wasn't beautiful what she had to tell-and mostly to that bloody box of bomb. And I'm simply asking each one of you, what's happened to you?"

He stopped his pacing and stuck his thumbs in his belt and seemed to be listening to the wheels turning in at least eleven other heads-only I stopped mine pretty quick, with Dave and Father and the Rape of Chicago coming up out of the dark on the turn and Mother and the Indiana Dunes and Jazz Limited just behind them, followed by the unthinkable thing the Spider doctor had flicked into existence when I flopped as a nurse, because I can't stand that to be done to my mind by anybody but myself.

I stopped them by using the old infallible Entertainers' gimmick, a fast survey of the most interesting topic there is-other people's troubles.

Offhand, Beau looked as if he had most troubles, shamed by his boss and his girl given her heart to a Soldier; he was hugging them to himself very quiet.

I didn't stop for the two ETs-they're too hard to figure-or for Doc; nobody can tell whether a fallen-down drunk's at the black or bright end of his cycle; you just know it's cycling.

Maud ought to be suffering as much as Beau, called names and caught out in a panic, which always hurts her because she's plus three hundred years more future than the rest of us and figures she ought to be that much wiser, which she isn't always-not to mention she's over fifty years old, though her home-century cosmetic science keeps her looking and acting teenage most of the time. She'd backed away from the bronze chest so as not to stand out, and now Lili came from behind the piano and stood beside her.

Lili had the opposite of troubles, a great big glow for Bruce, proud as a promised princess watching her betrothed. Erich frowned when he saw her, for he seemed proud too, proud of the way his *Kamerad* had taken command of us panicky whacks *Führer*-fashion. Sid still looked mostly grateful and inclined to let Bruce keep on talking.

Even Kaby and Mark, those two dragons hot for battle, standing a little in front and to one side of us by the bronze chest, like its guardians, seemed willing to listen. They made me realize one reason Sid had for letting Bruce run on, although the path his talk was leading us down was flashing with danger signals: When it was over, there'd still be the problem of what to do with the bomb, and a real opposition shaping up between Soldiers and Entertainers, and Sid was hoping a solution would turn up in the meantime or at least was willing to put off the evil day.

But beyond all that, and like the rest of us, I could tell from the way Sid was squinting his browy eyes and chewing his beardy lip that he was shaken and moved by what Bruce had said. This New Boy had dipped into our hearts and counted our kicks so beautifully, better than most of us could have done, and then somehow turned them around so that we had to think of what messes and heels and black sheep and lost lambs we were-well, we wanted to keep on listening.

Chapter 8
A Place to Stand

Give me a place to stand, and I will move the world.

—Archimedes

Bruce's voice had a faraway touch and he was looking up left at the Void as he said, "Have you ever really wondered why the two sides of this war are called the Snakes and the Spiders? Snakes may be clear enough-you always call the enemy something dirty. But Spiders-our name for ourselves? Bear with me, Ilhilihis; I know that no being is created dirty or malignant by Nature, but this is a matter of anthropoid feelings and folkways. Yes, Mark, I know that some of your legions have nicknames like the Drunken Lions and the Snails, and that's about as insulting as calling the British Expeditionary Force the Old Contemptibles.

"No, you'd have to go to bands of vicious youths in cities slated for ruin to find a habit of naming like ours, and even they would try to brighten up the black a bit. But simply-Spiders. And Snakes, for that's their name for themselves too, you know. Spiders and Snakes. What are our masters, that we give them names like that?"

It gave me the shivers and set my mind working in a dozen directions and I couldn't stop it, although it made the shivers worse.

Illy beside me now —I'd never given it a thought before, but he did have eight legs of a sort, and I remembered thinking of him as a spider monkey, and hadn't the Lunans had wisdom and atomic power and a billion years in which to get the Change War rolling?

Or suppose, in the far future, Terra's own spiders evolved intelligence and a cruel cannibal culture. They'd be able to keep their existence secret. I had no idea of who or what would be on Earth in Sevensee's day, and wouldn't it be perfect black hairy poisoned spider-mentality to spin webs secretly through the world of thought and all of space and time?

And Beau-wasn't there something real Snaky about him, the way he moved and all?

Spiders and Snakes. *Spinne und Schlange*, as Erich called them. S & S. But SS stood for the Nazi *Schutzstaffel*, the Black Shirts, and what if some of those cruel, crazy Jerries had discovered time travel and —I brought myself up with a jerk and asked myself, "Greta, how nuts can you get?"

From where he was on the floor, the front of the bar his sounding board, Doc shrieked up at Bruce like one of the damned from the pit, "Don't speak against the Spiders! Don't blaspheme! They can hear the Unborn whisper. Others whip only the skin, but they whip the naked brain and heart," and Erich called out, "That's enough, Bruce!"

But Bruce didn't spare him a look and said, "But whatever the Spiders are and no matter how much whip they use, it's plain as the telltale on the Maintainer that the Change War is not only going against them, but getting away from them. Dwell for a bit on the current flurry of stupid slugging and panicky anachronism, when we all know that anachronism is what gets the Change Winds out of control. This punch-drunk pounding on the Cretan-Dorian fracas as if it were the only battle going and the only way to work things. Whisking Constantine from Britain to the Bosporus by rocket, sending a pocket submarine back to sail with the Armada against Drake's woodensides —I'll wager you hadn't heard those! And now, to save Rome, an atomic bomb.

"Ye gods, they could have used Greek fire or even dynamite, but a fission weapon.... I leave you to imagine what gaps and scars that will make in what's left of history-the smothering of Greece and the vanishment of Provence and the troubadours and the Papacy's Irish Captivity won't be in it!"

The cut on his cheek had opened again and was oozing a little, but he didn't pay any attention to it, and neither did we, as his lips thinned in irony and he said, "But I'm forgetting that this is a cosmic war and that the Spiders are conducting operations on billions, trillions of planets and inhabited gas clouds through millions of ages and that we're just one little world-one little solar system, Sevensee-and we can hardly expect our inscrutable masters, with all their pressing preoccupations and far-flung responsibilities, to be especially understanding or tender in their treatment of our pet books and centuries, our favorite prophets and periods, or unduly concerned about preserving any of the trifles that we just happen to hold dear.

"Perhaps there are some sentimentalists who would rather die forever than go on living in a world without the *Summa*, the Field Equations, *Process and Reality*, *Hamlet*, Matthew, Keats, and the *Odyssey*, but our masters are practical creatures, ministering to the needs of those rugged souls who want to go on living no matter what."

Erich's "Bruce, I'm telling you that's enough," was lost in the quickening flow of the New Boy's words. "I won't spend much time on the minor signs of our major crack-up —the canceling of leaves, the sharper shortages, the loss of the Express Room, the use of Recuperation Stations for ops and all the other frantic patchwork-last operation but one, we were saddled with three Soldiers from outside the Galaxy and, no fault of theirs, they were no earthly use. Such little things might happen at a bad spot in any war and are perhaps only local. But there's a big thing."

He paused again, to let us wonder, I guess. Maud must have worked her way over to me, for I felt her dry little hand on my arm and she whispered out of the side of her mouth, "What do we do now?"

"We listen," I told her the same way. I felt a little impatient with her need to be doing something about things.

She cocked a gold-dusted eyebrow at me and murmured, "You, too?"

I didn't get to ask her me, too, what? Crush on Bruce? Nuts! —because just then Bruce's voice took up again in the faraway range.

"Have you ever asked yourselves how many operations the fabric of history can stand before it's all stitches, whether too much Change won't one day wear out the past? And the present and the future, too, the whole bleeding business. Is the law of the Conservation of Reality any more than a thin hope given a long name, a prayer of theoreticians? Change Death is as certain as Heat Death, and far faster. Every operation leaves reality a bit cruder, a bit uglier, a bit more makeshift, and a whole lot less rich in those details and feelings that are our heritage, like the crude penciled sketch on canvas when you've stripped off the paint.

"If that goes on, won't the cosmos collapse into an outline of itself, then nothing? How much thinning can reality stand, having more and more Doublegangers cut out of it? And there's another thing about every operation-it wakes up the Zombies a little more, and as its Change Winds die, it leaves them a little more disturbed and nightmare-ridden and frazzled. Those of you who have been on operations in heavily worked-over temporal areas will know what I mean-that look they give you out of the sides of their eyes as if to say, 'You again? For Christ's sake, go away. We're the dead. We're the ones who don't want to wake up, who don't want to be Demons and hate to be Ghosts. Stop torturing us.'"

I looked around at the Ghostgirls; I couldn't help it. They'd somehow got together on the control divan, facing us, their backs to the Maintainers. The Countess had dragged along the bottle of wine Erich had fetched her earlier and they were passing it back and forth. The Countess had a big rose splotch across the ruffled white lace of her blouse.

Bruce said, "There'll come a day when all the Zombies and all the Unborn wake up and go crazy together and figuratively come marching at us in their numberless hordes, saying, 'We've had enough.'"

But I didn't turn back to Bruce right away. Phryne's chiton had slipped off one shoulder and she and the Countess were sitting sagged forward, elbows on knees, legs spread-at least, as far as the Countess's hobble skirt would let her-and swayed toward each other a little. They were still surprisingly solid, although they hadn't had any personal attention for a half hour, and they were looking up over my head with half-shut eyes and they seemed, so help me, to be listening to what Bruce was saying and maybe hearing some of it.

"We make a careful distinction between Zombies and Unborn, between those troubled by our operations whose lifelines lie in the past and those whose lifelines lie in the future. But is there any distinction any longer? Can we tell the difference between the past and the future? Can we any longer locate the now, the real now of the cosmos? The Places have their own nows, the now of the Big Time we're on, but that's different and it's not made for real living.

"The Spiders tell us that the real now is somewhere in the last half of the 20th Century, which means that several of us here are also alive in the cosmos, have lifelines along which the now is traveling. But do you swallow that story quite so easily, Ilhilihis, Sevensee? How does it strike the servants of the Triple Goddess? The Spiders of Octavian Rome? The Demons of Good Queen Bess? The gentlemen Zombies of the Greater South? Do the Unborn man the starships, Maud?

"The Spiders also tell us that, although the fog of battle makes the now hard to pin down precisely, it will return with the unconditional surrender of the Snakes and the establishment of cosmic peace, and roll on as majestically toward the future as before, quickening the continuum with its passage. Do you really believe that? Or do you believe, as I do, that we've used up all the future as well as the past, wasted it in premature experience, and that we've had the real now smudged out of existence, stolen from us forever, the precious now of true growth, the child-moment in which all life lies, the moment like a newborn baby that is the only home for hope there is?"

He let that start to sink in, then took a couple of quick steps and went on, his voice rising over Erich's "Bruce, for the last time —" and seeming to pick up a note of hope from the very word he had used, "But although things look terrifyingly black, there remains a chance-the slimmest chance, but still a chance-of saving the cosmos from Change Death and restoring reality's richness and giving the Ghosts good sleep and perhaps even regaining the real now. We have the means right at hand. What if the power of time traveling were used not for war and destruction, but for healing, for the mutual enrichment of the ages, for quiet communication and growth, in brief, to bring a peace message —"

But my little commandant is quite an actor himself and knows a wee bit about the principles of scene-stealing, and he was not going to let Bruce drown him out as if he were just another extra playing a Voice from the Mob. He darted across our front, between us and the bar, took a running leap, and landed bang on the bloody box of bomb.

A bit later, Maud was silently showing me the white ring above her elbow where I'd grabbed her and Illy was teasing a clutch of his tentacles out of my other hand and squeaking reproachfully, "Greta girl, don't ever do that."

Erich was standing on the chest and I noticed that his boots carefully straddled the circle of skulls, and I should have known anyway you could hardly push them in the right order by jumping on them, and he was pointing at Bruce and saying, "—and that means mutiny, my young sir. *Um Gottes willen*, Bruce, listen to me and step down before you say anything worse. I'm older than you, Bruce. Mark's older. Trust in your *Kameraden*. Guide yourself by their knowledge."

He had got my attention, but I had much rather have him black my eye.

"You older than me?" Bruce was grinning. "When your twelve-years' advantage was spent in soaking up the wisdom of a race of sadistic dreamers gone paranoid, in a world whose thought-stream had already been muddied by one total war? Mark older than me? When all his ideas and loyalties are those of a wolf pack of unimaginative sluggers two thousand years younger than I am? Either of you older because you have more of the killing cynicism that is all the wisdom the Change World ever gives you? Don't make me laugh!

"I'm an Englishman, and I come from an epoch when total war was still a desecration and the flowers and buds of thoughts not yet whacked off or blighted. I'm a poet and poets are wiser than anyone because they're the only people who have the guts to think and feel at the same time. Right, Sid? When I talk to all of you about a peace message, I want you to think about it concretely in terms of using the Places to bring help across the mountains of time when help is really needed, not to bring help that's undeserved or knowledge that's premature or contaminating, sometimes not to bring anything at all, but just to check with infinite tenderness and concern that everything's safe and the glories of the universe unfolding as they were intended to —"

"Yes, you are a poet, Bruce," Erich broke in. "You can tootle soulfully on the flute and make us drip tears. You can let out the stops on the big organ pipes and make us tremble as if at Jehovah's footsteps. For the last twenty minutes, you have been giving us some very *charmante* poetry. But what are you? An Entertainer? Or are you a Soldier?"

Right then —I don't know what it was, maybe Sid clearing his throat —I could sense our feelings beginning to turn against Bruce. I got the strangest feeling of reality clamping down and bright colors going dull and dreams vanishing. Yet it was only then I also realized how much Bruce had moved us, maybe some of us to the verge of mutiny, even. I was mad at Erich for what he was doing, but I couldn't help admiring his cockiness.

I was still under the spell of Bruce's words and the more-than-words behind them, but then Erich would shift around a bit and one of his heels would kick near the death's-head pushbuttons and I wanted to stamp with spike heels on every death's-head button on his uniform. I didn't know exactly what I felt yet.

"Yes, I'm a Soldier," Bruce told him, "and I hope you won't ever have to worry about my courage, because it's going to take more courage than any operation we've ever planned, ever dreamed of, to carry the peace message to the other Places and to the wound-spots of the cosmos. Perhaps it will be a fast wicket and we'll be bowled down before we score a single run, but who cares? We may at least see our real masters when they come to smash us, and for me that will be a deep satisfaction. And we may do some smashing of our own."

"So you're a Soldier," Erich said, his smile showing his teeth. "Bruce, I'll admit that the half-dozen operations you've been on were rougher than anything I drew in my first hundred sleeps. For that, I am all honest sympathy. But that you should let them get you into such a state that love and a girl can turn you upside down and start you babbling about peace messages —"

"Yes, by God, love and a girl have changed me!" Bruce shouted at him, and I looked around at Lili and I remembered Dave saying, "I'm going to Spain," and I wondered if anything would ever again make my face flame like that. "Or, rather, they've made me stand up for what I've believed in all along. They've made me —"

"*Wunderbar,*" Erich called and began to do a little sissy dance on the bomb that set my teeth on edge. He bent his wrists and elbows at arty angles and stuck out a hip and ducked his head simperingly and blinked his eyes very fast. "Will you invite me to the wedding, Bruce? You'll have to get another best man, but I will be the flower girl and throw pretty little posies to all the distinguished guests. Here, Mark. Catch, Kaby. One for you, Greta. *Danke schön. Ach, zwei Herzen in dreivierteltakt ... ta-ta ... ta-ta ... ta-ta-ta-ta-ta...*"

"What the hell do you think a woman is?" Bruce raged. "Something to mess around with in your spare time?"

Erich kept on humming "Two Hearts in Waltz Time" —and jigging around to it, damn him-but he slipped in a nod to Bruce and a "Precisely." So I knew where I stood, but it was no news to me.

"Very well," Bruce said, "let's leave this Brown Shirt *maricón* to amuse himself and get down to business. I made all of you a proposal and I don't have to tell you how serious it is or how serious Lili and I are about it. We not only must infiltrate and subvert other Places, which luckily for us are made for infiltration, we also must make contact with the Snakes and establish working relationships with their Demons at our level as one of our first steps."

That stopped Erich's jig and got enough of a gasp from some of us to make it seem to come from practically everybody. Erich used it to work a change of pace.

"Bruce! We've let you carry this foolery further than we should. You seem to have the idea that because anything goes in the Place-dueling, drunkenness, *und so weiter* —you can say what you have and it will all be forgotten with the hangover. Not so. It is true that among such a set of monsters and free spirits as ourselves, and working as secret agents to boot, there cannot be the obvious military discipline that would obtain in a Terran army.

"But let me tell you, Bruce, let me grind it home into you-Sid and Kaby and Mark will bear me out in this, as officers of equivalent rank-that the Spider line of command stretches into and through this Place just as surely as the word of *der Führer* rules Chicago. And as I shouldn't have to emphasize to you, Bruce, the Spiders have punishments that would make my countrymen in Belsen and Buchenwald-well, pale a little. So while there is still a shadow of justification for our interpreting your remarks as utterly tasteless clowning —"

"Babble on," Bruce said, giving him a loose downward wave of his hand without looking. "I made you people a proposal." He paused. "How do you stand, Sidney Lessingham?"

Then I felt my legs getting weak, because Sid didn't answer right away. The old boy swallowed and started to look around at the rest of us. Then the feeling of reality clamping down got something awful, because he didn't look around, but straightened his back a little. Just then, Mark cut in fast.

"It grieves me, Bruce, but I think you are possessed. Erich, he must be confined."

Kaby nodded, almost absently. "Confine or kill the coward, whichever is easier, whip the woman, and let's get on to the Egyptian battle."

"Indeed, yes," Mark said. "I died in it. But now perhaps no longer."

Kaby said to him, "I like you, Roman."

Bruce was smiling, barely, and his eyes were moving and fixing. "You, Ilhilihis?"

Illy's squeak box had never sounded mechanical to me before, but it did as he answered, "I'm a lot deeper into borrowed time than the rest of you, tra-la-la, but Papa still loves living. Include me very much out, Brucie."

"Miss Davies?"

Beside me, Maud said flatly, "Do you think I'm a fool?" Beyond her, I saw Lili and I thought, "My God, I might look as proud if I were in her shoes, but I sure as hell wouldn't look as confident."

Bruce's eyes hadn't quite come to Beau when the gambler spoke up. "I have no cause to like you, sir, rather the opposite. But this Place has come to bore me more than Boston and I have always found it difficult to resist a long shot. A very long one, I fear. I am with you, sir."

There was a pain in my chest and a roaring in my ears and through it I heard Sevensee grunting, " —sicka these lousy Spiders. Deal me in."

And then Doc reared up in front of the bar and he'd lost his hat and his hair was wild and he grabbed an empty fifth by the neck and broke the bottom of it all jagged against the bar and he waved it and screeched, "*Ubivaytye Pauki —i Nyemetzi!*"

And right behind his words, Beau sang out fast the English of it, "Kill the Spiders-and the Germans!"

And Doc didn't collapse then, though I could see he was hanging onto the bar tight with his other hand, and the Place got stiller, inside and out, than I've ever known it, and Bruce's eyes were finally moving back toward Sid.

But the eyes stopped short of Sid and I heard Bruce say, "Miss Forzane?" and I thought, "That's funny," and I started to look around at the Countess, and felt all the eyes and I realized, "Hey, that's me! But this can't happen to me. To the others, yes, but not to me. I just work here. Not to Greta, no, no, no!"

But it had, and the eyes didn't let go, and the silence and the feeling of reality were Godawful, and I said to myself, "Greta, you've got to say something, if only a suitable four-letter word," and then suddenly I knew what the silence was like. It was like that of a big city if there were some way of shutting off all the noise in one second. It was like Erich's singing when the piano had deserted him. It was as if the Change Winds should ever die completely ... and I knew beforehand what had happened when I turned my back on them all.

The Ghostgirls were gone. The Major Maintainer hadn't merely been switched to Introvert. It was gone, too.

Chapter 9
A Locked Room

"We examined the moss between the bricks, and found it undisturbed."

"You looked among D — —'s papers, of course, and into the books of the library?"

"Certainly; we opened every package and parcel; we not only opened every book, but we turned over every leaf in each volume...."

—Poe

Three hours later, Sid and I plumped down on the couch nearest the kitchen, though too tired to want to eat for a while yet. A tighter search than I could ever have cooked up had shown that the Maintainer was not in the Place.

Of course it had to be in the Place, as we kept telling each other for the first two hours. It had to be, if circumstances and the theories we lived by in the Change World meant anything. A Maintainer is what maintains a Place. The Minor Maintainer takes care of oxygen, temperature, humidity, gravity, and other little life-cycle and matter-cycle things generally, but it's the Major Maintainer that keeps the walls from buckling and the ceiling from falling in. It is little, but oh my, it does so much.

It doesn't work by wires or radio or anything complicated like that. It just hooks into local space-time.

I have been told that its inside working part is made up of vastly tough, vastly hard giant molecules, each one of which is practically a vest-pocket cosmos in itself. Outside, it looks like a portable radio with a few more dials and some telltales and switches and plug-ins for earphones and a lot of other sensory thingumajigs.

But the Maintainer was gone and the Void hadn't closed in, yet. By this time, I was so fagged, I didn't care much whether it did or not.

One thing for sure, the Maintainer had been switched to Introvert before it was spirited away or else its disappearance automatically produced Introversion, take your choice, because we sure were Introverted-real nasty martinet-schoolmaster grip of reality on my thoughts that I knew, without trying, liquor wouldn't soften, not a breath of Change Wind, absolutely stifling, and the gray of the Void seeming so much inside my head that I think I got a glimmering of what the science boys mean when they explain to me that the Place is a kind of interweaving of the material and the mental —a Giant Monad, one of them called it.

Anyway, I said to myself, "Greta, if this is Introversion, I want no part of it. It is not nice to be cut adrift from the cosmos and know it. A lifeboat in the middle of the Pacific and a starship between galaxies are not in it for loneliness."

I asked myself why the Spiders had ever equipped Maintainers with Introversion switches anyway, when we couldn't drill with them and weren't supposed to use them except in an emergency so tight that it was either Introvert or surrender to the Snakes, and for the first time the obvious explanation came to me:

Introversion must be the same as scuttling, its main purpose to withhold secrets and materiel from the enemy. It put a place into a situation from which even the Spider high command couldn't rescue it, and there was nothing left but to sink down, down (out? up?), down into the Void.

If that was the case, our chances of getting back were about those of my being a kid again playing in the Dunes on the Small Time.

I edged a little closer to Sid and sort of squunched under his shoulder and rubbed my cheek against the smudged, gold-worked gray velvet. He looked down and I said, "A long way to Lynn Regis, eh, Siddy?"

"Sweetling, thou spokest a mouthful," he said. He knows very well what he is doing when he mixes his language that way, the wicked old darling.

"Siddy," I said, "why this gold-work? It'd be a lot smoother without it."

"Marry, men must prick themselves out and, 'faith I know not, but it helps if there's metal in it."

"And girls get scratched." I took a little sniff. "But don't put this doublet through the cleaner yet. Until we get out of the woods, I want as much you around as possible."

"Marry, and why should I?" he asked blankly, and I think he wasn't fooling me. The last thing time travelers find out is how they do or don't smell. Then his face clouded and he looked as though he wanted to squunch under my shoulder. "But 'faith, sweetling, your forest has a few more trees than Sherwood."

"Thou saidst it," I agreed, and wondered about the look. He oughtn't to be interested in my girlishness now. I knew I was a mess, but he had stuck pretty close to me during the hunt and you never can tell. Then I remembered that he was the other one who hadn't declared himself when Bruce was putting it to us, and it probably troubled his male vanity. Not me, though —I was still grateful to the Maintainer for getting me out of that spot, whatever other it had got us all into. It seemed ages ago.

We'd all jumped to the conclusion that the two Ghostgirls had run away with the Maintainer, I don't know where or why, but it looked so much that way. Maud had started yipping about how she'd never trusted Ghosts and always known that some day they'd start doing things on their own, and Kaby had got it firmly fixed in her head, right between the horns, that Phryne, being a Greek, was the ringleader and was going to wreak havoc on us all.

But when we were checking Stores the first time, I had noticed that the Ghostgirl envelopes looked flat. Ectoplasm doesn't take up much space when it's folded, but I had opened one anyway, then another, and then called for help.

Every last envelope was empty. We had lost over a thousand Ghostgirls, Sid's whole stock.

Well, at least it proved what none of us had ever seen or heard of being demonstrated: that there is a spooky link —a sort of Change Wind contact-between a Ghost and its lifeline; and when that umbilicus, I've heard it called, is cut, the part away from the lifeline dies.

Interesting, but what had bothered me was whether we Demons were going to evaporate too, because we are as much Doublegangers as the Ghosts and our apron strings had been cut just as surely. We're more solid, of course, but that would only mean we'd take a little longer. Very logical.

I remember I had looked up at Lili and Maud-us girls had been checking the envelopes; it's one of the proprieties we frequently maintain and anyway, if men check them, they're apt to trot out that old wheeze about "instant women" which I'm sick to death of hearing, thank you.

Anyway, I had looked up and said, "It's been nice knowing you," and Lili had said, "Twenty-three, skiddoo," and Maud had said, "Here goes nothing," and we had shook hands all around.

We figured that Phryne and the Countess had faded at the same time as the other Ghostgirls, but an idea had been nibbling at me and I said, "Siddy, do you suppose it's just barely possible that, while we were all looking at Bruce, those two Ghostgirls would have been able to work the Maintainer and get a Door and lam out of here with the thing?"

"Thou speakst my thoughts, sweetling. All weighs against it: Imprimis, 'tis well known that Ghosts cannot lay plots or act on them. Secundo, the time forbade getting a Door. Tercio-and here's the real meat of it-the Place folds without the Maintainer. Quadro, 'twere folly to depend on not one of-how many of us? ten, elf-not looking around in all the time it would have taken them —"

"I looked around once, Siddy. They were drinking and they had got to the control divan under their own power. Now when was that? Oh, yes, when Bruce was talking about Zombies."

"Yes, sweetling. And as I was about to cap my argument with quinquo when you 'gan prattle, I could have sworn none could touch the Maintainer, much less work it and purloin it, without my certain knowledge. Yet..."

"Eftsoons yet," I seconded him.

Somebody must have got a door and walked out with the thing. It certainly wasn't in the Place. The hunt had been a lulu. Something the size of a portable typewriter is not easy to hide and we had been inside everything from Beau's piano to the renewer link of the Refresher.

We had even fluoroscoped everybody, though it had made Illy writhe like a box of worms, as he'd warned us; he said it tickled terribly and I insisted on smoothing his fur for five minutes afterward, although he was a little standoffish toward me.

Some areas, like the bar, kitchen and Stores, took a long while, but we were thorough. Kaby helped Doc check Surgery: since she last made the Place, she has been stationed in a Field Hospital (it turns out the Spiders actually are mounting operations from them) and learned a few nice new wrinkles.

However, Doc put in some honest work on his own, though, of course, every check was observed by at least three people, not including Bruce or Lili. When the Maintainer vanished, Doc had pulled out of his glassy-eyed drunk in a way that would have surprised me if I hadn't seen it happen to him before, but when we finished Surgery and got on to the Art Gallery, he had started to putter and I noticed him hold out his coat and duck his head and whip out a flask and take a swig and by now he was well on his way toward another peak.

The Art Gallery had taken time too, because there's such a jumble of strange stuff, and it broke my heart but Kaby took her ax and split a beautiful blue woodcarving of a Venusian medusa because, although there wasn't a mark in the paw-polished surface, she claimed it was just big enough. Doc cried a little and we left him fitting the pieces together and mooning over the other stuff.

After we'd finished everything else, Mark had insisted on tackling the floor. Beau and Sid both tried to explain to him how this is a one-sided Place, that there is nothing, but nothing, under the floor; it just gets a lot harder than the diamonds crusting it as soon as you get a quarter inch down-that being the solid equivalent of the Void. But Mark was knuckle-headed (like all Romans, Sid assured me on the q.t.) and broke four diamond-plus drills before he was satisfied.

Except for some trick hiding places, that left the Void, and things don't vanish if you throw them at the Void-they half melt and freeze forever unless you can fish them out. Back of the Refresher, at about eye-level, are three Venusian coconuts that a Hittite strongman threw there during a major brawl. I try not to look at them because they are so much like witch heads they give me the woolies. The parts of the Place right up against the Void have strange spatial properties which one of the gadgets in Surgery makes use of in a way that gives me the worse woolies, but that's beside the point.

During the hunt, Kaby and Erich had used their Callers as direction finders to point out the Maintainer, just as they're used in the cosmos to locate the Door-and sometimes in the Big

Places, people tell me. But the Callers only went wild-like a compass needle whirling around without stopping-and nobody knew what that meant.

The trick hiding places were the Minor Maintainer, a cute idea, but it is no bigger than the Major and has its own mysterious insides and had obviously kept on doing its own work, so that was out for several reasons, and the bomb chest, though it seemed impossible for anyone to have opened it, granting they knew the secret of its lock, even before Erich jumped on it and put it in the limelight double. But when you've ruled out everything else, the word impossible changes meaning.

Since time travel is our business, a person might think of all sorts of tricks for sending the Maintainer into the past or future, permanently or temporarily. But the Place is strictly on the Big Time and everybody that should know tells me that time traveling *through* the Big Time is out. It's this way: the Big Time is a train, and the Little Time is the countryside and we're on the train, unless we go out a Door, and as Gertie Stein might put it, you can't time travel through the time you time travel in when you time travel.

I'd also played around with the idea of some fantastically obvious hiding place, maybe something that several people could pass back and forth between them, which would mean a conspiracy, and, of course, if you assume a big enough conspiracy, you can explain anything, including the cosmos itself. Still, I'd got a sort of shell-game idea about the Soldiers' three big black shakos and I hadn't been satisfied until I'd got the three together and looked in them all at the same time.

"Wake up, Greta, and take something. I can't stand here forever." Maud had brought us a tray of hearty snacks from then and yon, and I must say they were tempting; she whips up a mean hors d'oeuvre.

I looked them over and said, "Siddy, I want a hot dog."

"And I want a venison pasty! Out upon you, you finical jill, you o'erscrupulous jade, you whimsic and tyrannous poppet!"

I grabbed a handful and snuggled back against him.

"Go on, call me some more, Siddy," I told him. "Real juicy ones."

Chapter 10
Motives and Opportunities

> My thought, whose murder yet is but fantastical,
> Shakes so my single state of man that function
> Is smother'd in surmise, and nothing is
> But what is not.

—Macbeth

My big bad waif from King's Lynn had set the tray on his knees and started to wolf the food down. The others were finishing up. Erich, Mark and Kaby were having a quietly furious argument I couldn't overhear at the end of the bar nearest the bronze chest, and Illy was draped over the piano like a real octopus, listening in.

Beau and Sevensee were pacing up and down near the control divan and throwing each other a word now and then. Beyond them, Bruce and Lili were sitting on the opposite couch from us, talking earnestly about something. Maud had sat down at the other end of the bar and was knitting-it's one of the habits like chess and quiet drinking, or learning to talk by squeak box, that we pick up to pass the time in the Place in the long stretches between parties. Doc was fiddling around the Gallery, picking things up and setting them down, still managing to stay on his feet at any rate.

Lili and Bruce stood up, still gabbing intensely at each other, and Illy began to pick out with one tentacle a little tune in the high keys that didn't sound like anything on God's earth. "Where do they get all the energy?" I wondered.

As soon as I asked myself that, I knew the answer and I began to feel the same way myself. It wasn't energy; it was nerves, pure and simple.

Change is like a drug, I realized-you get used to the facts never staying the same, and one picture of the past and future dissolving into another maybe not very different but still different, and your mind being constantly goosed by strange moods and notions, like nightclub lights of shifting color with weird shadows between shining right on your brain.

The endless swaying and jogging is restful, like riding on a train.

You soon get to like the movement and to need it without knowing, and when it suddenly stops and you're just you and the facts you think from and feel from are exactly the same when you go back to them-boy, that's rough, as I found out now.

The instant we got Introverted, everything that ordinarily leaks into the Place, wake or sleep, had stopped coming, and we were nothing but ourselves and what we meant to each other and what we could make of that, an awfully lonely, scratchy situation.

I decided I felt like I'd been dropped into a swimming pool full of cement and held under until it hardened.

I could understand the others bouncing around a bit. It was a wonder they didn't hit the Void. Maud seemed to be standing it the best; maybe she'd got a little preparation from the long watches between stars; and then she is older than all of us, even Sid, though with a small "o" in "older."

The restless work of the search for the Maintainer had masked the feeling, but now it was beginning to come full force. Before the search, Bruce's speech and Erich's interruptions had done a passable masking job too. I tried to remember when I'd first got the feeling and decided it was after Erich had jumped on the bomb, about the time he mentioned poetry. Though I couldn't be sure. Maybe the Maintainer had been Introverted even earlier, when I'd turned to look at the Ghostgirls. I wouldn't have known. Nuts!

Believe me, I could feel that hardened cement on every inch of me. I remembered Bruce's beautiful picture of a universe without Big Change and decided it was about the worst idea going. I went on eating, though I wasn't so sure now it was a good idea to keep myself strong.

"Does the Maintainer have an Introversion telltale? Siddy!"

"'Sdeath, chit, and you love me, speak lower. Of a sudden, I feel not well, as if I'd drunk a butt of Rhenish and slept inside it. Marry yes, blue. In short flashes, saith the manual. Why ask'st thou?"

"No reason. God, Siddy, what I'd give for a breath of Change Wind."

"Thou can'st say that eftsoons," he groaned. I must have looked pretty miserable myself, for he put his arm around my shoulders and whispered gruffly, "Comfort thyself, sweetling, that while we suffer thus sorely, we yet cannot die the Change Death."

"What's that?" I asked him.

I didn't want to bounce around like the others. I had a suspicion I'd carry it too far. So, to keep myself from going batty, I started to rework the business of who had done what to the Maintainer.

During the hunt, there had been some pretty wild suggestions tossed around as to its disappearance or at least its Introversion: a feat of Snake science amounting to sorcery; the Spider high command bunkering the Places from above, perhaps in reaction to the loss of the Express Room, in such a hurry that they hadn't even time to transmit warnings; the hand of the Late Cosmicians, those mysterious hypothetical beings who are supposed to have successfully resisted the extension of the Change War into the future much beyond Sevensee's epoch-unless the Late Cosmicians are the ones fighting the Change War.

One thing these suggestions had steered very clear of was naming any one of us as a suspect, whether acting as Snake spy, Spider political police, agent of-who knows, after Bruce? —a secret Change World Committee of Public Safety or Spider revolutionary underground, or strictly on our own. Just as no one had piped a word, since the Maintainer had been palmed, about the split between Erich's and Bruce's factions.

Good group thinking probably, to sink differences in the emergency, but that didn't apply to what I did with my own thoughts.

Who wanted to escape so bad they'd Introvert the Place, cutting off all possible contact and communication either way with the cosmos and running the very big risk of not getting back to the cosmos at all?

Leaving out what had happened since Bruce had arrived and stirred things up, Doc seemed to me to have the strongest motive. He knew that Sid couldn't keep covering up for him forever and that Spider punishments for derelictions of duty are not just the clink of a firing squad, as Erich had reminded us. But Doc had been flat on the floor in front of the bar from the time Bruce had jumped on top of it, though I certainly hadn't had my eye on him every second.

Beau? Beau had said he was bored with the Place at a time when what he said counted, so he'd hardly lock himself in it maybe forever, not to mention locking Bruce in with himself and the babe he had a yen for.

Sid loves reality, Changing or not, and every least thing in it, people especially, more than any man or woman I've ever known-he's like a big-eyed baby who wants to grab every object and put it in his mouth-and it was hard to imagine him ever cutting himself off from the cosmos.

Maud, Kaby, Mark and the two ETs? None of them had any motive I knew of, though Sevensee's being from the very far future did tie in with that idea about the Late Cosmicians, and there did seem to be something developing between the Cretan and the Roman that could make them want to be Introverted together.

"Stick to the facts, Greta," I reminded myself with a private groan.

That left Erich, Bruce, Lili and myself.

Erich, I thought-now we're getting somewhere. The little commandant has the nervous system of a coyote and the courage of a crazy tomcat, and if he thought it would help him settle his battle with Bruce better to be locked in with him, he'd do it in a second.

But even before Erich had danced on the bomb, he'd been heckling Bruce from the crowd. Still, there would have been time between heckles for him to step quietly back from us, Introvert the Maintainer and ... well, that was nine-tenths of the problem.

If I was the guilty party, I was nuts and that was the best explanation of all. Gr-r-r!

Bruce's motives seemed so obvious, especially the mortal (or was it immortal?) danger he'd put himself in by inciting mutiny, that it seemed a shame he'd been in full view on the bar so long. Surely, if the Maintainer had been Introverted before he jumped on the bar, we'd all have noticed the flashing blue telltale. For that matter, I'd have noticed it when I looked back at the Ghostgirls-if it worked as Sid claimed, and he said he had never seen it in operation, just read in the manual-oh, 'sdeath!

But Bruce didn't need opportunity, as I'm sure all the males in the Place would have told me right off, because he had Lili to pull the job for him and she had as much opportunity as any of the rest of us. Myself, I have large reservations to this woman-putty-in-the-hands-of-the-man-she-loves-madly theory, but I had to admit there was something to be said for it in this case, and it had seemed quite natural to me when the rest of us had decided, by unspoken agreement, that neither Lili's nor Bruce's checks counted when we were hunting for the Maintainer.

That took care of all of us and left only the mysterious stranger, intruding somehow through a Door (how'd he get it without using our Maintainer?) or from an unimaginable hiding place or straight out of the Void itself. I know that last is impossible-nothing can step out of nothing-but if anything ever looked like it was specially built for something not at all nice to come looming out of, it's the Void-misty, foggily churning, slimy gray....

"Wait a second," I told myself, "and hang onto this, Greta. It should have smacked you in the face at the start."

Whatever came out of the Void, or, more to the point, whoever slipped back from our crowd to the Maintainer, Bruce would have seen them. He was looking at the Maintainer past our heads the whole time, and whatever happened to it, he saw it.

Erich wouldn't have, even after he was on the bomb, because he'd been stagewise enough to face Bruce most of the time to build up his role as tribune of the people.

But Bruce would have-unless he got so caught up in what he was saying....

No, kid, a Demon is always an actor, no matter how much he believes in what he's saying, and there never was an actor yet who wouldn't instantly notice a member of the audience starting to walk out on his big scene.

So Bruce knew, which made him a better actor than I'd have been willing to grant, since it didn't look as if anyone else had thought of what had just occurred to me, or they'd have gone over and put it to him.

Not me, though —I don't work that way. Besides, I didn't feel up to it-Nervy Anna enfold me, I felt like pure hell.

"Maybe," I told myself encouragingly, "the Place is Hell," but added, "Be your age, Greta-be a real rootless, ruleless, ruthless twenty-nine."

Chapter 11
The Western Front, 1917

The barrage roars and lifts. Then, clumsily bowed
With bombs and guns and shovels and battle gear,
Men jostle and climb to meet the bristling fire.
Lines of gray, muttering faces, masked with fear,
They leave their trenches, going over the top,
While time ticks blank and busy on their wrists

—Sassoon

"Please don't, Lili."

"I shall, my love."

"Sweetling, wake up! Hast the shakes?"

I opened my eyes a little and lied to Siddy with a smile and locked my hands together tight and watched Bruce and Lili quarrel nobly near the control divan and wished I had a great love to blur my misery and provide me with a passable substitute for Change Winds.

Lili won the argument, judging from the way she threw her head back and stepped away from Bruce's arms while giving him a proud, tender smile. He walked off a few steps; praise be, he didn't shrug his shoulders at us like an old husband, though his nerves were showing and he didn't seem to be standing Introversion well at all, as who of us were?

Lili rested a hand on the head of the control divan and pressed her lips together and looked around at us, mostly with her eyes. She'd wound a gray silk bandeau around her bangs. Her short gray silk dress without a waistline made her look, not so much like a flapper, though she looked like that all right, as like a little girl, except the neckline was scooped low enough to show she wasn't.

Her gaze hesitated and then stopped at me and I got a sunk feeling of what was coming, because women are always picking on me for an audience. Besides, Sid and I were the centrist party of two in our fresh-out-of-the-shell Place politics.

She took a deep breath and stuck out her chin and said in a voice that was even a little higher and Britisher than she usually uses, "We girls have often cried, 'Shut the Door!' But now the Door is jolly well shut for keeps!"

I knew I'd guessed right and I felt crawly with embarrassment, because I know about this love business of thinking you're the other person and trying to live their life-and grab their glory, though you don't know that-and carry their message for them, and how it can foul things up. Still, I couldn't help admitting what she said wasn't too bad a start-unpleasantly apt to be true, at any rate.

"My fiance believes we may yet be able to open the Door. I do not. He thinks it is a bit premature to discuss the peculiar pickle in which we all find ourselves. I do not."

There was a rasp of laughter from the bar. The militarists were reacting. Erich stepped out, looking very happy. "So now we have to listen to women making speeches," he called. "What is this Place, anyhow? Sidney Lessingham's Saturday Evening Sewing Circle?"

Beau and Sevensee, who'd stopped their pacing halfway between the bar and the control divan, turned toward Erich, and Sevensee looked a little burlier, a little more like half a horse, than satyrs in mythology book illustrations. He stamped-medium hard, I'd say-and said, "Ahh, go flya kite." I'd found out he'd learned English from a Demon who'd been a longshoreman with syndicalist-anarchist sympathies. Erich shut up for a moment and stood there grinning, his hands on his hips.

Lili nodded to the satyr and cleared her throat, looking scared. But she didn't speak; I could see she was thinking and feeling something, and her face got ugly and haggard, as if she were in a Change Wind that hadn't reached me yet, and her mouth went into a snarl to fight tears, but some spurted out, and when she did speak her voice was an octave lower and it wasn't just London talking but New York too.

"I don't know how Resurrection felt to you people, because I'm new and I loathe asking questions, but to me it was pure torture and I wished only I'd had the courage to tell Suzaku, 'I wish to remain a Zombie, if you don't mind. I'd rather the nightmares.' But I accepted Resurrection because I've been taught to be polite and because there is the Demon in me I don't understand that always wishes to live, and I found that I still felt like a Zombie, although I could flit about, and that I still had the nightmares, except they'd grown a deal vivider.

"I was a young girl again, seventeen, and I suppose every woman wishes to be seventeen, but I wasn't seventeen inside my head —I was a woman who had died of Bright's disease in New York in 1929 and also, because a Big Change blew my lifeline into a new drift, a woman who had died of the same disease in Nazi-occupied London in 1955, but rather more slowly because, as you can fancy, the liquor was in far shorter supply. I had to live with both those sets of memories and the Change World didn't blot them out any more than I'm told it does those of any Demon, and it didn't even push them into the background as I'd hoped it would.

"When some Change Fellow would say to me, 'Hallo, beautiful, how about a smile?' or 'That's a posh frock, kiddo,' I'd be back at Bellevue looking down at my swollen figure and the light getting like spokes of ice, or in that dreadful gin-steeped Stepney bedroom with Phyllis coughing herself to death beside me, or at best, for a moment, a little girl in Glamorgan looking at the Roman road and wondering about the wonderful life that lay ahead."

I looked at Erich, remembering he had a long nasty future back in the cosmos himself, and at any rate he wasn't smiling, and I thought maybe he's getting a little humility, knowing someone else has two of those futures, but I doubted it.

"Because, you see," Lili kept forcing it out, "all my three lives I'd been a girl who fell in love with a great young poet she'd never met, the voice of the new youth and all youth, and she'd told her first big lie to get in the Red Cross and across to France to be nearer him, and it was all danger and dark magics and a knight in armor, and she pictured how she'd find him wounded but not seriously, with a little bandage around his head, and she'd light a fag for him and smile lightly, never letting him guess what she felt, but only being her best self and watching to see if that made something happen to him....

"And then the Boche machine guns cut him down at Passchendaele and there couldn't ever have been bandages big enough and the girl stayed seventeen inside and messed about and tried to be wicked, though she wasn't very good at that, and to drink, and she had a bit more talent there, though drinking yourself to death is not nearly as easy as it sounds, even with a kidney weakness to help. But she turned the trick.

"Then a cock crows. She wakes with a tearing start from the gray dreams of death that fill her lifeline. It's cold daybreak. There's the smell of a French farm. She feels her ankles and they're not at all like huge rubber boots filled with water. They're not swollen the least bit. They're young legs.

"There's a little window and the tops of a row of trees that may be poplars when there's more light, and what there is shows cots like her own and heads under blankets, and hanging uniforms make large shadows and a girl is snoring. There's a very distant rumble and it moves the window a bit. Then she remembers they're Red Cross girls many, many kilometers from Passchendaele and that Bruce Marchant is going to die at dawn today.

"In a few more minutes, he's going over the top where there's a crop-headed machine-gunner in field gray already looking down the sights and swinging the gun a bit. But she isn't going to die today. She's going to die in 1929 and 1955.

"And just as she's going mad, there's a creaking and out of the shadows tiptoes a Jap with a woman's hairdo and the whitest face and the blackest eyebrows. He's wearing a rose robe and a black sash which belts to his sides two samurai swords, but in his right hand he has a strange silver pistol. And he smiles at her as if they were brother and sister and lovers at the same time and he says, '*Voulez-vous vivre, mademoiselle?*' and she stares and he bobs his head and says, 'Missy wish live, yes, no?'"

Sid's paw closed quietly around my shaking hands. It always gets me to hear about anyone's Resurrection, and although mine was crazier, it also had the Krauts in it. I hoped she wouldn't go through the rest of the formula and she didn't.

"Five minutes later, he's gone down a stairs more like a ladder to wait below and she's dressing in a rush. Her clothes resist a little, as if they were lightly gummed to the hook and the stained wall, and she hates to touch them. It's getting lighter and her cot looks as if someone were still sleeping there, although it's empty, and she couldn't bring herself to put her hand on the place if her new life depended on it.

"She climbs down and her long skirt doesn't bother her because she knows how to swing it. Suzaku conducts her past a sentry who doesn't see them and a puffy-faced farmer in a smock coughing and spitting the night out of his throat. They cross the farmyard and it's filled with rose light and she sees the sun is up and she knows that Bruce Marchant has just bled to death.

"There's an empty open touring car chugging loudly, waiting for someone; it has huge muddy wheels with wooden spokes and a brass radiator that says 'Simplex.' But Suzaku leads her past it to a dunghill and bows apologetically and she steps through a Door."

I heard Erich say to the others at the bar, "How touching! Now shall I tell everyone about my operation?" But he didn't get much of a laugh.

"That's how Lilian Foster came into the Change World with its steel-engraved nightmares and its deadly pace and deadlier lassitudes. I was more alive than I ever had been before, but it was the kind of life a corpse might get from unending electrical shocks and I couldn't summon any purpose or hope and Bruce Marchant seemed farther away than ever.

"Then, not six hours ago, a Soldier in a black uniform came through the Door and I thought, 'It can't be, but it does look like his photographs,' and then I thought I heard someone say the name Bruce, and then he shouted as if to all the world that he was Bruce Marchant, and I knew there was a Resurrection beyond Resurrection, a true resurrection. Oh, Bruce —"

She looked at him and he was crying and smiling and all the young beauty flooded back into her face, and I thought, "It has to be Change Winds, but it can't be. Face it without slobbering, Greta-there's something that works bigger miracles than Change."

And she went on, "And then the Change Winds died when the Snakes vaporized the Maintainer or the Ghostgirls Introverted it and all three of them vanished so swiftly and silently that even Bruce didn't notice-those are the best explanations I can summon and I fancy one of them is true. At all events, the Change Winds died and my past and even my futures became something I could bear lightly, because I have someone to bear them with me, and because at last I have a true future stretching out ahead of me, an unknown future which I shall create by living. Oh, don't you see that all of us have it now, this big opportunity?"

"*Hussa* for Sidney's suffragettes and the W.C.T.U.!" Erich cheered. "Beau, will you play us a medley of 'Hearts and Flowers' and 'Onward, Christian Soldiers'? I'm deeply moved, Lili. Where do the rest of us queue up for the Great Love Affair of the Century?"

Chapter 12
A Big Opportunity

Now is a bearable burden. What buckles the back is the added weight of the past's mistakes and the future's fears.

I had to learn to close the front door to tomorrow and the back door to yesterday and settle down to here and now.

—Anonymous

Nobody laughed at Erich's screwball sarcasms and still I thought, "Yes, perish his hysterical little gray head, but he's half right-Lili's got the big thing now and she wants to serve it up to the rest of us on a platter, only love doesn't cook and cut that way."

Those weren't bad ideas she had about the Maintainer, though, especially the one about the Ghostgirls doing the Introverting-it would explain why there couldn't be Introversion drill, the manual stuff about blue flashes being window-dressing, and something disappearing without movement or transition is the sort of thing that might not catch the attention-and I guess they gave the others something to think about too, for there wasn't any follow-up to Erich's frantic sniping.

But I honestly didn't see where there was this big opportunity being stuck away in a gray sack in the Void and I began to wonder and I got the strangest feeling and I said to myself, "Hang onto your hat, Greta. It's hope."

"The dreadful thing about being a Demon is that you have all time to range through," Lili was saying with a smile. "You can never shut the back door to yesterday or the front door to tomorrow and simply live in the present. But now that's been done for us: the Door is shut, we need never again rehash the past or the future. The Spiders and Snakes can never find us, for who ever heard of a Place that was truly lost being rescued? And as those in the know have told me, Introversion is the end as far as those outside are concerned. So we're safe from the Spiders and Snakes, we need never be slaves or enemies again, and we have a Place in which to live our new lives, the Place prepared for us from the beginning."

She paused. "Surely you understand what I mean? Sidney and Beauregard and Dr. Pyeshkov are the ones who explained it to me. The Place is a balanced aquarium, just like the cosmos. No one knows how many ages of Big Time it has been in use, without a bit of new material being brought in-only luxuries and people-and not a bit of waste cast off. No one knows how many more ages it may not sustain life. I never heard of Minor Maintainers wearing out. We have all the future, all the security, anyone can hope for. We have a Place to live together."

You know, she was dead right and I realized that all the time I'd had the conviction in the back of my mind that we were going to suffocate or something if we didn't get a Door open pretty quick. I should have known differently, if anybody should, because I'd once been in the Place without a Door for as long as a hundred sleeps during a foxhole stretch of the Change War and we'd had to start cycling our food and it had been okay.

And then, because it is also the way my mind works, I started to picture in a flash the consequences of our living together all by ourselves like Lili said.

I began to pair people off; I couldn't help it. Let's see, four women, six men, two ETs.

"Greta," I said, "you're going to be Miss Polly Andry for sure. We'll have a daily newspaper and folk-dancing classes, we'll shut the bar except evenings, Bruce'll keep a rhymed history of the Place."

I even thought, though I knew this part was strictly silly, about schools and children. I wondered what Siddy's would look like, or my little commandant's. "Don't go near the Void, dears." Of course that would be specially hard on the two ETs, but Sevensee at least wasn't so different and the genetics boys had made some wonderful advances and Maud ought to know about them and there were some amazing gadgets in Surgery when Doc sobered up. The patter of little hoofs...

"My fiance spoke to you about carrying a peace message to the rest of the cosmos," Lili added, "and bringing an end to the Big Change, and healing all the wounds that have been made in the Little Time."

I looked at Bruce. His face was set and strained, as will happen to the best of them when a girl starts talking about her man's business, and I don't know why, but I said to myself, "She's crucifying him, she's nailing him to his purpose as a woman will, even when there's not much point to it, as now."

And Lili went on, "It was a wonderful thought, but now we cannot carry or send any message and I believe it is too late in any event for a peace message to do any good. The cosmos is too raveled by change, too far gone. It will dissolve, fade, 'leave not a rack behind.' We're the survivors. The torch of existence has been put in our hands.

"We may already be all that's left in the cosmos, for have you thought that the Change Winds may have died at their source? We may never reach another cosmos, we may drift forever in the Void, but who of us has been Introverted before and who knows what we can or cannot do? We're a seed for a new future to grow from. Perhaps all doomed universes cast off seeds like this Place. It's a seed, it's an embryo, let it grow."

She looked swiftly at Bruce and then at Sid and she quoted, " 'Come, my friends, 'tis not too late to seek a newer world'."

I squeezed Sid's hand and I started to say something to him, but he didn't know I was there; he was listening to Lili quote Tennyson with his eyes entranced and his mouth open, as if he were imagining new things to put into it-oh, Siddy!

And then I saw the others were looking at her the same way. Ilhilihis was seeing finer feather forests than long-dead Luna's grow. The greenhouse child Maud ap-Ares Davies was stowing away on a starship bound for another galaxy, or thinking how different her life might have been, the children she might have had, if she'd stayed on the planets and out of the Change World. Even Erich looked as though he might be blitzing new universes, and Mark subduing them, for an eight-legged *Führer-imperator*. Beau was throbbing up a wider Mississippi in a bigger-than-life sidewheeler.

Even I —well, I wasn't dreaming of a Greater Chicago. "Let's not go hog-wild on this sort of thing," I told myself, but I did look up at the Void and I got a shiver because I imagined it drawing away and the whole Place starting to grow.

"I truly meant what I said about a seed," Lili went on slowly. "I know, as you all do, that there are no children in the Change World, that there cannot be, that we all become instantly sterile, that what they call a curse is lifted from us girls and we are no longer in bondage to the moon."

She was right, all right-if there's one thing that's been proved a million times in the Change World, it's that.

"But we are no longer in the Change World," Lili said softly, "and its limitations should no longer apply to us, including that one. I feel deeply certain of it, but —" she looked around slowly —"we are four women here and I thought one of us might have a surer indication."

My eyes followed hers around like anybody's would. In fact, everybody was looking around except Maud, and she had the silliest look of surprise on her face and it stayed there, and then, very carefully, she got down from the bar stool with her knitting. She looked at the half-finished pink bra with the long white needles stuck in it and her eyes bugged bigger yet, as if she were expecting it to turn into a baby sweater right then and there. Then she walked across the Place to Lili and stood beside her. While she was walking, the look of surprise changed to a quiet smile. The only other thing she did was throw her shoulders back a little.

I was jealous of her for a second, but it was a double miracle for her, considering her age, and I couldn't grudge her that. And to tell the truth, I was a little frightened, too. Even with Dave, I'd been bothered about this business of having babies.

Yet I stood up with Siddy —I couldn't stop myself and I guess he couldn't either-and hand in hand we walked to the control divan. Beau and Sevensee were there and Bruce, of course, and then, so help me, those Soldiers to the death, Kaby and Mark, started over from the bar and I couldn't see anything in their eyes about the greater glory of Crete and Rome, but something, I think, about each other, and after a moment Illy slowly detached himself from the piano and followed, lightly trailing his tentacles on the floor.

I couldn't exactly see him hoping for little Illies in this company, unless it was true what the jokes said about Lunans, but maybe he was being really disinterested and maybe he wasn't; maybe he was simply figuring that Illy ought to be on the side with the biggest battalions.

I heard dragging footsteps behind us and here came Doc from the Gallery, carrying in his folded arms an abstract sculpture as big as a newborn baby. It was an agglomeration of perfect shiny gray spheres the size of golf balls, shaping up to something like a large brain, but with holes showing through here and there. He held it out to us like an infant to be admired and worked his lips and tongue as if he were trying very hard to say something, though not a word came out that you could understand, and I thought, "Maxey AlekseMaxey AlekseDoc from the Gallery, carrying in his folded arms an abstract sculpture as big as a newborn baby. It was an agglomeration of perfect shiny gray spheres the size of golf balls, shaping up to something like a large brain, but with holes showing through here and there. He held it out to us like an infant to be admired and worked his lips and tongue as if he were trying very hard to say something, though not a word came out that you could understand, and I thought, "Maxey AlekseMaxey Aleksevich may be speechless drunk and have all sorts of holes in his head, but he's got the right instincts, bless his soulful little Russian heart."

We were all crowded around the control divan like a football team huddling. The Peace Packers, it came to me. Sevensee would be fullback or center and Illy left end-what a receiver! The right number, too. Erich was alone at the bar, but now even he —"Oh, no, this can't be," I thought-even he came toward us. Then I saw that his face was working the worst ever. He stopped halfway and managed to force a smile, but it was the worst, too. "That's my little commandant," I thought, "no team spirit."

"So now Lili and Bruce-yes, and *Grossmutterchen* Maud-have their little nest," he said, and he wouldn't have had to push his voice very hard to get a screech. "But what are the rest of us supposed to be-cowbirds?"

He crooked his neck and flapped his hands and croaked, "Cuc-koo! Cuc-koo!" And I said to myself, "I often thought you were crazy, boy, but now I know."

"*Teufelsdreck!* —yes, Devil's dirt! —but you all seem to be infected with this dream of children. Can't you see that the Change World is the natural and proper end of evolution? —a period of enjoyment and measuring, an ultimate working out of things, which women call destruction —'Help, I'm being raped!' 'Oh, what are they doing to my children?' —but which men know as fulfillment.

"You're given good parts in *Götterdämmerung* and you go up to the author and tap him on the shoulder and say, 'Excuse me, Herr Wagner, but this Twilight of the Gods is just a bit morbid. Why don't you write an opera for me about the little ones, the dear little blue-eyed curly-tops? A plot? Oh, boy meets girl and they settle down to breed, something like that.'

"Devil's dirt doubled and damned! Have you thought what life will be like without a Door to go out of to find freedom and adventure, to measure your courage and keenness? Do you want to grow long gray beards hobbling around this asteroid turned inside out? Putter around indoors to the end of your days, mooning about little baby cosmoses? —incidentally, with a live bomb for company. The cave, the womb, the little gray home in the nest-is that what you want? It'll grow? Oh, yes, like the city engulfing the wild wood, a proliferation of *Kinder, Kirche, Küche* —I should live so long!

"Women! —how I hate their bright eyes as they look at me from the fireside, bent-shouldered, rocking, deeply happy to be old, and say, 'He's getting weak, he's giving out, soon I'll have to put him to bed and do the simplest things for him.' Your filthy Triple Goddess, Kaby, the birther, bride, and burier of man! Woman, the enfeebler, the fetterer, the crippler! Woman! —and the curly-headed little cancers she wants!"

He lurched toward us, pointing at Lili. "I never knew one who didn't want to cripple a man if you gave her the chance. Cripple him, swaddle him, clip his wings, grind him to sausage to mold another man, hers, a doll man. You hid the Maintainer, you little smother-hen, so you could have your nest and your Brucie!"

He stopped, gasping, and I expected someone to bop him one on the schnozzle, and I think he did, too. I turned to Bruce and he was looking, I don't know how, sorry, guilty, anxious, angry, shaken, inspired, all at once, and I wished people sometimes had simple suburban reactions like magazine stories.

Then Erich made the mistake, if it was one, of turning toward Bruce and slowly staggering toward him, pawing the air with his hands as if he were going to collapse into his arms, and saying, "Don't let them get you, Bruce. Don't let them tie you down. Don't let them clip you-your words or your deeds. You're a Soldier. Even when you talked about a peace message, you talked about doing some smashing of your own. No matter what you think and feel, Bruce, no matter how much lying you do and how much you hide, you're really not on their side."

That did it.

It didn't come soon enough or, I think, in the right spirit to please me, but I will say it for Bruce that he didn't muck it up by tipping or softening his punch. He took one step forward and his shoulders spun and his fist connected sweet and clean.

As he did it, he said only one word, "Loki!" and darn if that didn't switch me back to a campfire in the Indiana Dunes and my mother telling me out of the Elder Saga about the malicious, sneering, all-spoiling Norse god and how, when the other gods came to trap him in his hideaway by the river, he was on the point of finishing knotting a mysterious net big enough, I had imagined, to snare the whole universe, and that if they'd come a minute later, he would have.

Erich was stretched on the floor, his head hitched up, rubbing his jaw and glaring at Bruce. Mark, who was standing beside me, moved a little and I thought he was going to do something, maybe even clobber Bruce in the old spirit of you can't do that to my buddy, but he just shook his head and said, "*Omnia vincit amor.*" I nudged him and said, "Meaning?" and he said, "Love licks everything."

I'd never have expected it from a Roman, but he was half right at any rate. Lili had her victory: Bruce clearing the field for the marriage by laying out the woman-hating boy friend who would be trying to get him to go out nights. At that moment, I think Bruce wanted Lili and a life with her more than he wanted to reform the Change World. Sure, us women have our little victories-until the legions come or the Little Corporal draws up his artillery or the Panzers roar down the road.

Erich scrambled to his feet and stood there in a half-slump, half-crouch, still rubbing his jaw and glaring at Bruce over his hand, but making no move to continue the fight, and I studied his face and said to myself, "If he can get a gun, he's going to shoot himself, I know."

Bruce started to say something and hesitated, like I would have in his shoes, and just then Doc got one of his unpredictable inspirations and went weaving out toward Erich, holding out the sculpture and making deaf-and-dumb noises like he had to us. Erich looked at him as if he were going to kill him, and then grabbed the sculpture and swung it up over his head and smashed it down on the floor, and for a wonder, it didn't shatter. It just skidded along in one piece and stopped inches from my feet.

That thing not breaking must have been the last straw for Erich. I swear I could see the red surge up through his eyes toward his brain. He swung around into the Stores sector and ran the few steps between him and the bronze bomb chest.

Everything got very slow motion for me, though I didn't do any moving. Almost every man started out after Erich. Bruce didn't, though, and Siddy turned back after the first surge forward, while Illy squunched down for a leap, and it was between Sevensee's hairy shanks and Beau's scissoring white pants that I saw that under-the-microscope circle of death's heads and watched Erich's finger go down on them in the order Kaby had given: one, three, five, six, two, four, seven. I was able to pray seven distinct times that he'd make a mistake.

He straightened up. Illy landed by the box like a huge silver spider and his tentacles whipped futilely across its top. The others surged to a frightened halt around them.

Erich's chest was heaving, but his voice was cool and collected as he said, "You mentioned something about our having a future, Miss Foster. Now you can make that more specific. Unless we get back to the cosmos and dump this box, or find a Spider A-tech, or manage to call headquarters for guidance on disarming the bomb, we have a future exactly thirty minutes long."

Chapter 13
The Tiger is Loose

But whence he was, or of what wombe ybore,
Of beasts, or of the earth, I have not red:
But certes was with milke of wolves and tygres fed.

—Spenser

I guess when they really push the button or throw the switch or spring the trap or focus the beam or what have you, you don't faint or go crazy or anything else convenient. I didn't. Everything, everybody, every move that was made, every word that was spoken, was painfully real to me, like a hand twisting and squeezing things deep inside me, and I saw every least detail spotlighted and magnified like I had the seven skulls.

Erich was standing beyond the bomb chest; little smiles were ruffling his lips. I'd never seen him look so sharp. Illy was beside him, but not on his side, you understand. Mark, Sevensee and Beau were around the chest to the nearer side. Beau had dropped to a knee and was scanning the chest minutely, terror-under-control making him bend his head a little closer than he needed to for clear vision, but with his hands locked together behind his back, I guess to restrain the impulse to push any and everything that looked like a disarming button.

Doc was sprawled face down on the nearest couch, out like a light, I suppose.

Us four girls were still by the control divan. With Kaby, that surprised me, because she didn't look scared or frozen, but almost as intensely alive as Erich.

Sid had turned back, as I'd said, and had one hand stretched out toward but not touching the Minor Maintainer, and a look on his beardy face as if he were calling down death and destruction on every boozy rogue who had ever gone up from King's Lynn to Cambridge and London, and I realized why: if he'd thought of the Minor Maintainer a second sooner, he could have pinned Erich down with heavy gravity before he could touch the buttons.

Bruce was resting one hand on the head of the control divan and was looking toward the group around the chest, toward Erich, I think, as if Erich had done something rather wonderful for him, though I can't imagine myself being tickled at being included in anybody's suicide surprise party. Bruce looked altogether too dreamy, Brahma blast him, for someone who must have the same steel-spiked thought in his head that I know darn well the rest of us had: that in twenty-nine minutes or so, the Place would be a sun in a bag.

Erich was the first to get down to business, as I'd have laid any odds he would be. He had the jump on us and he wasn't going to lose it.

"Well, when are you going to start getting Lili to tell us where she hid the Maintainer? It has to be her-she was too certain it was gone forever when she talked. And Bruce must have seen from the bar who took the Maintainer, and who would he cover up for but his girl?"

There he was plagiarizing my ideas, but I guess I was willing to sign them over to him in full if he got us the right pail of water for that time-bomb.

He glanced at his wrist. "According to my Caller, you have twenty-nine and a half minutes, including the time it will take to get a Door or contact headquarters. When are you going to get busy on the girl?"

Bruce laughed a little-deprecatingly, so help me-and started toward him. "Look here, old man," he said, "there's no need to trouble Lili, or to fuss with headquarters, even if you could. Really not at all. Not to mention that your surmises are quite unfounded, old chap, and I'm a bit surprised at your advancing them. But that's quite all right because, as it happens, I'm an atomics technician and I even worked on that very bomb. To disarm it, you just have to fiddle a bit with some of the ankhs, those hoopy little crosses. Here, let me —"

Allah il allah, but it must have struck everybody as it did me as being just too incredible an assertion, too bloody British a bare-faced bluff, for Erich didn't have to say a word; Mark and Sevensee grabbed Bruce by the arms, one on each side, as he stooped toward the bronze chest, and they weren't gentle about it. Then Erich spoke.

"Oh, no, Bruce. Very sporting of you to try to cover up for your girl friend, but we aren't going to let ourselves be blown to stripped atoms twenty-eight minutes too soon while you monkey with the buttons, the very thing Benson-Carter warned against, and pray for a guess-work miracle. It's too thin, Bruce, when you come from 1917 and haven't been on the Big Time for a hundred sleeps and were calling for an A-tech yourself a few hours ago. Much too thin. Bruce, something is going to happen that I'm afraid you won't like, but you're going to have to put up with it. That is, unless Miss Foster decides to be cooperative."

"I say, you fellows, let me go," Bruce demanded, struggling experimentally. "I know it's a bit thick to swallow and I did give you the wrong impression calling for an A-tech, but I just wanted to capture your attention then; I didn't want to have to work on the bomb. Really, Erich, would they have ordered Benson-Carter to pick us up unless one of us were an A-tech? They'd be sure to include one in the bally operation."

"When they're using patchwork tactics?" Erich grinningly quoted back at him.

Kaby spoke up beside me and said, "Benson-Carter was a magician of matter and he was going on the operation disguised as an old woman. We have the cloak and hood with the other garments," and I wondered how this cold fish of a she-officer could be the same girl who was giving Mark slurpy looks not ten minutes ago.

"Well?" Erich asked, glancing at his Caller and then swinging his eyes around at us as if there must be some of the old *Wehrmacht* iron somewhere. We all found ourselves looking at Lili and she was looking so sharp herself, so ready to jump and so at bay, that it was all *I* needed, at any rate, to make Erich's theory about the Maintainer a rock-bottom certainty.

Bruce must have realized the way our minds were working, for he started to struggle in earnest and at the same time called, "For God's sake, don't do anything to Lili! Let me loose, you idiots! Everything's true I told you—I can save you from that bomb. Sevensee, you took my side against the Spiders; you've nothing to lose. Sid, you're an Englishman. Beau, you're a gentleman and you love her, too-for God's sake, stop them!"

Beau glanced up over his shoulder at Bruce and the others surging around close to his ankles and he had on his poker face. Sid I could tell was once more going through the purgatory of decision. Beau reached his own decision first and I'll say it for him that he acted on it fast and intelligently. Right from his kneeling position and before he'd even turned his head quite back, he jumped Erich.

But other things in this cosmos besides Man can pick sides and act fast. Illy landed on Beau midway and whipped his tentacles around him tight and they went wobbling around like a drunken white-and-silver barber pole. Beau got his hands each around a tentacle, and at the same time his face began to get purple, and I winced at what they were both going through.

Maybe Sevensee had a hoof in Sid's purgatory, because Bruce shook loose from the satyr and tried to knock out Mark, but the Roman twisted his arm and kept him from getting in a good punch.

Erich didn't make a move to mix into either fight, which is my little commandant all over. Using his fists on anybody but me is beneath him.

Then Sid made his choice, but there was no way for me to tell what it was, for, as he reached for the Minor Maintainer, Kaby contemptuously snatched it away from his hands and gave him a knee in the belly that doubled me up in sympathy and sent him sprawling on his knees toward the fighters. On the return, Kaby gave Lili, who'd started to grab too, an effortless backhand smash that set her down on the divan.

Erich's face lit up like an electric sign and he kept his eyes fixed on Kaby.

She crouched a little, carrying her weight on the balls of her feet and firmly cradling the Minor Maintainer in her left arm, like a basketball captain planning an offensive. Then she waved her free hand decisively to the right. I didn't get it, but Erich did and Mark too, for Erich jumped for the Refresher sector and Mark let go of Bruce and followed him, ducking around Sevensee's arms, who was coming back into the fight on which side I don't know. Illy un-whipped from Beau and copied Erich and Mark with one big spring.

Then Kaby twisted a dial as far as it would go and Bruce, Beau, Sevensee and poor Siddy were slammed down and pinned to the floor by about eight gravities.

It should have been lighter near us —I hoped it was, but you couldn't tell from watching Siddy; he went flat on his face, spread-eagled, one hand stretched toward me so close, I could have touched it (but not let go!), and his mouth was open against the floor and he was gasping through a corner of it and I could see his spine trying to sink through his belly. Bruce just managed to get his head and one shoulder up a bit, and they all made me think of a Doré illustration of the *Inferno* where the cream of the damned are frozen up to their necks in ice in the innermost circle of Hell.

The gravity didn't catch me, although I could feel it in my left arm. I was mostly in the Refresher sector, but I dropped down flat too, partly out of a crazy compassion I have, but mostly because I didn't want to take a chance of having Kaby knock me down.

Erich, Mark and Illy had got clear and they headed toward us. Maud picked the moment to make her play; she hadn't much choice of times, if she wanted to make one. The Old Girl was looking it for once, but I guess the thought of her miracle must have survived alongside the fear of sacked sun and must have meant a lot to her, for she launched out fast, all set to straight-arm Kaby into the heavy gravity and grab the Minor Maintainer with the other hand.

Chapter 14
"Now Will You Talk?"

Like diamonds, we are cut with our own dust.

—Webster

Cretans have eyes under their back hair, or let's face it, Entertainers aren't Soldiers. Kaby weaved to one side and flicked a helpful hand and poor old Maud went where she'd been going to send Kaby. It sickened me to see the gravity take hold and yank her down.

I could have jumped up and made it four in a row for Kaby, but I'm not a bit brave when things like my life are at stake.

Lili was starting to get up, acting a little dazed. Kaby gently pushed her down again and quietly said, "Where is it?" and then hauled off and slapped her across the face. What got me was the matter-of-fact way Kaby did it. I can understand somebody getting mad and socking someone, or even deliberately working up a rage so as to be able to do something nasty, but this cold-blooded way turns my stomach.

Lili looked as if half her face were about to start bleeding, but she didn't look dazed any more and her jaw set. Kaby grabbed Lili's pearl necklace and twisted it around her neck and it broke and the pearls went bouncing around like ping-pong balls, so Kaby yanked down Lili's gray silk bandeau until it was around the neck and tightened that. Lili started to choke through her tight-pressed lips. Erich, Mark and Illy had come up and crowded around, but they seemed to be content with the job Kaby was doing.

"Listen, slut," she said, "we have no time. You have a healing room in this place. I can work the things."

"Here it comes," I thought, wishing I could faint. On top of everything, on top of death even, they had to drag in the nightmare personally stylized for me, the horror with my name on it. I wasn't going to be allowed to blow up peacefully. They weren't satisfied with an A-bomb. They had to write my private hell into the script.

"There is a thing called an Invertor," Kaby said exactly as I'd known she would, but as I didn't really hear it just then —a mental split I'll explain in a moment. "It opens you up so they can cure your insides without cutting your skin or making you bleed anywhere. It turns the big parts of you inside out, but not the blood tubes. All your skin-your eyes, ears, nose, toes, all of it-becoming the lining of a little hole that's half-filled with your hair.

"Meantime, your insides are exposed for whatever the healer wants to do to them. You live for a while on the air inside the hole. First the healer gives you an air that makes you sleep, or you go mad in about fifty heartbeats. We'll see what ten heartbeats do to you without the sleepy air. Now will you talk?"

I hadn't been listening to her, though, not the real me, or I'd have gone mad without getting the treatment. I once heard Doc say your liver is more mysterious and farther away from you than the stars, because although you live with your liver all your life, you never see it or learn to point to it instinctively, and the thought of someone messing around with that intimate yet unknown part of you is just too awful.

I knew I had to do something quick. Hell, at the first hint of Introversion, before Kaby had even named it, Illy had winced so that his tentacles were all drawn up like fat feather-sausages. Erich had looked at him questioningly, but that lousy Looney had un-endeared himself to me by squeaking, "Don't mind me, I'm just sensitive. Get on with the girl. Make her tell."

Yes, I knew I had to do something, and here on the floor that meant thinking hard and in high gear about something else. The screwball sculpture Erich had tried to smash was a foot from my nose and I saw a faint trail of white stuff where it had skidded. I reached out and touched the trail; it was finely gritty, like powdered glass. I tipped up the sculpture and the part on which it had skidded wasn't marred at all, not even dulled; the gray spheres were as glisteningly bright as ever. So I knew the trail was diamond dust rubbed off the diamonds in the floor by something even harder.

That told me the sculpture was something special and maybe Doc had had a real idea in his pickled brain when he'd been pushing the thing at all of us and trying to tell us something. He hadn't managed to say anything then, but he had earlier when he'd been going to tell us what to do about the bomb, and maybe there was a connection.

I twisted my memory hard and let it spring back and I got "Inversh ...bosh ..." Bosh, indeed! Bosh and inverse bosh to all boozers, Russki or otherwise.

So I quick tried the memory trick again and this time I got "glovsh" and then I grasped and almost sneezed on diamond dust as I watched the pieces fit themselves together in my mind like a speeded-up movie reel.

It all hung on that black right-hand hussar's glove Lili had produced for Bruce. Only she couldn't have found it in Stores, because we'd searched every fractional pigeonhole later on and there hadn't been any gloves there, not even the left-hand mate there would have been. Also, Bruce had had two left-hand gloves to start with, and we had been through the whole Place with a fine-tooth comb, and there had been only the two black gloves on the floor where Bruce had kicked them off the bar-those two and those two only, the left-hand glove he'd brought from outside and the right-hand glove Lili had produced for him.

So a left-hand glove had disappeared-the last I'd seen of it, Lili had been putting it on her tray-and a right-hand glove had appeared. Which could only add up to one thing: Lili had turned the left-hand glove into an identical right. She couldn't have done it by turning it inside out the ordinary way, because the lining was different.

But as I knew only too sickeningly well, there was an extraordinary way to turn things inside out, things like human beings. You merely had to put them on the Invertor in Surgery and flick the switch for full Inversion.

Or you could flick it for partial Inversion and turn something into a perfect three-dimensional mirror image of itself, just what a right-hand glove is of a left. Rotation through the fourth dimension, the science boys call it; I've heard of it being used in surgery on the highly asymmetric Martians, and even to give a socially impeccable right hand to a man who'd lost one, by turning an amputated right arm into an amputated left.

Ordinarily, nothing but live things are ever Inverted in Surgery and you wouldn't think of doing it to an inanimate object, especially in a Place where the Doc's a drunk and the Surgery hasn't been used for hundreds of sleeps.

But when you've just fallen in love, you think of wonderful crazy things to do for people. Drunk with love, Lili had taken Bruce's extra left-hand glove into Surgery, partially Inverted it, and got a right-hand glove to give him.

What Doc had been trying to say with his "Inversh ...bosh ..." was "Invert the box," meaning we should put the bronze chest through full Inversion to get at the bomb inside to disarm it. Doc too had got the idea from Lili's trick with the glove. What an inside-out tactical atomic bomb would look like, I could not imagine and did not particularly care to see. I might have to, though, I realized.

But the fast-motion film was still running in my head. Later on, Lili had decided like I had that her lover was going to lose out in his plea for mutiny unless she could give him a really captive audience-and maybe, even then, she had been figuring on creating the nest for Bruce's chicks and ...all those other things we'd believed in for a while. So she'd taken the

Major Maintainer and remembered the glove, and not many seconds later, she had set down on a shelf of the Art Gallery an object that no one would think of questioning-except someone who knew the Gallery by heart.

I looked at the abstract sculpture a foot from my nose, at the clustered gray spheres the size of golf balls. I had known that the inside of the Maintainer was made up of vastly tough, vastly hard giant molecules, but I hadn't realized they were quite *that* big.

I said to myself, "Greta, this is going to give you a major psychosis, but you're the one who has to do it, because no one is going to listen to your deductions when they're all practically living on negative time already."

I got up as quietly as if I were getting out of a bed I shouldn't have been in-there are some things Entertainers are good at-and Kaby was just saying "you go mad in about fifty heartbeats." Everybody on their feet was looking at Lili. Sid seemed to have moved, but I had no time for him except to hope he hadn't done anything that might attract attention to me.

I stepped out of my shoes and walked rapidly to Surgery-there's one good thing about this hardest floor anywhere, it doesn't creak. I walked through the Surgery screen that is like a wall of opaque, odorless cigarette smoke and I concentrated on remembering my snafued nurse's training, and before I had time to panic, I had the sculpture positioned on the gleaming table of the Invertor.

I froze for a moment when I reached for the Inversion switch, thinking of the other time and trying to remember what it had been that bothered me so much about an inside-out brain being bigger and not having eyes, but then I either thumbed my nose at my nightmare or kissed my sanity good-by, I don't know which, and twisted the switch all the way over, and there was the Major Maintainer winking blue about three times a second as nice as you could want it.

It must have been working as sweet and steady as ever, all the time it was Inverted, except that, being inside out, it had hocused the direction finders.

Chapter 15
Lord Spider

> black legged spiders
> with red hearts of hell

—marquis

"Jesu!" I turned and Sid's face was sticking through the screen like a tinted bas-relief hanging on a gray wall and I got the impression he had peered unexpectedly through a slit in an arras into Queen Elizabeth's bedroom.

He didn't have any time to linger on the sensation, even if he'd wanted to, for an elbow with a copper band thrust through the screen and dug his ribs and Kaby marched Lili in by the neck. Erich, Mark and Illy were right behind. They caught the blue flashes and stopped dead, staring at the long-lost. Erich spared me one look which seemed to say, so you did it, not that it matters. Then he stepped forward and picked it up and held it solidly to his left side in the double right-angle made by fingers, forearm and chest, and reached for the Introversion switch with a look on his face as if he were opening a fifth of whisky.

The blue light died and Change Winds hit me like a stiff drink that had been a long, long time in coming, like a hot trumpet note out of nowhere.

I felt the changing pasts blowing through me, and the uncertainties whistling past, and ice-stiff reality softening with all its duties and necessities, and the little memories shredding away and dancing off like autumn leaves, leaving maybe not even ghosts behind, and all the crazy moods like Mardi Gras dancers pouring down an evening street, and something inside me had the nerve to say it didn't care whether Greta Forzane's death was riding in those Winds because they felt so good.

I could tell it was hitting the others the same way. Even battered, tight-lipped Lili seemed to be saying, you're making me drink the stuff and I hate you for it, but I do love it. I guess we'd all had the worry that even finding and Extroverting the Maintainer wouldn't put us back in touch with the cosmos and give us those Winds we hate and love.

The thing that cut through to us as we stood there glowing was not the thought of the bomb, though that would have come in a few seconds more, but Sid's voice. He was still standing in the screen, except that now his face was out the other side and we could just see parts of his gray-doubleted back, but, of course, his "Jesu!" came through the screen as if it weren't there.

At first I couldn't figure out who he could be talking to, but I swear I never heard his voice so courtly obsequious before, so strong and yet so filled with awe and an under-note of, yes, sheer terror.

"Lord, I am filled from top to toe with confusion that you should so honor my poor Place," he said. "Poor say I and mine, when I mean that I have ever busked it faithfully for you, not dreaming that you would ever condescend ...yet knowing that your eye was certes ever upon me ...though I am but as a poor pinch of dust adrift between the suns ...I abase myself. Prithee, how may I serve thee, sir? I know not e'en how most suitably to address thee, Lord ...King ... Emperor Spider!"

I felt like I was getting very small, but not a bit less visible, worse luck, and even with the Change Winds inside me to give me courage, I thought this was really too much, coming on top of everything else; it was simply unfair.

At the same time, I realized it was to be expected that the big bosses would have been watching us with their unblinking beady black eyes ever since we had Introverted waiting to pounce if we should ever come out of it. I tried to picture what was on the other side of the screen and I didn't like the assignment.

But in spite of being petrified, I had a hard time not giggling, like the zany at graduation exercises, at the way the other ones in Surgery were taking it.

I mean the Soldiers. They each stiffened up like they had the old ramrod inside them, and their faces got that important look, and they glanced at each other and the floor without lowering their heads, as if they were measuring the distance between their feet and mentally chalking alternate sets of footprints to step into. The way Erich and Kaby held the Major and Minor Maintainers became formal; the way they checked their Callers and nodded reassuringly was positively esoteric. Even Illy somehow managed to look as if he were on parade.

Then from beyond the screen came what was, under the circumstances, the worst noise I've ever heard, a seemingly wordless distant-sounding howling and wailing, with a note of menace that made me shake, although it also had a nasty familiarity about it I couldn't place. Sid's voice broke into it, loud, fast and frightened.

"Your pardon, Lord, I did not think ...certes, the gravity ...I'll attend to it on the instant." He whipped a hand and half a head back through the screen, but without looking back and snapped his fingers, and before I could blink, Kaby had put the Minor Maintainer in his hand.

Sid went completely out of sight then and the howling stopped, and I thought that if that was the way a Lord Spider expressed his annoyance at being subjected to incorrect gravity, I hoped the bosses wouldn't start any conversations with me.

Erich pursed his lips and threw the other Soldiers a nod and the four of them marched through the screen as if they'd drilled a lifetime for this moment. I had the wild idea that Erich might give me his arm, but he strode past me as if I were ...an Entertainer.

I hesitated a moment then, but I had to see what was happening outside, even if I got eaten up for it. Besides, I had a bit of the thought that if these formalities went on much longer, even a Lord Spider was going to discover just how immune he was to confined atomic blast.

I walked through the screen with Lili beside me.

The Soldiers had stopped a few feet in front of it. I looked around ahead for whatever it was going to turn out to be, prepared to drop a curtsy or whatever else, bar nothing, that seemed expected of me.

I had a hard time spotting the beast. Some of the others seemed to be having trouble too. I saw Doc weaving around foolishly by the control divan, and Bruce and Beau and Sevensee and Maud on their feet beyond it, and I wondered whether we were dealing with an invisible monster; ought to be easy enough for the bosses to turn a simple trick like invisibility.

Then I looked sharply left where everyone else, even glassy-eyed Doc, was coming to look, into the Door sector, only there wasn't any monster there or even a Door, but just Siddy holding the Minor Maintainer and grinning like when he is threatening to tickle me, only more fiendishly.

"Not a move, masters," he cried, his eyes dancing, "or I'll pin the pack of you down, marry and amen I will. It is my firm purpose to see the Place blasted before I let this instrument out of my hands again."

My first thought was, "'Sblood but Siddy is a real actor! I don't care if he didn't study under anyone later than Burbage, that just proves how good Burbage is."

Sid had convinced us not only that the real Spiders had arrived, but earlier that the gravity in the edge of Stores had been a lot heavier than it actually was. He completely fooled all those Soldiers, including my swelled-headed victorious little commandant, and I kind of filed away the timing of that business of reaching out the hand and snapping the fingers without looking, it was so good.

"Beauregard!" Sid called. "Get to the Major Maintainer and call headquarters. But don't come through Door, marry go by Refresher. I'll not trust a single Demon of you in this sector with me until much more has been shown and settled."

"Siddy, you're wonderful," I said, starting toward him. "As soon as I got the Maintainer unsnarled and looked around and saw your sweet old face —"

"Back, tricksy trull! Not the breadth of one scarlet toenail nearer me, you Queen of Sleights and High Priestess of Deception!" he bellowed. "You least of all do I trust. Why you hid the Maintainer, I know not, 'faith, but later you'll discover the truth to me or I'll have your gizzard."

I could see there was going to have to be a little explaining.

Doc, touched off, I guess, by Sid waving his hand at me, threw back his head and let off one of those shuddery Siberian wolf-howls he does so blamed well. Sid waved toward him sharply and he shut up, beaming toothily, but at least I knew who was responsible for the Spider wail of displeasure that Sid had either called for or more likely got as a gift of the gods and used in his act.

Beau came circling around fast and Erich shoved the Major Maintainer into his hands without making any fuss. The four Soldiers were looking pretty glum after losing their grand review.

Beau dumped some junk off one of the Art Gallery's sturdy taborets and set the Major Maintainer on it carefully but fast, and quickly knelt in front of it and whipped on some earphones and started to tune. The way he did it snatched away from me my inward glory at my big Inversion brainwave so fast, I might never have had it, and there was nothing in my mind again but the bronze bomb chest.

I wondered if I should suggest Inverting the thing, but I said to myself, "Uh-uh, Greta, you got no diploma to show them and there probably isn't time to try two things, anyway."

Then Erich for once did something I wanted him to, though I didn't care for its effect on my nerves, by looking at his Caller and saying quietly, "Nine minutes to go, if Place time and cosmic time are synching."

Beau was steady as a rock and working adjustments so fine that I couldn't even see his fingers move.

Then, at the other end of the Place, Bruce took a few steps toward us. Sevensee and Maud followed a bit behind him. I remembered Bruce was another of our nuts with a private program for blowing up the place.

"Sidney," he called, and then, when he'd got Sid's attention, "Remember, Sidney, you and I both came down to London from Peterhouse."

I didn't get it. Then Bruce looked toward Erich with a devil-may-care challenge and toward Lili as if he were asking her forgiveness for something. I couldn't read her expression; the bruises were blue on her throat and her cheek was puffy.

Then Bruce once more shot Erich that look of challenge and he spun and grabbed Sevensee by a wrist and stuck out a foot-even half-horses aren't too sharp about infighting, I guess, and the satyr had every right to feel at least as confused as I felt-and sent him stumbling into Maud, and the two of them tumbled to the floor in a jumble of hairy legs and pearl-gray frock. Bruce raced to the bomb chest.

Most of us yelled, "Stop him, Sid, pin him down," or something like that—I know I did because I was suddenly sure that he'd been asking Lili's pardon for blowing the two of them up-and all the rest of us too, the love-blinded stinker.

Sid had been watching him all the time and now he lifted his hand to the Minor Maintainer, but then he didn't touch any of the dials, just watched and waited, and I thought, "Shaitan shave us! Does Siddy want in on death, too? Ain't he satisfied with all he knows about life?"

Bruce had knelt and was twisting some things on the front of the chest, and it was all as bright as if he were under a bank of Klieg lights, and I was telling myself I wouldn't know anything when the fireball fired, and not believing it, and Sevensee and Maud had got unscrambled and were starting for Bruce, and the rest of us were yelling at Sid, except that Erich was just looking at Bruce very happily, and Sid was still not doing anything, and it was unbearable except just then I felt the little arteries start to burst in my brain like a string of fire-crackers and the old aorta pop, and for good measure, a couple of valves come unhinged in my ticker, and I was thinking, "Well, now I know what it's like to die of heart failure and high blood pressure," and having a last quiet smile at having cheated the bomb, when Bruce jumped up and back from the chest.

"That does it!" he announced cheerily. "She's as safe as the Bank of England."

Sevensee and Maud stopped themselves just short of knocking him down and I said to myself, "Hey, let's get a move on! I thought heart attacks were fast."

Before anyone else could speak, Beau did. He had turned around from the Major Maintainer and pulled aside one of the earphones.

"I got headquarters," he said crisply. "They told me how to disarm the bomb —I merely said I thought we ought to know. What did you do, sir?" he called to Bruce.

"There's a row of four ankhs just below the lock. The first to your left you give a quarter turn to the right, the second a quarter turn to the left, same for the fourth, and you don't touch the third."

"That is it, sir," Beau confirmed.

The long silence was too much for me; I guess I must have the shortest span for unspoken relief going. I drew some nourishment out of my restored arteries into my brain cells and yelled, "Siddy, I know I'm a tricksy trull and the High Vixen of all Foxes, but what the Hell is Peterhouse?"

"The oldest college at Cambridge," he told me rather coolly.

Chapter 16
The Possibility-Binders

"Familiar with infinite universe sheafs and open-ended postulate systems? —the notion that everything is possible-and I mean everything-and everything has happened. *Everything.*"

—Heinlein

An hour later, I was nursing a weak highball and a black eye in the sleepy-time darkness on the couch farthest from the piano, half watching the highlighted party going on around it and the bar, while the Place waited for rendezvous with Egypt and the Battle of Alexandria.

Sid had swept all our outstanding problems into one big bundle and, since his hand held the joker of the Minor Maintainer, he had settled them all as high-handedly as if they'd been those of a bunch of schoolkids.

It amounted to this:

We'd been Introverted when most of the damning things had happened, so presumably only we knew about them, and we were all in so deep one way or another that we'd all have to keep quiet to protect our delicate complexions.

Well, Erich's triggering the bomb did balance rather neatly Bruce's incitement to mutiny, and there was Doc's drinking, while everybody who had declared for the peace message had something to hide. Mark and Kaby I felt inclined to trust anywhere, Maud for sure, and Erich in this particular matter, damn him. Illy I didn't feel at all easy about, but I told myself there always has to be a fly in the ointment —a darn big one this time, and furry.

Sid didn't mention his own dirty linen, but he knew we knew he'd flopped badly as boss of the Place and only recouped himself by that last-minute flimflam.

Remembering Sid's trick made me think for a moment about the real Spiders. Just before I snuck out of Surgery, I'd had a vivid picture of what they must look like, but now I couldn't get it again. It depressed me, not being able to remember-oh, I probably just imagined I'd had a picture, like a hophead on a secret-of-the-universe kick. Me ever find out anything about the Spiders? —except for nervous notions like I'd had during the recent fracas? —what a laugh!

The funniest thing (ha-ha!) was that I had ended up the least-trusted person. Sid wouldn't give me time to explain how I'd deduced what had happened to the Maintainer, and even when Lili spoke up and admitted hiding it, she acted so bored I don't think everybody believed her-although she did spill the realistic detail that she hadn't used partial Inversion on the glove; she'd just turned it inside out to make it a right and then done a full Inversion to get the lining back inside.

I tried to get Doc to confirm that he'd reasoned the thing out the same way I had, but he said he had been blacked out the whole time, except during the first part of the hunt, and he didn't remember having any bright ideas at all. Right now, he was having Maud explain to him twice, in detail, everything that had happened. I decided that it was going to take a little more work before my reputation as a great detective was established.

I looked over the edge of the couch and just made out in the gloom one of Bruce's black gloves. It must have been kicked there. I fished it up. It was the right-hand one. My big clue, and was I sick of it! Got mittens, God forbid! I slung it away and, like a lurking octopus, Illy shot up a tentacle from the next couch, where I hadn't known he was resting, and snatched the glove like it was a morsel of underwater garbage. These ETs can seem pretty shuddery non-human at times.

I thought of what a cold-blooded, skin-saving louse Illy had been, and about Sid and his easy suspicions, and Erich and my black eye, and how, as usual, I'd got left alone in the end. My men!

Bruce had explained about being an A-tech. Like a lot of us, he'd had several widely different jobs during his first weeks in the Change World and one of them had been as secretary to a group of the minor atomics boys from the Manhattan-Project-Earth-Satellite days. I gathered he'd also absorbed some of his bothersome ideas from them. I hadn't quite decided yet what species of heroic heel he belonged to, but he was thick with Mark and Erich again. Everybody's men!

Sid didn't have to argue with anybody; all the wild compulsions and mighty resolves were dead now, anyway until they'd had a good long rest. I sure could use one myself, I knew.

The party at the piano was getting wilder. Lili had been dancing the black bottom on top of it and now she jumped down into Sid's and Sevensee's arms, taking a long time about it. She'd been drinking a lot and her little gray dress looked about as innocent on her as diapers would on Nell Gwyn. She continued her dance, distributing her marks of favor equally between Sid, Erich and the satyr. Beau didn't mind a bit, but serenely pounded out "Tonight's the Night"—which she'd practically shouted to him not two minutes ago.

I was glad to be out of the party. Who can compete with a highly experienced, utterly disillusioned seventeen-year-old really throwing herself away for the first time?

Something touched my hand. Illy had stretched a tentacle into a furry wire to return me the black glove, although he ought to have known I didn't want it. I pushed it away, privately calling Illy a washed-out moronic tarantula, and right away I felt a little guilty. What right had I to be critical of Illy? Would my own character have shown to advantage if I'd been locked in with eleven octopoids a billion years away? For that matter, where did I get off being critical of anyone?

Still, I was glad to be out of the party, though I kept on watching it. Bruce was drinking alone at the bar. Once Sid had gone over to him and they'd had one together and I'd heard Bruce reciting from Rupert Brooke those deliberately corny lines, "For England's the one land, I know, Where men with Splendid Hearts may go; and Cambridgeshire, of all England, The Shire for Men who Understand;" and I'd remembered that Brooke too had died young in World War One and my ideas had got fuzzy. But mostly Bruce was just calmly drinking by himself. Every once in a while Lili would look at him and stop dead in her dancing and laugh.

I'd figured out this Bruce-Lili-Erich business as well as I cared to. Lili had wanted the nest with all her heart and nothing else would ever satisfy her, and now she'd go to hell her own way and probably die of Bright's disease for a third time in the Change World. Bruce hadn't wanted the nest or Lili as much as he wanted the Change World and the chances it gave for Soldierly cavorting and poetic drunks; Lili's seed wasn't his idea of healing the cosmos; maybe he'd make a real mutiny some day, but more likely he'd stick to bar-room epics.

His and Lili's infatuation wouldn't die completely, no matter how rancid it looked right now. The real-love angle might go, but Change would magnify the romance angle and it might seem to them like a big thing of a sort if they met again.

Erich had his *Kamerad*, shaped to suit him, who'd had the guts and cleverness to disarm the bomb he'd had the guts to trigger. You have to hand it to Erich for having the nerve to put us all in a situation where we'd have to find the Maintainer or fry, but I don't know anything disgusting enough to hand to him.

I had tried a while back. I had gone up behind him and said, "Hey, how's my wicked little commandant? Forgotten your *und so weiter?*" and as he turned, I clawed my nails and slammed him across the cheek. That's how I got the black eye. Maud wanted to put an electronic leech on it, but I took the old handkerchief in ice water. Well, at any rate Erich had his scratches to match Bruce's, not as deep, but four of them, and I told myself maybe they'd get infected —I hadn't washed my hands since the hunt. Not that Erich doesn't love scars.

Mark was the one who helped me up after Erich knocked me down.

"You got any omnias for that?" I snapped at him.

"For what?" Mark asked.

"Oh, for everything that's been happening to us," I told him disgustedly.

He seemed to actually think for a moment and then he said, *"Omnia mutantur, nihil interit."*

"Meaning?" I asked him.

He said, "All things change, but nothing is really lost."

It would be a wonderful philosophy to stand with against the Change Winds. Also damn silly. I wondered if Mark really believed it. I wished I could. Sometimes I come close to thinking it's a lot of baloney trying to be any decent kind of Demon, even a good Entertainer. Then I tell myself, "That's life, Greta. You've got to love through it somehow." But there are times when some of these cookies are not too easy to love.

Something brushed the palm of my hand again. It was Illy's tentacle, with the tendrils of the tip spread out like a little bush. I started to pull my hand away, but then I realized the Loon was simply lonely. I surrendered my hand to the patterned gossamer pressures of feather-talk.

Right away I got the words, "Feeling lonely, Greta girl?"

It almost floored me, I tell you. Here I was understanding feather-talk, which I just didn't, and I was understanding it in English, which didn't make sense at all.

For a second, I thought Illy must have spoken, but I knew he hadn't, and for a couple more seconds I thought he was working telepathy on me, using the feather-talk as cues. Then I tumbled to what was happening: he was playing English on my palm like on the keyboard of his squeakbox, and since I could play English on a squeakbox myself, my mind translated automatically.

Realizing this almost gave my mind stage fright, but I was too fagged to be hocused by self-consciousness. I just lay back and let the thoughts come through. It's good to have someone talk to you, even an underweight octopus, and without the squeaks Illy didn't sound so silly; his phrasing was soberer.

"Feeling sad, Greta girl, because you'll never understand what's happening to us all," Illy asked me, "because you'll never be anything but a shadow fighting shadows-and trying to love shadows in between the battles? It's time you understood we're not really fighting a war at all, although it looks that way, but going through a kind of evolution, though not exactly the kind Erich had in mind.

"Your Terran thought has a word for it and a theory for it —a theory that recurs on many worlds. It's about the four orders of life: Plants, Animals, Men and Demons. Plants are energy-binders —they can't move through space or time, but they can clutch energy and transform it. Animals are space-binders —they can move through space. Man (Terran or ET, Lunan or non-Lunan) is a time-binder —he has memory.

"Demons are the fourth order of evolution, possibility-binders —they can make all of what might be part of what is, and that is their evolutionary function. Resurrection is like the metamorphosis of a caterpillar into a butterfly: a third-order being breaks out of the chrysalis of its lifeline into fourth-order life. The leap from the ripped cocoon of an unchanging reality is like the first animal's leap when he ceases to be a plant, and the Change World is the core of meaning behind the many myths of immortality.

"All evolution looks like a war at first-octopoids against monopoids, mammals against reptiles. And it has a necessary dialectic: there must be the thesis-we call it Snake-and the antithesis-Spider-before there can be the ultimate synthesis, when all possibilities are fully realized in one ultimate universe. The Change War isn't the blind destruction it seems.

"Remember that the Serpent is your symbol of wisdom and the Spider your sign for patience. The two names are rightly frightening to you, for all high existence is a mixture of horror and delight. And don't be surprised, Greta girl, at the range of my words and thoughts; in a way, I've had a billion years to study Terra and learn her languages and myths.

"Who are the real Spiders and Snakes, meaning who were the first possibility-binders? Who was Adam, Greta girl? Who was Cain? Who were Eve and Lilith?

"In binding all possibility, the Demons also bind the mental with the material. All fourth-order beings live inside and outside all minds, throughout the whole cosmos. Even this Place is, after its fashion, a giant brain: its floor is the brainpan, the boundary of the Void is the cortex of gray matter-yes, even the Major and Minor Maintainers are analogues of the pineal and pituitary glands, which in some form sustain all nervous systems.

"There's the real picture, Greta girl."

The feather-talk faded out and Illy's tendril tips merged into a soft pad on which I fingered, "Thanks, Daddy Longlegs."

Chewing over in my mind what Illy had just told me, I looked back at the gang around the piano. The party seemed to be breaking up; at least some of them were chopping away at it. Sid had gone to the control divan and was getting set to tune in Egypt. Mark and Kaby were there with him, all bursting with eagerness and the vision of tanks on ranks of mounted Zombie bowmen going up in a mushroom cloud; I thought of what Illy had told me and I managed a smile-seems we've got to win and lose all the battles, every which way.

Mark had just put on his Parthian costume, groaning cheerfully, "Trousers again!" and was striding around under a hat like a fur-lined ice-cream cone and with the sleeves of his metal-stuffed candys flapping over his hands. He waved a short sword with a heart-shaped guard at Bruce and Erich and told them to get a move on.

Kaby was going along on the operation wearing the old-woman disguise intended for Benson-Carter. I got a half-hearted kick out of knowing she was going to have to cover that chest and hobble.

Bruce and Erich weren't taking orders from Mark just yet. Erich went over and said something to Bruce at the bar, and Bruce got down and went over with Erich to the piano, and Erich tapped Beau on the shoulder and leaned over and said something to him, and Beau nodded and yanked "Limehouse Blues" to a fast close and started another piece, something slow and nostalgic.

Erich and Bruce waved to Mark and smiled, as if to show him that whether he came over and stood with them or not, the legate and the lieutenant and the commandant were very much together. And while Sevensee hugged Lili with a simple enthusiasm that made me wonder why I've wasted so much imagination on genetic treatments for him, Erich and Bruce sang:

"To the legion of the lost ones, to the cohort of the damned,
To our brothers in the tunnels outside time,
Sing three Change-resistant Zombies, raised from death and robot-crammed,
And Commandos of the Spiders —
Here's to crime!
We're three blind mice on the wrong time-track,
Hush-hush-hush!
We've lost our now and will never get back,
Hush-hush-hush!
Change Commandos out on the spree,
Damned through all possibility,
Ghostgirls, think kindly on such as we,
Hush-hush-hush!"*

While they were singing, I looked down at my charcoal skirt and over at Maud and Lili and I thought, "Three gray hustlers for three black hussars, that's our speed." Well, I'd never thought of myself as a high-speed job, winning all the races —I wouldn't feel comfortable that way. Come to think of it, we've got to lose and win all the races in the long run, the way the course is laid out.

I fingered to Illy, "That's the picture, all right, Spider boy."

No Great Magic

The troupers of the Big Time
lack no art to sway a crowd —
or to change all history!

I

> To bring the dead to life
> Is no great magic.
> Few are wholly dead:
> Blow on a dead man's embers
> And a live flame will start.
> —Graves

I dipped through the filmy curtain into the boys' half of the dressing room and there was Sid sitting at the star's dressing table in his threadbare yellowed undershirt, the lucky one, not making up yet but staring sternly at himself in the bulb-framed mirror and experimentally working his features a little, as actors will, and kneading the stubble on his fat chin.

I said to him quietly, "Siddy, what are we putting on tonight? Maxwell Anderson's *Elizabeth the Queen* or Shakespeare's *Macbeth*? It says *Macbeth* on the callboard, but Miss Nefer's getting ready for Elizabeth. She just had me go and fetch the red wig."

He tried out a few eyebrow rears-right, left, both together-then turned to me, sucking in his big gut a little, as he always does when a gal heaves into hailing distance, and said, "Your pardon, sweetling, what sayest thou?"

Sid always uses that kook antique patter backstage, until I sometimes wonder whether I'm in Central Park, New York City, nineteen hundred and three quarters, or somewhere in Southwark, Merry England, fifteen hundred and same. The truth is that although he loves every last fat part in Shakespeare and will play the skinniest one with loyal and inspired affection, he thinks Willy S. penned Falstaff with nobody else in mind but Sidney J. Lessingham. (And no accent on the ham, please.)

I closed my eyes and counted to eight, then repeated my question.

He replied, "Why, the Bard's tragical history of the bloody Scot, certes." He waved his hand toward the portrait of Shakespeare that always sits beside his mirror on top of his reserve makeup box. At first that particular picture of the Bard looked too nancy to me —a sort of peeping-tom schoolteacher-but I've grown used to it over the months and even palsy-feeling.

He didn't ask me why I hadn't asked Miss Nefer my question. Everybody in the company knows she spends the hour before curtain-time getting into character, never parting her lips except for that purpose-or to bite your head off if you try to make the most necessary conversation.

"Aye, 'tiz *Macbeth* tonight," Sid confirmed, returning to his frowning-practice: left eyebrow up, right down, reverse, repeat, rest. "And I must play the ill-starred Thane of Glamis."

I said, "That's fine, Siddy, but where does it leave us with Miss Nefer? She's already thinned her eyebrows and beaked out the top of her nose for Queen Liz, though that's as far as she's got. A beautiful job, the nose. Anybody else would think it was plastic surgery instead of putty. But it's going to look kind of funny on the Thaness of Glamis."

Sid hesitated a half second longer than he usually would —I thought, *his timing's off tonight* —and then he harrumphed and said, "Why, Iris Nefer, decked out as Good Queen Bess, will speak a prologue to the play —a prologue which I have myself but last week writ." He owled his eyes. "'Tis an experiment in the new theater."

I said, "Siddy, prologues were nothing new to Shakespeare. He had them on half his other plays. Besides, it doesn't make sense to use Queen Elizabeth. She was dead by the time he whipped up *Macbeth*, which is all about witchcraft and directed at King James."

He growled a little at me and demanded, "Prithee, how comes it your peewit-brain bears such a ballast of fusty book-knowledge, chit?"

I said softly, "Siddy, you don't camp in a Shakespearean dressing room for a year, tete-a-teting with some of the wisest actors ever, without learning a little. Sure I'm a mental case, a poor little A & A existing on your sweet charity, and don't think I don't appreciate it, but —"

"A-and-A, thou sayest?" he frowned. "Methinks the gladsome new forswearers of sack and ale call themselves AA."

"Agoraphobe and Amnesiac," I told him. "But look, Siddy, I was going to sayest that I do know the plays. Having Queen Elizabeth speak a prologue to *Macbeth* is as much an anachronism as if you put her on the gantry of the British moonship, busting a bottle of champagne over its schnozzle."

"Ha!" he cried as if he'd caught me out. "And saying there's a new Elizabeth, wouldn't that be the bravest advertisement ever for the Empire? —perchance rechristening the pilot, copilot and astrogator Drake, Hawkins and Raleigh? And the ship *The Golden Hind*? Tilly fally, lady!"

He went on, "My prologue an anachronism, quotha! The groundlings will never mark it. Think'st thou wisdom came to mankind with the stenchful rocket and the sundered atomy? More, the Bard himself was topfull of anachronism. He put spectacles on King Lear, had clocks tolling the hour in Caesar's Rome, buried that Roman 'stead o' burning him and gave Czechoslovakia a seacoast. Go to, doll."

"Czechoslovakia, Siddy?"

"Bohemia, then, what skills it? Leave me now, sweet poppet. Go thy ways. I have matters of import to ponder. There's more to running a repertory company than reading the footnotes to Furness."

Martin had just slouched by calling the Half Hour and looking in his solemnity, sneakers, levis and dirty T-shirt more like an underage refugee from Skid Row than Sid's newest recruit, assistant stage manager and hardest-worked juvenile-though for once he'd remembered to shave. I was about to ask Sid who was going to play Lady Mack if Miss Nefer wasn't, or, if she were going to double the roles, shouldn't I help her with the change? She's a slow dresser and the Elizabeth costumes are pretty realistically stayed. And she would have trouble getting off that nose, I was sure. But then I saw that Siddy was already slapping on the alboline to keep the grease paint from getting into his pores.

Greta, you ask too many questions, I told myself. *You get everybody riled up and you rack your own poor ricketty little mind;* and I hied myself off to the costumery to settle my nerves.

The costumery, which occupies the back end of the dressing room, is exactly the right place to settle the nerves and warm the fancies of any child, including an unraveled adult who's saving what's left of her sanity by pretending to be one. To begin with there are the regular costumes for Shakespeare's plays, all jeweled and spangled and brocaded, stage armor, great Roman togas with weights in the borders to make them drape right, velvets of every color to rest your cheek against and dream, and the fantastic costumes for the other plays we favor; Ibsen's *Peer Gynt*, Shaw's *Back to Methuselah* and Hilliard's adaptation of Heinlein's *Children of Methuselah*, the Capek brothers' *Insect People*, O'Neill's *The Fountain*, Flecker's *Hassan*, *Camino Real*, *Children of the Moon*, *The Beggar's Opera*, *Mary of Scotland*, *Berkeley Square*, *The Road to Rome*.

There are also the costumes for all the special and variety performances we give of the plays: *Hamlet* in modern dress, *Julius Caesar* set in a dictatorship of the 1920's, *The Taming of the Shrew* in caveman furs and leopard skins, where Petruchio comes in riding a dinosaur, *The Tempest* set on another planet with a spaceship wreck to start it off *Karrumph!* —which means a half dozen spacesuits, featherweight but looking ever so practical, and the weirdest sort of extraterrestrial-beast outfits for Ariel and Caliban and the other monsters.

Oh, I tell you the stuff in the costumery ranges over such a sweep of space and time that you sometimes get frightened you'll be whirled up and spun off just anywhere, so that you have to clutch at something very real to you to keep it from happening and to remind you where you *really* are-as I did now at the subway token on the thin gold chain around my neck (Siddy's first gift to me that I can remember) and chanted very softly to myself, like a charm or a prayer, closing my eyes and squeezing the holes in the token: "Columbus Circle, Times Square, Penn Station, Christopher Street...."

But you don't ever get *really* frightened in the costumery. Not exactly, though your goose-hairs get wonderfully realistically tingled and your tummy chilled from time to time-because you know it's all make-believe, a lifesize doll world, a children's dress-up world. It gets you thinking of far-off times and scenes as *pleasant* places and not as black hungry mouths that might gobble you up and keep you forever. It's always safe, always *just in the theatre, just on the stage*, no matter how far it seems to plunge and roam ... and the best sort of therapy for a pot-holed mind like mine, with as many gray ruts and curves and gaps as its cerebrum, that can't remember one single thing before this last year in the dressing room and that can't ever push its shaking body out of that same motherly fatherly room, except to stand in the wings for a scene or two and watch the play until the fear gets too great and the urge to take just one peek at *the audience* gets too strong ... and I remember what happened the two times I *did* peek, and I have to come scuttling back.

The costumery's good occupational therapy for me, too, as my pricked and calloused finger-tips testify. I think I must have stitched up or darned half the costumes in it this last twelve-month, though there are so many of them that I swear the drawers have accordion pleats and the racks extend into the fourth dimension-not to mention the boxes of props and the shelves of scripts and prompt-copies and other books, including a couple of encyclopedias and the many thick volumes of Furness's *Variorum Shakespeare*, which as Sid had guessed I'd been boning up on. Oh, and I've sponged and pressed enough costumes, too, and even refitted them to newcomers like Martin, ripping up and resewing seams, which can be a punishing job with heavy materials.

In a less sloppily organized company I'd be called wardrobe mistress, I guess. Except that to anyone in show business that suggests a crotchety old dame with lots of authority and scissors hanging around her neck on a string. Although I got my crochets, all right, I'm not that old. Kind of childish, in fact. As for authority, everybody outranks me, even Martin.

Of course to somebody *outside* show business, wardrobe mistress might suggest a yummy gal who spends her time dressing up as Nell Gwyn or Anitra or Mrs. Pinchwife or Cleopatra or even Eve (we got a legal costume for it) and inspiring the boys. I've tried that once or twice. But Siddy frowns on it, and if Miss Nefer ever caught me at it I think she'd whang me.

And in a normaller company it would be the wardrobe room, too, but costumery is my infantile name for it and the actors go along with my little whims.

I don't mean to suggest our company is completely crackers. To get as close to Broadway even as Central Park you got to have something. But in spite of Sid's whip-cracking there is a comforting looseness about its efficiency-people trade around the parts they play without fuss, the bill may be changed a half hour before curtain without anybody getting hysterics, nobody gets fired for eating garlic and breathing it in the leading lady's face. In short, we're a team. Which is funny when you come to think of it, as Sid and Miss Nefer and Bruce and Maudie are British (Miss Nefer with a touch of Eurasian blood, I romance); Martin and Beau and me are American (at least I *think* I am) while the rest come from just everywhere.

Besides my costumery work, I fetch things and run inside errands and help the actresses dress and the actors too. The dressing room's very coeducational in a halfway respectable way. And every once in a while Martin and I police up the whole place, me skittering about with dustcloth and wastebasket, he wielding the scrub-brush and mop with such silent grim efficiency that it always makes me nervous to get through and duck back into the costumery to collect myself.

Yes, the costumery's a great place to quiet your nerves or improve your mind or even dream your life away. But this time I couldn't have been there eight minutes when Miss Nefer's Eliz-abeth-angry voice came skirling, "Girl! Girl! Greta, where is my ruff with silver trim?" I laid my hands on it in a flash and loped it to her, because Old Queen Liz was known to slap even her Maids of Honor around a bit now and then and Miss Nefer is a bear on getting into character—a real Paul Muni.

She was all made up now, I was happy to note, at least as far as her face went—I hate to see that spooky eight-spoked faint tattoo on her forehead (I've sometimes wondered if she got it acting in India or Egypt maybe).

Yes, she was already all made up. This time she'd been going extra heavy on the burrowing-into-character bit, I could tell right away, even if it was only for a hacked-out anachronistic prologue. She signed to me to help her dress without even looking at me, but as I got busy I looked at *her* eyes. They were so cold and sad and lonely (maybe because they were so far away from her eyebrows and temples and small tight mouth, and so shut away from each other by that ridge of nose) that I got the creeps. Then she began to murmur and sigh, very softly at first, then loudly enough so I got the sense of it.

"Cold, so cold," she said, still seeing things far away though her hands were working smoothly with mine. "Even a gallop hardly fires my blood. Never was such a Januarius, though there's no snow. Snow will not come, or tears. Yet my brain burns with the thought of Mary's death-warrant unsigned. There's my particular hell!—to doom, perchance, all future queens, or leave a hole for the Spaniard and the Pope to creep like old worms back into the sweet apple of England. Philip's tall black crooked ships massing like sea-going fortresses south-away—cragged castles set to march into the waves. Parma in the Lowlands! And all the while my bright young idiot gentlemen spurting out my treasure as if it were so much water, as if gold pieces were a glut of summer posies. Oh, alackanight!"

And I thought, *Cry Iced!—that's sure going to be one tyrannosaur of a prologue. And how you'll ever shift back to being Lady Mack beats me. Greta, if this is what it takes to do just a bit part, you'd better give up your secret ambition of playing walk-ons some day when your nerves heal.*

She was really getting to me, you see, with that characterization. It was as if I'd managed to go out and take a walk and sat down in the park outside and heard the President talking to himself about the chances of war with Russia and realized he'd sat down on a bench with its back to mine and only a bush between. You see, here we were, two females undignifiedly twisted together, at the moment getting her into that crazy crouch-deep bodice that's like a big icecream cone, and yet here at the same time was Queen Elizabeth the First of England, three hundred and umpty-ump years dead, coming back to life in a Central Park dressing room. It shook me.

She looked so much the part, you see-even without the red wig yet, just powdered pale makeup going back to a quarter of an inch from her own short dark bang combed and netted back tight. The age too. Miss Nefer can't be a day over forty-well, forty-two at most-but now she looked and talked and felt to my hands dressing her, well, at least a dozen years older. I guess when Miss Nefer gets into character she does it with each molecule.

That age point fascinated me so much that I risked asking her a question. Probably I was figuring that she couldn't do me much damage because of the positions we happened to be in at the moment. You see, I'd started to lace her up and to do it right I had my knee against the tail of her spine.

"How old, I mean how young might your majesty be?" I asked her, innocently wonderingly like some dumb serving wench.

For a wonder she didn't somehow swing around and clout me, but only settled into character a little more deeply.

"Fifty-four winters," she replied dismally. " 'Tiz Januarius of Our Lord's year One Thousand and Five Hundred and Eighty and Seven. I sit cold in Greenwich, staring at the table where Mary's death warrant waits only my sign manual. If I send her to the block, I open the doors to future, less official regicides. But if I doom her not, Philip's armada will come inching up the Channel in a season, puffing smoke and shot, and my English Catholics, thinking only of

Mary Regina, will rise and i' the end the Spaniard will have all. All history would alter. That must not be, even if I'm damned for it! And yet ...and yet...."

A bright blue fly came buzzing along (the dressing room has *some* insect life) and slowly circled her head rather close, but she didn't even flicker her eyelids.

"I sit cold in Greenwich, going mad. Each afternoon I ride, praying for some mischance, some prodigy, to wash from my mind away the bloody question for some little space. It skills not what: a fire, a tree a-failing, Davison or e'en Eyes Leicester tumbled with his horse, an assassin's ball clipping the cold twigs by my ear, a maid crying rape, a wild boar charging with dipping tusks, news of the Spaniard at Thames' mouth or, more happily, a band of strolling actors setting forth some new comedy to charm the fancy or some great unheard-of tragedy to tear the heart-though that were somewhat much to hope for at this season and place, even if Southwark be close by."

The lacing was done. I stood back from her, and really she looked so much like Elizabeth painted by Gheeraerts or on the Great Seal of Ireland or something-though the ash-colored plush dress trimmed in silver and the little silver-edge ruff and the black-silver tinsel-cloth cloak lined with white plush hanging behind her looked most like a winter riding costume-and her face was such a pale frozen mask of Elizabeth's inward tortures, that I told myself, *Oh, I got to talk to Siddy again, he's made some big mistake, the lardy old lackwit. Miss Nefer just can't be figuring on playing in Macbeth tonight.*

As a matter of fact I was nerving myself to ask *her* all about it direct, though it was going to take some real nerve and maybe be risking broken bones or at least a flayed cheek to break the ice of that characterization, when who should come by calling the Fifteen Minutes but Martin. He looked so downright goofy that it took my mind off Nefer-in-character for all of eight seconds.

His levied bottom half still looked like *The Lower Depths.* Martin is Village Stanislavsky rather than Ye Olde English Stage Traditions. But above that ...well, all it really amounted to was that he was stripped to the waist and had shaved off the small high tuft of chest hair and was wearing a black wig that hung down in front of his shoulders in two big braids heavy with silver hoops and pins. But just the same those simple things, along with his tarpaper-solarium tan and habitual poker expression, made him look so like an American Indian that I thought, *Hey Zeus! —he's all set to play Hiawatha, or if he'd just cover up that straight-line chest, a frowny Pocahontas.* And I quick ran through what plays with Indian parts we do and could only come up with *The Fountain.*

I mutely goggled my question at him, wiggling my hands like guppy fins, but he brushed me off with a solemn mysterious smile and backed through the curtain. I thought, *nobody can explain this but Siddy*, and I followed Martin.

History does not move in one current,
like the wind across bare seas,
but in a thousand streams and eddies,
like the wind over a broken landscape.
—Cary

The boys' half of the dressing room (two-thirds really) was bustling. There was the smell of spirit gum and Max Factor and just plain men. Several guys were getting dressed or un-, and Bruce was cussing Bloody-something because he'd just burnt his fingers unwinding from the neck of a hot electric bulb some crepe hair he'd wound there to dry after wetting and stretching it to turn it from crinkly to straight for his Banquo beard. Bruce is always getting to the theater late and trying shortcuts.

But I had eyes only for Sid. So help me, as soon as I saw him they bugged again. *Greta, I told myself, you're going to have to send Martin out to the drugstore for some anti-bug powder. "For the roaches, boy?" "No, for the eyes."*

Sid was made up and had his long mustaches and elf-locked Macbeth wig on-and his corset too. I could tell by the way his waist was sucked in before he saw me. But instead of dark kilts and that bronze-studded sweat-stained leather battle harness that lets him show off his beefy shoulders and the top half of his heavily furred chest-and which really does look great on Macbeth in the first act when he comes in straight from battle-but instead of that he was wearing, so help me, red tights cross-gartered with strips of gold-blue tinsel-cloth, a green doublet gold-trimmed and to top it a ruff, and he was trying to fit onto his front a bright silvered cuirass that would have looked just dandy maybe on one of the Pope's Swiss Guards.

I thought, *Siddy, Willy S. ought to reach out of his portrait there and bop you one on the koko for contemplating such a crazy-quilt desecration of just about his greatest and certainly his most atmospheric play.*

Just then he noticed me and hissed accusingly, "There thou art, slothy minx! Spring to and help stuff me into this monstrous chest-kettle."

"Siddy, what *is* all this?" I demanded as my hands automatically obeyed. "Are you going to play *Macbeth* for laughs, except maybe leaving the Porter a serious character? You think you're Red Skelton?"

"What monstrous brabble is this, you mad bitch?" he retorted, grunting as I bear-hugged his waist, shouldering the cuirass to squeeze it home.

"The clown costumes on all you men," I told him, for now I'd noticed that the others were in rainbow hues, Bruce a real eye-buster in yellow tights and violet doublet as he furiously bushed out and clipped crosswise sections of beard and slapped them on his chin gleaming brown with spirit gum. "I haven't seen any eight-inch polka-dots yet but I'm sure I will."

Suddenly a big grin split Siddy's face and he laughed out loud at me, though the laugh changed to a gasp as I strapped in the cuirass three notches too tight. When we'd got that adjusted he said, "I' faith thou slayest me, pretty witling. Did I not tell you this production is an experiment, a novelty? We shall but show *Macbeth* as it might have been costumed at the court of King James. In the clothes of the day, but gaudier, as was then the stage fashion. Hold, dove, I've somewhat for thee." He fumbled his grouch bag from under his doublet and dipped finger and thumb in it, and put in my palm a silver model of the Empire State Building, charm bracelet size, and one of the new Kennedy dimes.

As I squeezed those two and gloated my eyes on them, feeling securer and happier and friendlier for them though I didn't at the moment want to, I thought, *Well, Siddy's right about that, at least I've read they used to costume the plays that way, though I don't see how Shakespeare stood it. But it was dirty of them all not to tell me beforehand.*

But that's the way it is. Sometimes I'm the butt as well as the pet of the dressing room, and considering all the breaks I get I shouldn't mind. I smiled at Sid and went on tiptoes and necked out my head and kissed him on a powdery cheek just above an aromatic mustache. Then I wiped the smile off my face and said, "Okay, Siddy, play Macbeth as Little Lord Fauntleroy or Baby Snooks if you want to. I'll never squeak again. But the Elizabeth prologue's still an anachronism. And-this is the thing I came to tell you, Siddy-Miss Nefer's not getting ready for any measly prologue. She's set to play Queen Elizabeth all night and tomorrow morning too. Whatever you think, she doesn't know we're doing *Macbeth*. But who'll do Lady Mack if she doesn't? And Martin's not dressing for Malcolm, but for the Son of the Last of the Mohicans, I'd say. What's more —"

You know, something I said must have annoyed Sid, for he changed his mood again in a flash. "Shut your jaw, you crook brained cat, and begone!" he snarled at me. "Here's curtain time close upon us, and you come like a wittol scattering your mad questions like the crazed Ophelia her flowers. Begone, I say!"

"Yessir," I whipped out softly. I skittered off toward the door to the stage, because that was the easiest direction. I figured I could do with a breath of less grease-painty air. Then, "Oh, Greta," I heard Martin call nicely.

He'd changed his levis for black tights, and was stepping into and pulling up around him a very familiar dress, dark green and embroidered with silver and stage-rubies. He'd safety-pinned a folded towel around his chest-to make a bosom of sorts, I realized.

He armed into the sleeves and turned his back to me. "Hook me up, would you?" he entreated.

Then it hit me. They had no actresses in Shakespeare's day, they used boys. And the dark green dress was so familiar to me because —

"Martin," I said, halfway up the hooks and working fast-Miss Nefer's costume fitted him fine. "You're going to play —?"

"Lady Macbeth, yes," he finished for me. "Wish me courage, will you Greta? Nobody else seems to think I need it."

I punched him half-heartedly in the rear. Then, as I fastened the last hooks, my eyes topped his shoulder and I looked at our faces side by side in the mirror of his dressing table. His, in spite of the female edging and him being at least eight years younger than me, I think, looked wise, poised, infinitely resourceful with power in reserve, very very real, while mine looked like that of a bewildered and characterless child ghost about to scatter into air-and the edges of my charcoal sweater and skirt, contrasting with his strong colors, didn't dispel that last illusion.

"Oh, by the way, Greta," he said, "I picked up a copy of *The Village Times* for you. There's a thumbnail review of our *Measure for Measure*, though it mentions no names, darn it. It's around here somewhere...."

But I was already hurrying on. Oh, it was logical enough to have Martin playing Mrs. Macbeth in a production styled to Shakespeare's own times (though pedantically over-authentic, I'd have thought) and it really did answer all my questions, even why Miss Nefer could sink herself wholly in Elizabeth tonight if she wanted to. But it meant that I must be missing so much of what was going on right around me, in spite of spending 24 hours a day in the dressing room, or at most in the small adjoining john or in the wings of the stage just outside the dressing room door, that it scared me. Siddy telling everybody, "*Macbeth* tonight in Elizabethan costume, boys and girls," sure, that I could have missed-though you'd have thought he'd have asked my help on the costumes.

But Martin getting up in Mrs. Mack. Why, someone must have held the part on him twenty-eight times, cueing him, while he got the lines. And there must have been at least a couple of run-through rehearsals to make sure he had all the business and stage movements down pat, and Sid and Martin would have been doing their big scenes every backstage minute they could spare with Sid yelling, "Witling! Think'st *that's* a wifely buss?" and Martin would have been droning his lines last time he scrubbed and mopped....

Greta, they're hiding things from you, I told myself.

Maybe there was a 25th hour nobody had told me about yet when they did all the things they didn't tell me about.

Maybe they were things they didn't dare tell me because of my top-storey weakness.

I felt a cold draft and shivered and I realized I was at the door to the stage.

I should explain that our stage is rather an unusual one, in that it can face two ways, with the drops and set pieces and lighting all capable of being switched around completely. To your left, as you look out the dressing-room door, is an open-air theater, or rather an open-air place for the audience—a large upward-sloping glade walled by thick tall trees and with benches for over two thousand people. On that side the stage kind of merges into the grass and can be made to look part of it by a green groundcloth.

To your right is a big roofed auditorium with the same number of seats.

The whole thing grew out of the free summer Shakespeare performances in Central Park that they started back in the 1950's.

The Janus-stage idea is that in nice weather you can have the audience outdoors, but if it rains or there's a cold snap, or if you want to play all winter without a single break, as we've been doing, then you can put your audience in the auditorium. In that case, a big accordion-pleated wall shuts off the out of doors and keeps the wind from blowing your backdrop, which is on that side, of course, when the auditorium's in use.

Tonight the stage was set up to face the outdoors, although that draft felt mighty chilly.

I hesitated, as I always do at the door to the stage-though it wasn't the actual stage lying just ahead of me, but only backstage, the wings. You see, I always have to fight the feeling that if I go out the dressing room door, go out just eight steps, the world will change while I'm out there and I'll never be able to get back. It won't be New York City any more, but Chicago or Mars or Algiers or Atlanta, Georgia, or Atlantis or Hell and I'll never be able to get back to that lovely warm womb with all the jolly boys and girls and all the costumes smelling like autumn leaves.

Or, especially when there's a cold breeze blowing, I'm afraid that *I'll* change, that I'll grow wrinkled and old in eight footsteps, or shrink down to the witless blob of a baby, or forget altogether who I am—

—or, it occurred to me for the first time now, *remember* who I am. Which might be even worse.

Maybe that's what I'm afraid of.

I took a step back. I noticed something new just beside the door: a high-legged, short-keyboard piano. Then I saw that the legs were those of a table. The piano was just a box with yellowed keys. Spinet? Harpsichord?

"Five minutes, everybody," Martin quietly called out behind me.

I took hold of myself. Greta, I told myself-also for the first time, *you know that some day you're really going to have to face this thing, and not just for a quick dip out and back either. Better get in some practice.*

I stepped through the door.

Beau and Doc were already out there, made up and in costume for Ross and King Duncan. They were discreetly peering past the wings at the gathering audience. Or at the place where the audience ought to be gathering, at any rate-sometimes the movies and girlie shows and brainheavy beatnik bruhahas outdraw us altogether. Their costumes were the same kooky colorful ones as the others'. Doc had a mock-ermine robe and a huge gilt papier-mache crown. Beau was carrying a ragged black robe and hood over his left arm-he doubles the First Witch.

As I came up behind them, making no noise in my black sneakers, I heard Beau say, "I see some rude fellows from the City approaching. I was hoping we wouldn't get any of those. How should they scent us out?"

Brother, I thought, *where do you expect them to come from if not the City? Central Park is bounded on three sides by Manhattan Island and on the fourth by the Eighth Avenue Subway. And Brooklyn and Bronx boys have got pretty sharp scenters. And what's it get you insulting the woiking and non-woiking people of the woild's greatest metropolis? Be grateful for any audience you get, boy.*

But I suppose Beau Lassiter considers anybody from north of Vicksburg a "rude fellow" and is always waiting for the day when the entire audience will arrive in carriage and democrat wagons.

Doc replied, holding down his white beard and heavy on the mongrel Russo-German accent he miraculously manages to suppress on stage except when "Vot does it matter? Ve don't convinze zem, ve don't convinze nobody. *Nichevo.*"

Maybe, I thought, *Doc shares my doubts about making Macbeth plausible in rainbow pants.*

Still unobserved by them, I looked between their shoulders and got the first of my shocks.

It wasn't night at all, but afternoon. A dark cold lowering afternoon, admittedly. But afternoon all the same.

Sure, between shows I sometimes forget whether it's day or night, living inside like I do. But getting matinees and evening performances mixed is something else again.

It also seemed to me, although Beau was leaning in now and I couldn't see so well, that the glade was smaller than it should be, the trees closer to us and more irregular, and I couldn't see the benches. That was Shock Two.

Beau said anxiously, glancing at his wrist, "I wonder what's holding up the Queen?"

Although I was busy keeping up nerve-pressure against the shocks, I managed to think. *So he knows about Siddy's stupid Queen Elizabeth prologue too. But of course he would. It's only me they keep in the dark. If he's so smart he ought to remember that Miss Nefer is always the last person on stage, even when she opens the play.*

And then I thought I heard, through the trees, the distant drumming of horses' hoofs and the sound of a horn.

Now they do have horseback riding in Central Park and you can hear auto horns there, but the hoofbeats don't drum that wild way. And there aren't so many riding together. And no auto horn I ever heard gave out with that sweet yet imperious *ta-ta-ta-TA*.

I must have squeaked or something, because Beau and Doc turned around quickly, blocking my view, their expressions half angry, half anxious.

I turned too and ran for the dressing room, for I could feel one of my mind-wavery fits coming on. At the last second it had seemed to me that the scenery was getting skimpier, hardly more than thin trees and bushes itself, and underfoot feeling more like ground than a ground cloth, and overhead not theater roof but gray sky. *Shock Three and you're out, Greta*, my umpire was calling.

I made it through the dressing room door and nothing there was wavering or dissolving, praised be Pan. Just Martin standing with his back to me, alert, alive, poised like a cat inside that green dress, the prompt book in his right hand with a finger in it, and from his left hand long black tatters swinging-telling me he'd still be doubling Second Witch. And he was hissing, "Places, please, everybody. On stage!"

With a sweep of silver and ash-colored plush, Miss Nefer came past him, for once leading the last-minute hurry to the stage. She had on the dark red wig now. For me that crowned her characterization. It made me remember her saying, "My brain burns." I ducked aside as if she were majesty incarnate.

And then she didn't break her own precedent. She stopped at the new thing beside the door and poised her long white skinny fingers over the yellowed keys, and suddenly I remembered what it was called: a virginals.

She stared down at it fiercely, evilly, like a witch planning an enchantment. Her face got the secret fiendish look that, I told myself, the real Elizabeth would have had ordering the deaths of Ballard and Babington, or plotting with Drake (for all they say she didn't) one of his raids, that long long forefinger tracing crooked courses through a crabbedly drawn map of the Indies and she smiling at the dots of cities that would burn.

Then all her eight fingers came flickering down and the strings inside the virginals began to twang and hum with a high-pitched rendering of Grieg's "In the Hall of the Mountain King."

Then as Sid and Bruce and Martin rushed past me, along with a black swooping that was Maud already robed and hooded for Third Witch, I beat it for my sleeping closet like Peer Gynt himself dashing across the mountainside away from the cave of the Troll King, who only wanted to make tiny slits in his eyeballs so that forever afterwards he'd see reality just a little differently. And as I ran, the master-anachronism of that menacing mad march music was shrilling in my ears.

III

Sound a dumbe shew. Enter the three fatall sisters, with a rocke, a threed, and a pair of sheeres.

—Old Play

My sleeping closet is just a cot at the back end of the girls' third of the dressing room, with a three-panel screen to make it private.

When I sleep I hang my outside clothes on the screen, which is pasted and thumbtacked all over with the New York City stuff that gives me security: theater programs and restaurant menus, clippings from the *Times* and the *Mirror*, a torn-out picture of the United Nations building with a hundred tiny gay paper flags pasted around it, and hanging in an old hairnet a home-run baseball autographed by Willie Mays. Things like that.

Right now I was jumping my eyes over that stuff, asking it to keep me located and make me safe, as I lay on my cot in my clothes with my knees drawn up and my fingers over my ears so the louder lines from the play wouldn't be able to come nosing back around the trunks and tables and bright-lit mirrors and find me. Generally I like to listen to them, even if they're sort of sepulchral and drained of overtones by their crooked trip. But they're always tense-making. And tonight (I mean this afternoon) —no!

It's funny I should find security in mementos of a city I daren't go out into-no, not even for a stroll through Central Park, though I know it from the Pond to Harlem Meer-the Met Museum, the Menagerie, the Ramble, the Great Lawn, Cleopatra's Needle and all the rest. But that's the way it is. Maybe I'm like Jonah in the whale, reluctant to go outside because the whale's a terrible monster that's awful scary to look in the face and might really damage you gulping you a second time, yet reassured to know you're living in the stomach of that particular monster and not a seventeen tentacled one from the fifth planet of Aldebaran.

It's really true, you see, about me actually living in the dressing room. The boys bring me meals: coffee in cardboard cylinders and doughnuts in little brown grease-spotted paper sacks and malts and hamburgers and apples and little pizzas, and Maud brings me raw vegetables-carrots and parsnips and little onions and such, and watches to make sure I exercise my molars grinding them and get my vitamins. I take spit-baths in the little john. Architects don't seem to think actors ever take baths, even when they've browned themselves all over playing Pindarus the Parthian in *Julius Caesar*. And all my shut-eye is caught on this little cot in the twilight of my NYC screen.

You'd think I'd be terrified being alone in the dressing room during the wee and morning hours, let alone trying to sleep then, but that isn't the way it works out. For one thing, there's apt to be someone sleeping in too. Maudie especially. And it's my favorite time too for costume-mending and reading the *Variorum* and other books, and for just plain way-out dreaming. You see, the dressing room is the one place I really do feel safe. Whatever is out there in New York that terrorizes me, I'm pretty confident that it can never get in here.

Besides that, there's a great big bolt on the inside of the dressing room door that I throw whenever I'm all alone after the show. Next day they buzz for me to open it.

It worried me a bit at first and I had asked Sid, "But what if I'm so deep asleep I don't hear and you have to get in fast?" and he had replied, "Sweetling, a word in your ear: our own Beauregard Lassiter is the prettiest picklock unjailed since Jimmy Valentine and Jimmy Dale. I'll not ask where he learned his trade, but 'tis sober truth, upon my honor."

And Beau had confirmed this with a courtly bow, murmuring, "At your service, Miss Greta."

"How do you jigger a big iron bolt through a three-inch door that fits like Maudie's tights?" I wanted to know.

"He carries lodestones of great power and divers subtle tools," Sid had explained for him.

I don't know how they work it so that some Traverse-Three cop or park official doesn't find out about me and raise a stink. Maybe Sid just throws a little more of the temperament he uses to keep most outsiders out of the dressing-room. We sure don't get any janitors or scrubwomen, as Martin and I know only too well. More likely he squares someone. I do get the impression all the company's gone a little way out on a limb letting me stay here-that the directors of our theater wouldn't like it if they found out about me.

In fact, the actors are all so good about helping me and putting up with my antics (though they have their own, Danu digs!) that I sometimes think I must be related to one of them —a distant cousin or sister-in-law (or wife, my God!), because I've checked our faces side by side in the mirrors often enough and I can't find any striking family resemblances. Or maybe I was even an actress in the company. The least important one. Playing the tiniest roles like Lucius in *Caesar* and Bianca in *Othello* and one of the little princes in *Dick the Three Eyes* and Fleance and the Gentlewoman in *Macbeth*, though me doing even that much acting strikes me to laugh.

But whatever I am in that direction-if I'm anything-not one of the actors has told me a word about it or dropped the least hint. Not even when I beg them to tell me or try to trick them into it, presumably because it might revive the shock that gave me agoraphobia and amnesia in the first place, and maybe this time knock out my entire mind or at least smash the new mouse-in-a-hole consciousness I've made for myself.

I guess they must have got by themselves a year ago and talked me over and decided my best chance for cure or for just bumping along half happily was staying in the dressing room rather than being sent home (funny, could I have another?) or to a mental hospital. And then they must have been cocky enough about their amateur psychiatry and interested enough in me (the White Horse knows why) to go ahead with a program almost any psychiatrist would be bound to yike at.

I got so worried about the set up once and about the risks they might be running that, gritting down my dread of the idea, I said to Sid, "Siddy, shouldn't I see a doctor?"

He looked at me solemnly for a couple of seconds and then said, "Sure, why not? Go talk to Doc right now," tipping a thumb toward Doc Pyeskov, who was just sneaking back into the bottom of his makeup box what looked like a half pint from the flask I got. I did, incidentally. Doc explained to me Kraepelin's classification of the psychoses, muttering, as he absentmindedly fondled my wrist, that in a year or two he'd be a good illustration of Korsakov's Syndrome.

They've all been pretty darn good to me in their kooky ways, the actors have. Not one of them has tried to take advantage of my situation to extort anything out of me, beyond asking me to sew on a button or polish some boots or at worst clean the wash bowl. Not one of the boys has made a pass I didn't at least seem to invite. And when my crush on Sid was at its worst he shouldered me off by getting polite-something he only is to strangers. On the rebound I hit Beau, who treated me like a real Southern gentleman.

All this for a stupid little waif, whom anyone but a gang of sentimental actors would have sent to Bellevue without a second thought or feeling. For, to get disgustingly realistic, my most plausible theory of me is that I'm a stage-struck girl from Iowa who saw her twenties slipping away and her sanity too, and made the dash to Greenwich Village, and went so ape on Shakespeare after seeing her first performance in Central Park that she kept going back there night after night (Christopher Street, Penn Station, Times Square, Columbus Circle-see?) and hung around the stage door, so mousy but open-mouthed that the actors made a pet of her.

And then something very nasty happened to her, either down at the Village or in a dark corner of the Park. Something so nasty that it blew the top of her head right off. And she ran to the only people and place where she felt she could ever again feel safe. And she showed them the top of her head with its singed hair and its jagged ring of skull and they took pity.

My least plausible theory of me, but the one I like the most, is that I was born in the dressing room, cradled in the top of a flat theatrical trunk with my ears full of Shakespeare's lines before I ever said "Mama," let alone lamped a TV; hush-walked when I cried by whoever was off stage, old props my first toys, trying to eat crepe hair my first indiscretion, sticks of grease-paint my first crayons. You know, I really wouldn't be bothered by crazy fears about New York changing and the dressing room shifting around in space and time, if I could be sure I'd always be able to stay in it and that the same sweet guys and gals would always be with me and that the shows would always go on.

This show was sure going on, it suddenly hit me, for I'd let my fingers slip off my ears as I sentimentalized and wish-dreamed and I heard, muted by the length and stuff of the dressing room, the slow beat of a drum and then a drum note in Maudie's voice taking up that beat as she warned the other two witches, "A drum, a drum! Macbeth doth come."

Why, I'd not only missed Sid's history-making-and-breaking Queen Elizabeth prologue (kicking myself that I had, now it was over), I'd also missed the short witch scene with its famous "Fair is foul and foul is fair," the Bloody Sergeant scene where Duncan hears about Macbeth's victory, and we were well into the second witch scene, the one on the blasted heath where Macbeth gets it predicted to him he'll be king after Duncan and is tempted to speculate about hurrying up the process.

I sat up. I did hesitate a minute then, my fingers going back toward my ears, because *Macbeth* is specially tense-making and when I've had one of my mind-wavery fits I feel weak for a while and things are blurry and uncertain. Maybe I'd better take a couple of the barbiturate sleeping pills Maudie manages to get for me and-but *No, Greta,* I told myself, *you want to watch this show, you want to see how they do in those crazy costumes. You especially want to see how Martin makes out. He'd never forgive you if you didn't.*

So I walked to the other end of the empty dressing room, moving quite slowly and touching the edges here and there, the words of the play getting louder all the time. By the time I got to the door Bruce-Banquo was saying to the witches, "If you can look into the seeds of time, And say which grain will grow and which will not," —those lines that stir anyone's imagination with their veiled vision of the universe.

The overall lighting was a little dim (afternoon fading already? —a *late* matinee?) and the stage lights flickery and the scenery still a little spectral-flimsy. Oh, my mind-wavery fits can be lulus! But I concentrated on the actors, watching them through the entrance-gaps in the wings. They were solid enough.

Giving a solid performance, too, as I decided after watching that scene through and the one after it where Duncan congratulates Macbeth, with never a pause between the two scenes in true Elizabethan style. Nobody was laughing at the colorful costumes. After a while I began to accept them myself.

Oh, it was a different *Macbeth* than our company usually does. Louder and faster, with shorter pauses between speeches, the blank verse at times approaching a chant. But it had a lot of real guts and everybody was just throwing themselves into it, Sid especially.

The first Lady Macbeth scene came. Without exactly realizing it I moved forward to where I'd been when I got my three shocks. Martin is so intent on his career and making good that he has me the same way about it.

The Thaness started off, as she always does, toward the opposite side of the stage and facing a little away from me. Then she moved a step and looked down at the stage-parchment letter in her hands and began to read it, though there was nothing on it but scribble, and my heart sank because the voice I heard was Miss Nefer's. I thought (and almost said out loud) *Oh, dammit, he funked out, or Sid decided at the last minute he couldn't trust him with the part. Whoever got Miss Nefer out of the ice cream cone in time?*

Then she swung around and I saw that no, my God, it *was* Martin, no mistaking. He'd been using her voice. When a person first does a part, especially getting up in it without much rehearsing, he's bound to copy the actor he's been hearing doing it. And as I listened on, I realized it was fundamentally Martin's own voice pitched a trifle high, only some of the intonations and rhythms were Miss Nefer's. He was showing a lot of feeling and intensity too and real Martin-type poise. *You're off to a great start, kid*, I cheered inwardly. *Keep it up!*

Just then I looked toward the audience. Once again I almost squeaked out loud. For out there, close to the stage, in the very middle of the reserve section, was a carpet spread out. And sitting in the middle of it on some sort of little chair, with what looked like two charcoal braziers smoking to either side of her, was Miss Nefer with a string of extras in Elizabethan hats with cloaks pulled around them.

For a second it really threw me because it reminded me of the things I'd seen or thought I'd seen the couple of times I'd sneaked a peek through the curtain-hole at the audience in the indoor auditorium.

It hardly threw me for more than a second, though, because I remembered that the characters who speak Shakespeare's prologues often stay on stage and sometimes kind of join the audience and even comment on the play from time to time-Christopher Sly and attendant lords in *The Shrew*, for one. Sid had just copied and in his usual style laid it on thick.

Well, bully for you, Siddy, I thought, *I'm sure the witless New York groundlings will be thrilled to their cold little toes knowing they're sitting in the same audience as Good Queen Liz and attendant courtiers. And as for you, Miss Nefer*, I added a shade invidiously, *you just keep on sitting cold in Central Park, warmed by dry-ice smoke from braziers, and keep your mouth shut and everything'll be fine. I'm sincerely glad you'll be able to be Queen Elizabeth all night long. Just so long as you don't try to steal the scene from Martin and the rest of the cast, and the real play.*

I suppose that camp chair will get a little uncomfortable by the time the Fifth Act comes tramping along to that drumbeat, but I'm sure you're so much in character you'll never feel it.

One thing though: just don't scare me again pretending to work witchcraft-with a virginals or any other way.

Okay?

Swell.

Me, now, I'm going to watch the play.

IV

...to dream of new dimensions,
Cheating checkmate
by painting the king's robe
So that he slides like a queen;
—Graves

I swung back to the play just at the moment Lady Mack soliloquizes, "Come to my woman's breasts. And take my milk for gall, you murdering ministers." Although I knew it was just folded towel Martin was touching with his fingertips as he lifted them to the top half of his green bodice, I got carried away, he made it so real. I decided boys can play girls better than people think. Maybe they should do it a little more often, and girls play boys too.

Then Sid-Macbeth came back to his wife from the wars, looking triumphant but scared because the murder-idea's started to smoulder in him, and she got busy fanning the blaze like any other good little *hausfrau* intent on her husband rising in the company and knowing that she's the power behind him and that when there are promotions someone's always got to get the axe. Sid and Martin made this charming little domestic scene so natural yet gutsy too that I wanted to shout hooray. Even Sid clutching Martin to that ridiculous pot-chested cuirass didn't have one note of horseplay in it. Their bodies spoke. It was the McCoy.

After that, the play began to get real good, the fast tempo and exaggerated facial expressions actually helping it. By the time the Dagger Scene came along I was digging my fingernails into my sweaty palms. Which was a good thing-my eating up the play, I mean-because it kept me from looking at the audience again, even taking a fast peek. As you've gathered, audiences bug me. All those people out there in the shadows, watching the actors in the light, all those silent voyeurs as Bruce calls them. Why, they might be anything. And sometimes (to my mind-wavery sorrow) I think they are. Maybe crouching in the dark out there, hiding among the others, is the one who did the nasty thing to me that tore off the top of my head.

Anyhow, if I so much as glance at the audience, I begin to get ideas about it-and sometimes even if I don't, as just at this moment I thought I heard horses restlessly pawing hard ground and one whinny, though that was shut off fast. *Krishna kressed us!* I thought, *Skiddy can't have hired horses for Nefer-Elizabeth much as he's a circus man at heart. We don't have that kind of money. Besides —*

But just then Sid-Macbeth gasped as if he were sucking in a bucket of air. He'd shed the cuirass, fortunately. He said, "Is this a dagger which I see before me, the handle toward my hand?" and the play hooked me again, and I had no time to think about or listen for anything else. Most of the offstage actors were on the other side of the stage, as that's where they make their exits and entrances at this point in the Second Act. I stood alone in the wings, watching the play like a bug, frightened only of the horrors Shakespeare had in mind when he wrote it.

Yes, the play was going great. The Dagger Scene was terrific where Duncan gets murdered offstage, and so was the part afterwards where hysteria mounts as the crime's discovered.

But just at this point I began to catch notes I didn't like. Twice someone was late on entrance and came on as if shot from a cannon. And three times at least Sid had to throw someone a line when they blew up-in the clutches Sid's better than any prompt book. It began to look as if the play were getting out of control, maybe because the new tempo was so hot.

But they got through the Murder Scene okay. As they came trooping off, yelling "Well contented," most of them on my side for a change, I went for Sid with a towel. He always sweats like a pig in the Murder Scene. I mopped his neck and shoved the towel up under his doublet to catch the dripping armpits.

Meanwhile he was fumbling around on a narrow table where they lay props and costumes for quick changes. Suddenly he dug his fingers into my shoulder, enough to catch my attention at this point, meaning I'd show bruises tomorrow, and yelled at me under his breath, "And you love me, our crows and robes. Presto!"

I was off like a flash to the costumery. There were Mr. and Mrs. Mack's king-and-queen robes and stuff hanging and sitting just where I knew they'd have to be.

I snatched them up, thinking, *Boy, they made a mistake when they didn't tell about this special performance*, and I started back like Flash Two.

As I shot out the dressing room door the theater was very quiet. There's a short low-pitched scene on stage then, to give the audience a breather. I heard Miss Nefer say loudly (it had to be loud to get to me from even the front of the audience): "'Tis a good bloody play, Eyes," and some voice I didn't recognize reply a bit grudgingly, "There's meat in it and some poetry too, though rough-wrought." She went on, still as loudly as if she owned the theater, "'Twill make Master Kyd bite his nails with jealousy-ha, ha!"

Ha-ha yourself, you scene-stealing witch, I thought, as I helped Sid and then Martin on with their royal outer duds. But at the same time I knew Sid must have written those lines himself to go along with his prologue. They had the unmistakable rough-wrought Lessingham touch. Did he really expect the audience to make anything of that reference to Shakespeare's predecessor Thomas Kyd of *The Spanish Tragedy* and the lost *Hamlet*? And if they knew enough to spot that, wouldn't they be bound to realize the whole Elizabeth-Macbeth tie-up was anachronistic? But when Sid gets an inspiration he can be very bull-headed.

Just then, while Bruce-Banquo was speaking his broody low soliloquy on stage, Miss Nefer cut in again loudly with, "Aye, Eyes, a good bloody play. Yet somehow, methinks —I know not how—I've heard it before." Whereupon Sid grabbed Martin by the wrist and hissed, "Did'st hear? Oh, I like not that," and I thought, *Oh-ho, so now she's beginning to ad-lib.*

Well, right away they all went on stage with a flourish, Sid and Martin crowned and hand in hand. The play got going strong again. But there were still those edge-of-control undercurrents and I began to be more uneasy than caught up, and I had to stare consciously at the actors to keep off a wavery-fit.

Other things began to bother me too, such as all the doubling.

Macbeth's a great play for doubling. For instance, anyone except Macbeth or Banquo can double one of the Three Witches-or one of the Three Murderers for that matter. Normally we double at least one or two of the Witches and Murderers, but this performance there'd been more multiple-parting than I'd ever seen. Doc had whipped off his Duncan beard and thrown on a brown smock and hood to play the Porter with his normal bottle-roughened accents. Well, a drunk impersonating a drunk, pretty appropriate. But Bruce was doing the next-door-to-impossible double of Banquo and Macduff, using a ringing tenor voice for the latter and wearing in the murder scene a helmet with dropped visor to hide his Banquo beard. He'd be able to tear it off, of course, after the Murderers got Banquo and he'd made his brief appearance as a bloodied-up ghost in the Banquet Scene. I asked myself, *My God, has Siddy got all the other actors out in front playing courtiers to Elizabeth-Nefer? Wasting them that way? The whoreson rogue's gone nuts!*

But really it was plain frightening, all that frantic doubling and tripling with its suggestion that the play (and the company too, Freya forfend) was becoming a ricketty patchwork illusion with everybody racing around faster and faster to hide the holes. And the scenery-wavery stuff and the warped Park-sounds were scary too. I was actually shivering by the time Sid got to: "Light thickens; and the crow Makes wing to the rooky wood: Good things of day begin to droop and drowse; Whiles night's black agents to their preys do rouse." Those graveyard lines didn't help my nerves any, of course. Nor did thinking I heard Nefer-Elizabeth say from the audience, rather softly for her this time, "Eyes, I have heard that speech, I know not where. Think you 'tiz stolen?"

Greta, I told myself, *you need a miltown before the crow makes wing through your kooky head.*

I turned to go and fetch me one from my closet. And stopped dead.

Just behind me, pacing back and forth like an ash-colored tiger in the gloomy wings, looking daggers at the audience every time she turned at that end of her invisible cage, but ignoring me completely, was Miss Nefer in the Elizabeth wig and rig.

Well, I suppose I should have said to myself, *Greta, you imagined that last loud whisper from the audience. Miss Nefer's simply unkinked herself, waved a hand to the real audience and come back stage. Maybe Sid just had her out there for the first half of the play. Or maybe she just couldn't stand watching Martin give such a bang-up performance in her part of Lady Mack.*

Yes, maybe I should have told myself something like that, but somehow all I could think then-and I thought it with a steady mounting shiver-was, *We got two Elizabeths. This one is our witch Nefer. I know. I dressed her. And I know that devil-look from the virginals. But if this is our Elizabeth, the company Elizabeth, the stage Elizabeth ... who's the other?*

And because I didn't dare to let myself think of the answer to that question, I dodged around the invisible cage that the ash-colored skirt seemed to ripple against as the Tiger Queen turned and I ran into the dressing room, my only thought to get behind my New York City Screen.

Even little things are turning out to be great things and becoming intensely interesting.

Have you ever thought about the properties of numbers?

—The Maiden

Lying on my cot, my eyes crosswise to the printing, I looked from a pink Algonquin menu to a pale green New Amsterdam program, with a tiny doll of Father Knickerbocker dangling between them on a yellow thread. Really they weren't covering up much of anything. A ghostly hole an inch and a half across seemed to char itself in the program. As if my eye were right up against it, I saw in vivid memory what I'd seen the two times I'd dared a peek through the hole in the curtain: a bevy of ladies in masks and Nell Gwyn dresses and men in King Charles knee-breeches and long curled hair, and the second time a bunch of people and creatures just wild: all sorts and colors of clothes, humans with hoofs for feet and antennae springing from their foreheads, furry and feathery things that had more arms than two and in one case that many heads-as if they were dressed up in our *Tempest*, *Peer Gynt* and *Insect People* costumes and some more besides.

Naturally I'd had mind-wavery fits both times. Afterwards Sid had wagged a finger at me and explained that on those two nights we'd been giving performances for people who'd arranged a costume theater-party and been going to attend a masquerade ball, and 'zounds, when would I learn to guard my half-patched pate?

I don't know, I guess never, I answered now, quick looking at a Giants pennant, a Korvette ad, a map of Central Park, my Willie Mays baseball and a Radio City tour ticket. That was eight items I'd looked at this trip without feeling any inward improvement. They weren't reassuring me at all.

The blue fly came slowly buzzing down over my screen and I asked it, "What are you looking for? A spider?" when what should I hear coming back through the dressing room straight toward my sleeping closet but Miss Nefer's footsteps. No one else walks that way.

She's going to do something to you, Greta, I thought. *She's the maniac in the company. She's the one who terrorized you with the boning knife in the shrubbery, or sicked the giant tarantula on you at the dark end of the subway platform, or whatever it was, and the others are covering up for. She's going to smile the devil-smile and weave those white twig-fingers at you, all eight of them. And Birnam Wood'll come to Dunsinane and you'll be burnt at the stake by men in armor or drawn and quartered by eight-legged monkeys that talk or torn apart by wild centaurs or whirled through the roof to the moon without being dressed for it or sent burrowing into the past to stifle in Iowa 1948 or Egypt 4,008 B.C. The screen won't keep her out.*

Then a head of hair pushed over the screen. But it was black-bound-with-silver, Brahma bless us, and a moment later Martin was giving me one of his rare smiles.

I said, "Marty, do something for me. Don't ever use Miss Nefer's footsteps again. Her voice, okay, if you have to. But not the footsteps. Don't ask me why, just don't."

Martin came around and sat on the foot of my cot. My legs were already doubled up. He straightened out his blue-and-gold skirt and rested a hand on my black sneakers.

"Feeling a little wonky, Greta?" he asked. "Don't worry about me. Banquo's dead and so's his ghost. We've finished the Banquet Scene. I've got lots of time."

I just looked at him, queerly I guess. Then without lifting my head I asked him, "Martin, tell me the truth. Does the dressing room move around?"

I was talking so low that he hitched a little closer, not touching me anywhere else though.

"The Earth's whipping around the sun at 20 miles a second," he replied, "and the dressing room goes with it."

I shook my head, my cheek scrubbing the pillow, "I mean ... shifting," I said. "By itself."

"How?" he asked.

"Well," I told him, "I've had this idea-it's just a sort of fancy, remember-that if you wanted to time-travel and, well, do things, you could hardly pick a more practical machine than a dressing room and sort of stage and half-theater attached, with actors to man it. Actors can fit in anywhere. They're used to learning new parts and wearing strange costumes. Heck, they're even used to traveling a lot. And if an actor's a bit strange nobody thinks anything of it-he's almost expected to be foreign, it's an asset to him."

"And a theater, well, a theater can spring up almost anywhere and nobody ask questions, except the zoning authorities and such and they can always be squared. Theaters come and go. It happens all the time. They're transitory. Yet theaters are crossroads, anonymous meeting places, anybody with a few bucks or sometimes nothing at all can go. And theaters attract important people, the sort of people you might want to do something to. Caesar was stabbed in a theater. Lincoln was shot in one. And...."

My voice trailed off. "A cute idea," he commented.

I reached down to his hand on my shoe and took hold of his middle finger as a baby might. "Yeah," I said, "But Martin, is it true?"

He asked me gravely, "What do you think?"

I didn't say anything.

"How would you like to work in a company like that?" he asked speculatively.

"I don't really know," I said.

He sat up straighter and his voice got brisk. "Well, all fantasy aside, how'd you like to work in this company?" He asked, lightly slapping my ankle. "On the stage, I mean. Sid thinks you're ready for some of the smaller parts. In fact, he asked me to put it to you. He thinks you never take him seriously."

"Pardon me while I gasp and glow," I said. Then, "Oh Marty, I can't really imagine myself doing the tiniest part."

"Me neither, eight months ago," he said. "Now, look. Lady Macbeth."

"But Marty," I said, reaching for his finger again, "you haven't answered my question. About whether it's true."

"Oh that!" he said with a laugh, switching his hand to the other side. "Ask me something else."

"Okay," I said, "why am I bugged on the number eight? Because I'm permanently behind a private 8-ball?"

"Eight's a number with many properties," he said, suddenly as intently serious as he usually is. "The corners of a cube."

"You mean I'm a square?" I said. "Or just a brick? You know, 'She's a brick.'"

"But eight's most curious property," he continued with a frown, "is that lying on its side it signifies infinity. So eight erect is really —" and suddenly his made-up, naturally solemn face got a great glow of inspiration and devotion —"Infinity Arisen!"

Well, I don't know. You meet quite a few people in the theater who are bats on numerology, they use it to pick stage-names. But I'd never have guessed it of Martin. He always struck me as the skeptical, cynical type.

"I had another idea about eight," I said hesitatingly. "Spiders. That 8-legged asterisk on Miss Nefer's forehead —" I suppressed a shudder.

"You don't like her, do you?" he stated.

"I'm afraid of her," I said.

"You shouldn't be. She's a very great woman and tonight she's playing an infinitely more difficult part than I am. No, Greta," he went on as I started to protest, "believe me, you don't understand anything about it at this moment. Just as you don't understand about spiders, fearing them. They're the first to climb the rigging and to climb ashore too. They're the web-weavers, the line-throwers, the connectors, Siva and Kali united in love. They're the double mandala, the beginning and the end, infinity mustered and on the march —"

"They're also on my New York screen!" I squeaked, shrinking back across the cot a little and pointing at a tiny glinting silver-and-black thing mounting below my Willy-ball.

Martin gently caught its line on his finger and lifted it very close to his face. "Eight eyes too," he told me. Then, "Poor little god," he said and put it back.

"Marty? Marty?" Sid's desperate stage-whisper rasped the length of the dressing room.

Martin stood up. "Yes, Sid?"

Sid's voice stayed a whisper but went from desperate to ferocious. "You villainous elf-skin! Know you not the Cauldron Scene's been playing a hundred heartbeats? 'Tis 'most my entrance and we still mustering only two witches out of three! Oh, you nott-pated starveling!"

Before Sid had got much more than half of that out, Martin had slipped around the screen, raced the length of the dressing room, and I'd heard a lusty thwack as he went out the door. I couldn't help grinning, though with Martin racked by anxieties and reliefs over his first time as Lady Mack, it was easy to understand it slipping his mind that he was still doubling Second Witch.

VI

> I will vault credit
> and affect high pleasures
> Beyond death.
> —Ferdinand

I sat down where Martin had been, first pushing the screen far enough to the side for me to see the length of the dressing room and notice anyone coming through the door and any blurs moving behind the thin white curtain shutting off the boys' two-thirds.

I'd been going to think. But instead I just sat there, experiencing my body and the room around it, steadying myself or maybe readying myself. I couldn't tell which, but it was nothing to think about, only to feel. My heartbeat became a very faint, slow, solid throb. My spine straightened.

No one came in or went out. Distantly I heard Macbeth and the witches and the apparitions talk.

Once I looked at the New York Screen, but all the stuff there had grown stale. No protection, no nothing.

I reached down to my suitcase and from where I'd been going to get a miltown I took a dexedrine and popped it in my mouth. Then I started out, beginning to shake.

When I got to the end of the curtain I went around it to Sid's dressing table and asked Shakespeare, "Am I doing the right thing, Pop?" But he didn't answer me out of his portrait. He just looked sneaky-innocent, like he knew a lot but wouldn't tell, and I found myself think of a little silver-framed photo Sid had used to keep there too of a cocky German-looking young actor with "Erich" autographed across it in white ink. At least I supposed he was an actor. He looked a little like Erich von Stroheim, but nicer yet somehow nastier too. The photo had used to upset me, I don't know why. Sid must have noticed it, for one day it was gone.

I thought of the tiny black-and-silver spider crawling across the remembered silver frame, and for some reason it gave me the cold creeps.

Well, this wasn't doing me any good, just making me feel dismal again, so I quickly went out. In the door I had to slip around the actors coming back from the Cauldron Scene and the big bolt nicked my hip.

Outside Maud was peeling off her Third Witch stuff to reveal Lady Macduff beneath. She twitched me a grin.

"How's it going?" I asked.

"Okay, I guess," she shrugged. "What an audience! Noisy as highschool kids."

"How come Sid didn't have a boy do your part?" I asked.

"He goofed, I guess. But I've battened down my bosoms and playing Mrs. Macduff as a boy."

"How does a girl do that in a dress?" I asked.

"She sits stiff and thinks pants," she said, handing me her witch robe. "'Scuse me now. I got to find my children and go get murdered."

I'd moved a few steps nearer the stage when I felt the gentlest tug at my hip. I looked down and saw that a taut black thread from the bottom of my sweater connected me with the dressing room. It must have snagged on the big bolt and unraveled. I moved my body an inch or so, tugging it delicately to see what it felt like and I got the answers: Theseus's clew, a spider's line, an umbilicus.

I reached down close to my side and snapped it with my fingernails. The black thread leaped away. But the dressing room door didn't vanish, or the wings change, or the world end, and I didn't fall down.

After that I just stood there for quite a while, feeling my new freedom and steadiness, letting my body get used to it. I didn't do any thinking. I hardly bothered to study anything around me, though I did notice that there were more bushes and trees than set pieces, and that the flickery lightning was simply torches and that Queen Elizabeth was in (or back in) the audience. Sometimes letting your body get used to something is all you should do, or maybe can do.

And I did smell horse dung.

When the Lady Macduff Scene was over and the Chicken Scene well begun, I went back to the dressing room. Actors call it the Chicken Scene because Macduff weeps in it about "all my pretty chickens and their dam," meaning his kids and wife, being murdered "at one fell swoop" on orders of that chickenyard-raiding "hell-kite" Macbeth.

Inside the dressing room I steered down the boys' side. Doc was putting on an improbable-looking dark makeup for Macbeth's last faithful servant Seyton. He didn't seem as boozy-woozy as usual for Fourth Act, but just the same I stopped to help him get into a chain-mail shirt made of thick cord woven and silvered.

In the third chair beyond, Sid was sitting back with his corset loosened and critically survey-ing Martin, who'd now changed to a white wool nightgown that clung and draped beautifully, but not particularly enticingly, on him and his folded towel, which had slipped a bit.

From beside Sid's mirror, Shakespeare smiled out of his portrait at them like an intelligent big-headed bug.

Martin stood tall, spread his arms rather like a high priest, and intoned, *"Amici! Romani! Populares!"*

I nudged Doc. "What goes on now?" I whispered.

He turned a bleary eye on them. "I think they are rehearsing *Julius Caesar* in Latin." He shrugged. "It begins the oration of Antony."

"But why?" I asked. Sid does like to put every moment to use when the performance-fire is in people, but this project seemed pretty far afield-hyper-pedantic. Yet at the same time I felt my scalp shivering as if my mind were jumping with speculations just below the surface.

Doc shook his head and shrugged again.

Sid shoved a palm at Martin and roared softly, "'Sdeath, boy, thou'rt not playing a Roman statua but a Roman! Loosen your knees and try again."

Then he saw me. Signing Martin to stop, he called, "Come hither, sweetling." I obeyed quickly. He gave me a fiendish grin and said, "Thou'st heard our proposal from Martin. What sayest thou, wench?"

This time the shiver was in my back. It felt good. I realized I was grinning back at him, and I knew what I'd been getting ready for the last twenty minutes.

"I'm on," I said. "Count me in the company."

Sid jumped up and grabbed me by the shoulders and hair and bussed me on both cheeks. It was a little like being bombed.

"Prodigious!" he cried. "Thou'lt play the Gentlewoman in the Sleepwalking Scene tonight. Martin, her costume! Now sweet wench, mark me well." His voice grew grave and old. "When was it she last walked?"

The new courage went out of me like water down a chute. "But Siddy, I can't start *tonight*," I protested, half pleading, half outraged.

"Tonight or never! 'Tis an emergency-we're short-handed." Again his voice changed. "When was it she last walked?"

"But Siddy, I don't *know* the part."

"You must. You've heard the play twenty times this year past. When was it she last walked?"

Martin was back and yanking down a blonde wig on my head and shoving my arms into a light gray robe.

"I've never studied *the lines*," I squeaked at Sidney.

"Liar! I've watched your lips move a dozen nights when you watched the scene from the wings. Close your eyes, girl! Martin, unhand her. Close your eyes, girl, empty your mind, and listen, listen only. When was it she last walked?"

In the blackness I heard myself replying to that cue, first in a whisper, then more loudly, then full-throated but grave, "Since his majesty went into the field, I have seen her rise from her bed, throw her nightgown upon her, unlock her closet, take forth —"

"Bravissimo!" Siddy cried and bombed me again. Martin hugged his arm around my shoulders too, then quickly stooped to start hooking up my robe from the bottom.

"But that's only the first lines, Siddy," I protested.

"They're enough!"

"But Siddy, what if I blow up?" I asked.

"Keep your mind empty. You won't. Further, I'll be at your side, doubling the Doctor, to prompt you if you pause."

That ought to take care of two of me, I thought. Then something else struck me. "But Siddy," I quavered, "how do I play the Gentlewoman as a boy?"

"Boy?" he demanded wonderingly. "Play her without falling down flat on your face and I'll be past measure happy!" And he smacked me hard on the fanny.

Martin's fingers were darting at the next to the last hook. I stopped him and shoved my hand down the neck of my sweater and got hold of the subway token and the chain it was on and yanked. It burned my neck but the gold links parted. I started to throw it across the room, but instead I smiled at Siddy and dropped it in his palm.

"The Sleepwalking Scene!" Maud hissed insistently to us from the door.

I know death hath ten thousand several doors
For men to take their exits, and 'tis found
They go on such strange geometrical hinges,
You may open them both ways.
—The Duchess

There is this about an actor on stage: he can see the audience but he can't *look* at them, unless he's a narrator or some sort of comic. I wasn't the first (Grendel groks!) and only scared to death of becoming the second as Siddy walked me out of the wings onto the stage, over the groundcloth that felt so much like ground, with a sort of interweaving policeman-grip on my left arm.

Sid was in a dark gray robe looking like some dismal kind of monk, his head so hooded for the Doctor that you couldn't see his face at all.

My skull was pulse-buzzing. My throat was squeezed dry. My heart was pounding. Below that my body was empty, squirmy, electricity-stung, yet with the feeling of wearing ice cold iron pants.

I heard as if from two million miles, "When was it she last walked?" and then an iron bell somewhere tolling the reply —I guess it had to be my voice coming up through my body from my iron pants: "Since his majesty went into the field —" and so on, until Martin had come on stage, stary-eyed, a white scarf tossed over the back of his long black wig and a flaring candle two inches thick gripped in his right hand and dripping wax on his wrist, and started to do Lady Mack's sleepwalking half-hinted confessions of the murders of Duncan and Banquo and Lady Macduff.

So here is what I saw then without looking, like a vivid scene that floats out in front of your mind in a reverie, hovering against a background of dark blur, and sort of flashes on and off as you think, or in my case act. All the time, remember, with Sid's hand hard on my wrist and me now and then tolling Shakespearan language out of some lightless storehouse of memory I'd never known was there to belong to me.

There was a medium-size glade in a forest. Through the half-naked black branches shone a dark cold sky, like ashes of silver, early evening.

The glade had two horns, as it were, narrowing back to either side and going off through the forest. A chilly breeze was blowing out of them, almost enough to put out the candle. Its flame rippled.

Rather far back in the horn to my left, but not very far, were clumped two dozen or so men in dark cloaks they huddled around themselves. They wore brimmed tallish hats and pale stuff showing at their necks. Somehow I assumed that these men must be the "rude fellows from the City" I remembered Beau mentioning a million or so years ago. Although I couldn't see them very well, and didn't spend much time on them, there was one of them who had his hat off or excitedly pushed way back, showing a big pale forehead. Although that was all the conscious impression I had of his face, he seemed frighteningly familiar.

In the horn to my right, which was wider, were lined up about a dozen horses, with grooms holding tight every two of them, but throwing their heads back now and then as they strained against the reins, and stamping their front hooves restlessly. Oh, they frightened me, I tell you, that line of two-foot-long glossy-haired faces, writhing back their upper lips from teeth wide as piano keys, every horse of them looking as wild-eyed and evil as Fuseli's steed sticking its head through the drapes in his picture "The Nightmare."

To the center the trees came close to the stage. Just in front of them was Queen Elizabeth sitting on the chair on the spread carpet, just as I'd seen her out there before; only now I could see that the braziers were glowing and redly high-lighting her pale cheeks and dark red hair and the silver in her dress and cloak. She was looking at Martin-Lady Mack-most intently, her mouth grimaced tight, twisting her fingers together.

Standing rather close around her were a half dozen men with fancier hats and ruffs and wide-flaring riding gauntlets.

Then, through the trees and tall leafless bushes just behind Elizabeth, I saw an identical Elizabeth-face floating, only this one was smiling a demonic smile. The eyes were open very wide. Now and then the pupils darted rapid glances from side to side.

There was a sharp pain in my left wrist and Sid whisper-snarling at me, "Accustomed action!" out of the corner of his shadowed mouth.

I tolled on obediently, "It is an accustomed action with her, to seem thus washing her hands: I have known her continue in this a quarter of an hour."

Martin had set down the candle, which still flared and guttered, on a little high table so firm its thin legs must have been stabbed into the ground. And he was rubbing his hands together slowly, continually, tormentedly, trying to get rid of Duncan's blood which Mrs. Mack knows in her sleep is still there. And all the while as he did it, the agitation of the seated Elizabeth grew, the eyes flicking from side to side, hands writhing.

He got to the lines, "Here's the smell of blood still: all the perfumes of Arabia will not sweeten this little hand. Oh, oh, oh!"

As he wrung out those soft, tortured sighs, Elizabeth stood up from her chair and took a step forward. The courtiers moved toward her quickly, but not touching her, and she said loudly, "Tis the blood of Mary Stuart whereof she speaks-the pails of blood that will gush from her chopped neck. Oh, I cannot endure it!" And as she said that last, she suddenly turned about and strode back toward the trees, kicking out her ash-colored skirt. One of the courtiers turned with her and stooped toward her closely, whispering something. But although she paused a moment, all she said was, "Nay, Eyes, stop not the play, but follow me not! Nay, I say leave me, Leicester!" And she walked into the trees, he looking after her.

Then Sid was kicking my ankle and I was reciting something and Martin was taking up his candle again without looking at it saying with a drugged agitation, "To bed; to bed; there's knocking at the gate."

Elizabeth came walking out of the trees again, her head bowed. She couldn't have been in them ten seconds. Leicester hurried toward her, hand anxiously outstretched.

Martin moved offstage, torturedly yet softly wailing, "What's done cannot be undone."

Just then Elizabeth flicked aside Leicester's hand with playful contempt and looked up and she was smiling the devil-smile. A horse whinnied like a trumpeted snicker.

As Sid and I started our last few lines together I intoned mechanically, letting words free-fall from my mind to my tongue. All this time I had been answering Lady Mack in my thoughts, *That's what you think, sister.*

God cannot effect that anything which is past should not have been.

It is more impossible than rising the dead.

—Summa Theologica

The moment I was out of sight of the audience I broke away from Sid and ran to the dressing room. I flopped down on the first chair I saw, my head and arms trailed over its back, and I almost passed out. It wasn't a mind-wavery fit. Just normal faint.

I couldn't have been there long-well, not very long, though the battle-rattle and alarums of the last scene were echoing tinnily from the stage-when Bruce and Beau and Mark (who was playing Malcolm, Martin's usual main part) came in wearing their last-act stage-armor and carrying between them Queen Elizabeth flaccid as a sack. Martin came after them, stripping off his white wool nightgown so fast that buttons flew. I thought automatically, *I'll have to sew those.*

They laid her down on three chairs set side by side and hurried out. Unpinning the folded towel, which had fallen around his waist, Martin walked over and looked down at her. He yanked off his wig by a braid and tossed it at me.

I let it hit me and fall on the floor. I was looking at that white queenly face, eyes open and staring sightless at the ceiling, mouth open a little too with a thread of foam trailing from the corner, and at that ice-cream-cone bodice that never stirred. The blue fly came buzzing over my head and circled down toward her face.

"Martin," I said with difficulty, "I don't think I'm going to like what we're doing."

He turned on me, his short hair elfed, his fists planted high on his hips at the edge of his black tights, which now were all his clothes.

"You knew!" he said impatiently. "You knew you were signing up for more than acting when you said, 'Count me in the company.' "

Like a legged sapphire the blue fly walked across her upper lip and stopped by the thread of foam.

"But Martin …changing the past …dipping back and killing the real queen …replacing her with a double —"

His dark brows shot up. "The real-You think this is the real Queen Elizabeth?" He grabbed a bottle of rubbing alcohol from the nearest table, gushed some on a towel stained with grease-paint and, holding the dead head by its red hair (no, wig-the real one wore a wig too) scrubbed the forehead.

The white cosmetic came away, showing sallow skin and on it a faint tattoo in the form of an "S" styled like a yin-yang symbol left a little open.

"Snake!" he hissed. "Destroyer! The arch-enemy, the eternal opponent! God knows how many times people like Queen Elizabeth have been dug out of the past, first by Snakes, then by Spiders, and kidnapped or killed and replaced in the course of our war. This is the first big operation I've been on, Greta. But I know that much."

My head began to ache. I asked, "If she's an enemy double, why didn't she know a performance of Macbeth in her lifetime was an anachronism?"

"Foxholed in the past, only trying to hold a position, they get dulled. They turn half zombie. Even the Snakes. Even our people. Besides, she almost did catch on, twice when she spoke to Leicester."

"Martin," I said dully, "if there've been all these replacements, first by them, then by us, what's happened to the *real* Elizabeth?"

He shrugged. "God knows."

I asked softly, "But does He, Martin? Can He?"

He hugged his shoulders in, as if to contain a shudder. "Look, Greta," he said, "it's the Snakes who are the warpers and destroyers. We're restoring the past. The Spiders are trying to keep things as first created. We only kill when we must."

I shuddered then, for bursting out of my memory came the glittering, knife-flashing, night-shrouded, bloody image of my lover, the Spider soldier-of-change Erich von Hohenwald, dying in the grip of a giant silver spider, or spider-shaped entity large as he, as they rolled in a tangled ball down a flight of rocks in Central Park.

But the memory-burst didn't blow up my mind, as it had done a year ago, no more than snapping the black thread from my sweater had ended the world. I asked Martin, "Is that what the Snakes say?"

"Of course not! They make the same claims we do. But somewhere, Greta, you have to *trust*." He put out the middle finger of his hand.

I didn't take hold of it. He whirled it away, snapping it against his thumb.

"You're still grieving for that carrion there!" he accused me. He jerked down a section of white curtain and whirled it over the stiffening body. "If you must grieve, grieve for Miss Nefer! Exiled, imprisoned, locked forever in the past, her mind pulsing faintly in the black hole of the dead and gone, yearning for Nirvana yet nursing one lone painful patch of consciousness. And only to hold a fort! Only to make sure Mary Stuart is executed, the Armada licked, and that all the other consequences flow on. The Snakes' Elizabeth let Mary live ...and England die ... and the Spaniard hold North America to the Great Lakes and New Scandinavia."

Once more he put out his middle finger.

"All right, all right," I said, barely touching it. "You've convinced me."

"Great!" he said. "'By for now, Greta. I got to help strike the set."

"That's good," I said. He loped out.

I could hear the skirling sword-clashes of the final fight to the death of the two Macks, Duff and Beth. But I only sat there in the empty dressing room pretending to grieve for a devil-smiling snow tiger locked in a time-cage and for a cute sardonic German killed for insubordination that *I* had reported ...but really grieving for a girl who for a year had been a rootless child of the theater with a whole company of mothers and fathers, afraid of nothing more than subway bogies and Park and Village monsters.

As I sat there pitying myself beside a shrouded queen, a shadow fell across my knees. I saw stealing through the dressing room a young man in worn dark clothes. He couldn't have been more than twenty-three. He was a frail sort of guy with a weak chin and big forehead and eyes that saw everything. I knew at one he was the one who had seemed familiar to me in the knot of City fellows.

He looked at me and I looked from him to the picture sitting on the reserve makeup box by Siddy's mirror. And I began to tremble.

He looked at it too, of course, as fast as I did. And then he began to tremble too, though it was a finer-grained tremor than mine.

The sword-fight had ended seconds back and now I heard the witches faintly wailing, "Fair is foul, and foul is fair —" Sid has them echo that line offstage at the end to give a feeling of prophecy fulfilled.

Then Sid came pounding up. He's the first finished, since the fight ends offstage so Macduff can carry back a red-necked papier-mache head of him and show it to the audience. Sid stopped dead in the door.

Then the stranger turned around. His shoulders jerked as he saw Sid. He moved toward him just two or three steps at a time, speaking at the same time in breathy little rushes.

Sid stood there and watched him. When the other actors came boiling up behind him, he put his hands on the doorframe to either side so none of them could get past. Their faces peered around him.

And all this while the stranger was saying, "What may this mean? Can such things be? Are all the seeds of time ... wetted by some hell-trickle ... sprouted at once in their granary? Speak ... speak! You played me a play ... that I am writing in my secretest heart. Have you disjointed the frame of things ... to steal my unborn thoughts? Fair is foul indeed. Is all the world a stage? Speak, I say! Are you not my friend Sidney James Lessingham of King's Lynn ... singed by time's fiery wand ... sifted over with the ashes of thirty years? Speak, are you not he? Oh, there are more things in heaven and earth ... aye, and perchance hell too ... Speak, I charge you!"

And with that he put his hands on Sid's shoulders, half to shake him, I think, but half to keep from falling over. And for the one time I ever saw it, glib old Siddy had nothing to say.

He worked his lips. He opened his mouth twice and twice shut it. Then, with a kind of desperation in his face, he motioned the actors out of the way behind him with one big arm and swung the other around the stranger's narrow shoulders and swept him out of the dressing room, himself following.

The actors came pouring in then, Bruce tossing Macbeth's head to Martin like a football while he tugged off his horned helmet, Mark dumping a stack of shields in the corner, Maudie pausing as she skittered past me to say, "Hi Gret, great you're back," and patting my temple to show what part of me she meant. Beau went straight to Sid's dressing table and set the portrait aside and lifted out Sid's reserve makeup box.

"The lights, Martin!" he called.

Then Sid came back in, slamming and bolting the door behind him and standing for a moment with his back against it, panting.

I rushed to him. Something was boiling up inside me, but before it could get to my brain I opened my mouth and it came out as, "Siddy, you can't fool me, that was no dirty S-or-S. I don't care how much he shakes and purrs, or shakes a spear, or just plain shakes-Siddy, that was Shakespeare!"

"Aye, girl, I think so," he told me, holding my wrists together. "They can't find dolls to double men like that-or such is my main hope." A big sickly grin came on his face. "Oh, gods," he demanded, "with what words do you talk to a man whose speech you've stolen all your life?"

I asked him, "Sid, were we *ever* in Central Park?"

He answered, "Once-twelve months back. A one-night stand. They came for Erich. You flipped."

He swung me aside and moved behind Beau. All the lights went out.

Then I saw, dimly at first, the great dull-gleaming jewel, covered with dials and green-glowing windows, that Beau had lifted from Sid's reserve makeup box. The strongest green glow showed his intent face, still framed by the long glistening locks of the Ross wig, as he knelt before the thing-Major Maintainer, I remembered it was called.

"When now? Where?" Beau tossed impatiently to Sid over his shoulder.

"The forty-fourth year before our Lord's birth!" Sid answered instantly. "Rome!"

Beau's fingers danced over the dials like a musician's, or a safe-cracker's. The green glow flared and faded flickeringly.

"There's a storm in that vector of the Void."

"Circle it," Sid ordered.

"There are dark mists every way."

"Then pick the likeliest dark path!"

I called through the dark, "Fair is foul, and foul is fair, eh, Siddy?"

"Aye, chick," he answered me. "'Tis all the rule we have!"

Appointment in Tomorrow

Is it possible to have a world without moral values?
Or does lack of morality become a moral value, also?

The first angry rays of the sun-which, startlingly enough, still rose in the east at 24 hour intervals-pierced the lacy tops of Atlantic combers and touched thousands of sleeping Americans with unconscious fear, because of their unpleasant similarity to the rays from World War III's atomic bombs.

They turned to blood the witch-circle of rusty steel skeletons around Inferno in Manhattan. Without comment, they pointed a cosmic finger at the tarnished brass plaque commemorating the martyrdom of the Three Physicists after the dropping of the Hell Bomb. They tenderly touched the rosy skin and strawberry bruises on the naked shoulders of a girl sleeping off a drunk on the furry and radiantly heated floor of a nearby roof garden. They struck green magic from the glassy blot that was Old Washington. Twelve hours before, they had revealed things as eerily beautiful, and as ravaged, in Asia and Russia. They pinked the white walls of the Colonial dwelling of Morton Opperly near the Institute for Advanced Studies; upstairs they slanted impartially across the Pharoahlike and open-eyed face of the elderly physicist and the ugly, sleep-surly one of young Willard Farquar in the next room. And in nearby New Washington they made of the spire of the Thinkers' Foundation a blue and optimistic glory that outshone White House, Jr.

It was America approaching the end of the Twentieth Century. America of juke-box burlesque and your local radiation hospital. America of the mask-fad for women and Mystic Christianity. America of the off-the-bosom dress and the New Blue Laws. America of the Endless War and the loyalty detector. America of marvelous Maizie and the monthly rocket to Mars. America of the Thinkers and (a few remembered) the Institute. "Knock on titanium," "Whadya do for black-outs," "Please, lover, don't think when I'm around," America, as combat-shocked and crippled as the rest of the bomb-shattered planet.

Not one impudent photon of the sunlight penetrated the triple-paned, polarizing windows of Jorj Helmuth's bedroom in the Thinker's Foundation, yet the clock in his brain awakened him to the minute, or almost. Switching off the Educational Sandman in the midst of the phrase, "...applying tensor calculus to the nucleus," he took a deep, even breath and cast his mind to the limits of the world and his knowledge. It was a somewhat shadowy vision, but, he noted with impartial approval, definitely less shadowy than yesterday morning.

Employing a rapid mental scanning technique, he next cleared his memory chains of false associations, including those acquired while asleep. These chores completed, he held his finger on a bedside button, which rotated the polarizing window panes until the room slowly filled with a muted daylight. Then, still flat on his back, he turned his head until he could look at the remarkably beautiful blonde girl asleep beside him.

Remembering last night, he felt a pang of exasperation, which he instantly quelled by taking his mind to a higher and dispassionate level from which he could look down on the girl and even himself as quaint, clumsy animals. Still, he grumbled silently, Caddy might have had enough consideration to clear out before he awoke. He wondered if he shouldn't have used his hypnotic control of the girl to smooth their relationship last night, and for a moment the word that would send her into deep trance trembled on the tip of his tongue. But no, that special power of his over her was reserved for far more important purposes.

Pumping dynamic tension into his 20-year-old muscles and confidence into his 60-year-old mind, the 40-year-old Thinker rose from bed. No covers had to be thrown off; the nuclear heating unit made them unnecessary. He stepped into his clothing-the severe tunic, tights and sockassins of the modern business man. Next he glanced at the message tape beside his phone, washed down with ginger ale a vita-amino-enzyme tablet, and walked to the window. There, gazing along the rows of newly planted mutant oaks lining Decontamination Avenue, his smooth face broke into a smile.

It had come to him, the next big move in the intricate game making up his life-and mankind's. Come to him during sleep, as so many of his best decisions did, because he regularly employed the time-saving technique of somno-thought, which could function at the same time as somno-learning.

He set his who?-where? robot for "Rocket Physicist" and "Genius Class." While it worked, he dictated to his steno-robot the following brief message:

Dear Fellow Scientist:

A project is contemplated that will have a crucial bearing on man's future in deep space. Ample non-military Government funds are available. There was a time when professional men scoffed at the Thinkers. Then there was a time when the Thinkers perforce neglected the professional men. Now both times are past. May they never return! I would like to consult you this afternoon, three o'clock sharp, Thinkers' Foundation I.

Jorj Helmuth

Meanwhile the who?-where? had tossed out a dozen cards. He glanced through them, hesitated at the name "Willard Farquar," looked at the sleeping girl, then quickly tossed them all into the addresso-robot and plugged in the steno-robot.

The buzz-light blinked green and he switched the phone to audio.

"The President is waiting to see Maizie, sir," a clear feminine voice announced. "He has the general staff with him."

"Martian peace to him," Jorj Helmuth said. "Tell him I'll be down in a few minutes."

Huge as a primitive nuclear reactor, the great electronic brain loomed above the knot of hush-voiced men. It almost filled a two-story room in the Thinkers' Foundation. Its front was an orderly expanse of controls, indicators, telltales, and terminals, the upper ones reached by a chair on a boom.

Although, as far as anyone knew, it could sense only the information and questions fed into it on a tape, the human visitors could not resist the impulse to talk in whispers and glance uneasily at the great cryptic cube. After all, it had lately taken to moving some of its own controls-the permissible ones-and could doubtless improvise a hearing apparatus if it wanted to.

For this was the thinking machine beside which the Marks and Eniacs and Maniacs and Maddidas and Minervas and Mimirs were less than Morons. This was the machine with a million times as many synapses as the human brain, the machine that remembered by cutting delicate notches in the rims of molecules (instead of kindergarten paper-punching or the Coney Island shimmying of columns of mercury). This was the machine that had given instructions on building the last three-quarters of itself. This was the goal, perhaps, toward which fallible human reasoning and biased human judgment and feeble human ambition had evolved.

This was the machine that really thought —a million-plus!

This was the machine that the timid cyberneticists and stuffy professional scientists had said could not be built. Yet this was the machine that the Thinkers, with characteristic Yankee push, *had* built. And nicknamed, with characteristic Yankee irreverence and girl-fondness, "Maizie."

Gazing up at it, the President of the United States felt a chord plucked within him that hadn't been sounded for decades, the dark and shivery organ chord of his Baptist childhood. Here, in a strange sense, although his reason rejected it, he felt he stood face to face with the living God: infinitely stern with the sternness of reality, yet infinitely just. No tiniest error or wilful misstep could ever escape the scrutiny of this vast mentality. He shivered.

The grizzled general-there was also one who was gray-was thinking that this was a very odd link in the chain of command. Some shadowy and usually well-controlled memories from World War II faintly stirred his ire. Here he was giving orders to a being immeasurably more intelligent than himself. And always orders of the "Tell me how to kill that man" rather than the "Kill that man" sort. The distinction bothered him obscurely. It relieved him to know that Maizie had built-in controls which made her always the servant of humanity, or of humanity's right-minded leaders-even the Thinkers weren't certain which.

The gray general was thinking uneasily, and, like the President, at a more turbid level, of the resemblance between Papal infallibility and the dictates of the machine. Suddenly his bony wrists began to tremble. He asked himself: Was this the Second Coming? Mightn't an incarnation be in metal rather than flesh?

The austere Secretary of State was remembering what he'd taken such pains to make everyone forget: his youthful flirtation at Lake Success with Buddhism. Sitting before his *guru*, his teacher, feeling the Occidental's awe at the wisdom of the East, or its pretense, he had felt a little like this.

The burly Secretary of Space, who had come up through United Rockets, was thanking his stars that at any rate the professional scientists weren't responsible for this job. Like the grizzled general, he'd always felt suspicious of men who kept telling you how to do things, rather than doing them themselves. In World War III he'd had his fill of the professional physicists, with their eternal taint of a misty sort of radicalism and free-thinking. The Thinkers were better-more disciplined, more human. They'd called their brain-machine Maizie, which helped take the curse off her. Somewhat.

The President's Secretary, a paunchy veteran of party caucuses, was also glad that it was the Thinkers who had created the machine, though he trembled at the power that it gave them over the Administration. Still, you could do business with the Thinkers. And nobody (not even the Thinkers) could do business (that sort of business) with Maizie!

Before that great square face with its thousands of tiny metal features, only Jorj Helmuth seemed at ease, busily entering on the tape the complex Questions of the Day that the high officials had handed him: logistics for the Endless War in Pakistan, optimum size for next year's sugar-corn crop, current thought trends in average Soviet minds-profound questions, yet many of them phrased with surprising simplicity. For figures, technical jargon, and layman's language were alike to Maizie; there was no need to translate into mathematical shorthand, as with the lesser brain-machines.

The click of the taper went on until the Secretary of State had twice nervously fired a cigaret with his ultrasonic lighter and twice quickly put it away. No one spoke.

Jorj looked up at the Secretary of Space. "Section Five, Question Four-whom would that come from?"

The burly man frowned. "That would be the physics boys, Opperly's group. Is anything wrong?"

Jorj did not answer. A bit later he quit taping and began to adjust controls, going up on the boom-chair to reach some of them. Eventually he came down and touched a few more, then stood waiting.

From the great cube came a profound, steady purring. Involuntarily the six officials backed off a bit. Somehow it was impossible for a man to get used to the sound of Maizie starting to think.

Jorj turned, smiling. "And now, gentlemen, while we wait for Maizie to celebrate, there should be just enough time for us to watch the takeoff of the Mars rocket." He switched on a giant television screen. The others made a quarter turn, and there before them glowed the rich ochres and blues of a New Mexico sunrise and, in the middle distance, a silvery mighty spindle.

Like the generals, the Secretary of Space suppressed a scowl. Here was something that ought to be spang in the center of his official territory, and the Thinkers had locked him completely out of it. That rocket there-just an ordinary Earth satellite vehicle commandeered from the Army, but equipped by the Thinkers with Maizie-designed nuclear motors capable of the Mars journey and more. The first spaceship-and the Secretary of Space was not in on it!

Still, he told himself, Maizie had decreed it that way. And when he remembered what the Thinkers had done for him in rescuing him from breakdown with their mental science, in rescuing the whole Administration from collapse he realized he had to be satisfied. And that was without taking into consideration the amazing additional mental discoveries that the Thinkers were bringing down from Mars.

"Lord," the President said to Jorj as if voicing the Secretary's feeling, "I wish you people could bring a couple of those wise little devils back with you this trip. Be a good thing for the country."

Jorj looked at him a bit coldly. "It's quite unthinkable," he said. "The telepathic abilities of the Martians make them extremely sensitive. The conflicts of ordinary Earth minds would impinge on them psychotically, even fatally. As you know, the Thinkers were able to contact them only because of our degree of learned mental poise and errorless memory-chains. So for the present it must be our task alone to glean from the Martians their astounding mental skills. Of course, some day in the future, when we have discovered how to armor the minds of the Martians —"

"Sure, I know," the President said hastily. "Shouldn't have mentioned it, Jorj."

Conversation ceased. They waited with growing tension for the great violet flames to bloom from the base of the silvery shaft.

Meanwhile the question tape, like a New Year's streamer tossed out a high window into the night, sped on its dark way along spinning rollers. Curling with an intricate aimlessness curiously like that of such a streamer, it tantalized the silvery fingers of a thousand relays, saucily evaded the glances of ten thousand electric eyes, impishly darted down a narrow black alleyway of memory banks, and, reaching the center of the cube, suddenly emerged into a small room where a suave fat man in shorts sat drinking beer.

He flipped the tape over to him with practiced finger, eyeing it as a stockbroker might have studied a ticker tape. He read the first question, closed his eyes and frowned for five seconds. Then with the staccato self-confidence of a hack writer, he began to tape out the answer.

For many minutes the only sounds were the rustle of the paper ribbon and the click of the taper, except for the seconds the fat man took to close his eyes, or to drink or pour beer. Once, too, he lifted a phone, asked a concise question, waited half a minute, listened to an answer, then went back to the grind.

Until he came to Section Five, Question Four. That time he did his thinking with his eyes open.

The question was: "Does Maizie stand for Maelzel?"

He sat for a while slowly scratching his thigh. His loose, persuasive lips tightened, without closing, into the shape of a snarl.

Suddenly he began to tape again.

"Maizie does not stand for Maelzel. Maizie stands for amazing, humorously given the form of a girl's name. Section Six, Answer One: The mid-term election viewcasts should be spaced as follows...."

But his lips didn't lose the shape of a snarl.

Five hundred miles above the ionosphere, the Mars rocket cut off its fuel and slumped gratefully into an orbit that would carry it effortlessly around the world at that altitude. The pilot unstrapped himself and stretched, but he didn't look out the viewport at the dried-mud disc that was Earth, cloaked in its haze of blue sky. He knew he had two maddening months ahead of him in which to do little more than that. Instead, he unstrapped Sappho.

Used to free fall from two previous experiences, and loving it, the fluffy little cat was soon bounding about the cabin in curves and gyrations that would have made her the envy of all back-alley and parlor felines on the planet below. A miracle cat in the dream world of free fall. For a long time she played with a string that the man would toss out lazily. Sometimes she caught the string on the fly, sometimes she swam for it frantically.

After a while the man grew bored with the game. He unlocked a drawer and began to study the details of the wisdom he would discover on Mars this trip-priceless spiritual insights that would be balm to war-battered mankind.

The cat carefully selected a spot three feet off the floor, curled up on the air, and went to sleep.

Jorj Helmuth snipped the emerging answer tape into sections and handed each to the appropriate man. Most of them carefully tucked theirs away with little more than a glance, but the Secretary of Space puzzled over his.

"Who the devil would Maelzel be?" he asked.

A remote look came into the eyes of the Secretary of State. "Edgar Allen Poe," he said frowningly, with eyes half-closed.

The grizzled general snapped his fingers. "Sure! Maelzel's Chess player. Read it when I was a kid. About an automaton that was supposed to play chess. Poe proved it hid a man inside it."

The Secretary of Space frowned. "Now what's the point in a fool question like that?"

"You said it came from Opperly's group?" Jorj asked sharply.

The Secretary of Space nodded. The others looked at the two men puzzledly.

"Who would that be?" Jorj pressed. "The group, I mean."

The Secretary of Space shrugged. "Oh, the usual little bunch over at the Institute. Hindeman, Gregory, Opperly himself. Oh, yes, and young Farquar."

"Sounds like Opperly's getting senile," Jorj commented coldly. "I'd investigate."

The Secretary of Space nodded. He suddenly looked tough. "I will. Right away."

Sunlight striking through French windows spotlighted a ballet of dust motes untroubled by air-conditioning. Morton Opperly's living room was well-kept but worn and quite behind the times. Instead of reading tapes there were books; instead of steno-robots, pen and ink; while in place of a four by six TV screen, a Picasso hung on the wall. Only Opperly knew that the painting was still faintly radioactive, that it had been riskily so when he'd smuggled it out of his bomb-singed apartment in New York City.

The two physicists fronted each other across a coffee table. The face of the elder was cadaverous, large-eyed, and tender-fined down by a long life of abstract thought. That of the younger was forceful, sensuous, bulky as his body, and exceptionally ugly. He looked rather like a bear.

Opperly was saying, "So when he asked who was responsible for the Maelzel question, I said I didn't remember." He smiled. "They still allow me my absent-mindedness, since it nourishes their contempt. Almost my sole remaining privilege." The smile faded. "Why do you keep on teasing the zoo animals, Willard?" he asked without rancor. "I've maintained many times that we shouldn't truckle to them by yielding to their demand that we ask Maizie questions.

You and the rest have overruled me. But then to use those questions to convey veiled insults isn't reasonable. Apparently the Secretary of Space was bothered enough about this last one to pay me a 'copter call within twenty minutes of this morning's meeting at the Foundation. Why do you do it, Willard?"

The features of the other convulsed unpleasantly. "Because the Thinkers are charlatans who must be exposed," he rapped out. "We know their Maizie is no more than a tealeaf-reading fake. We've traced their Mars rockets and found they go nowhere. We know their Martian mental science is bunk."

"But we've already exposed the Thinkers very thoroughly," Opperly interposed quietly. "You know the good it did."

Farquar hunched his Japanese-wrestler shoulders. "Then it's got to be done until it takes."

Opperly studied the bowl of mutated flowers by the coffee pot. "I think you just want to tease the animals, for some personal reason of which you probably aren't aware."

Farquar scowled. "We're the ones in the cages."

Opperly continued his inspection of the flowers' bells. "All the more reason not to poke sticks through the bars at the lions and tigers strolling outside. No, Willard, I'm not counseling appeasement. But consider the age in which we live. It wants magicians." His voice grew especially tranquil. "A scientist tells people the truth. When times are good-that is, when the truth offers no threat-people don't mind. But when times are very, very bad...." A shadow darkened his eyes. "Well, we all know what happened to —" And he mentioned three names that had been household words in the middle of the century. They were the names on the brass plaque dedicated to the martyred three physicists.

He went on, "A magician, on the other hand, tells people what they wish were true-that perpetual motion works, that cancer can be cured by colored lights, that a psychosis is no worse than a head cold, that they'll live forever. In good times magicians are laughed at. They're a luxury of the spoiled wealthy few. But in bad times people sell their souls for magic cures, and buy perpetual motion machines to power their war rockets."

Farquar clenched his fist. "All the more reason to keep chipping away at the Thinkers. Are we supposed to beg off from a job because it's difficult and dangerous?"

Opperly shook his head. "We're to keep clear of the infection of violence. In my day, Willard, I was one of the Frightened Men. Later I was one of the Angry Men and then one of the Minds of Despair. Now I'm convinced that all my reactions were futile."

"Exactly!" Farquar agreed harshly. "You reacted. You didn't act. If you men who discovered atomic energy had only formed a secret league, if you'd only had the foresight and the guts to use your tremendous bargaining position to demand the power to shape mankind's future...."

"By the time you were born, Willard," Opperly interrupted dreamily, "Hitler was merely a name in the history books. We scientists weren't the stuff out of which cloak-and-dagger men are made. Can you imagine Oppenheimer wearing a mask or Einstein sneaking into the Old White House with a bomb in his briefcase?" He smiled. "Besides, that's not the way power is seized. New ideas aren't useful to the man bargaining for power-only established facts or lies are."

"Just the same, it would have been a good thing if you'd had a little violence in you."

"No," Opperly said.

"I've got violence in me," Farquar announced, shoving himself to his feet.

Opperly looked up from the flowers. "I think you have," he agreed.

"But what are we to do?" Farquar demanded. "Surrender the world to charlatans without a struggle?"

Opperly mused for a while. "I don't know what the world needs now. Everyone knows Newton as the great scientist. Few remember that he spent half his life muddling with alchemy, looking for the philosopher's stone. Which Newton did the world need then?"

"Now you are justifying the Thinkers!"

"No, I leave that to history."

"And history consists of the actions of men," Farquar concluded. "I intend to act. The Thinkers are vulnerable, their power fantastically precarious. What's it based on? A few lucky guesses. Faith-healing. Some science hocus-pocus, on the level of those juke-box burlesque acts between the strips. Dubious mental comfort given to a few nerve-torn neurotics in the Inner Cabinet-and their wives. The fact that the Thinkers' clever stage-managing won the President a doubtful election. The erroneous belief that the Soviets pulled out of Iraq and Iran because of the Thinkers' Mind Bomb threat. A brain-machine that's just a cover for Jan Tregarron's guesswork. Oh, yes, and that hogwash of 'Martian wisdom.' All of it mere bluff! A few pushes at the right times and points are all that are needed-and the Thinkers know it! I'll bet they're terrified already, and will be more so when they find that we're gunning for them. Eventually they'll be making overtures to us, turning to us for help. You wait and see."

"I am thinking again of Hitler," Opperly interposed quietly. "On his first half dozen big steps, he had nothing but bluff. His generals were against him. They knew they were in a cardboard fort. Yet he won every battle, until the last. Moreover," he pressed on, cutting Farquar short, "the power of the Thinkers isn't based on what they've got, but on what the world hasn't got-peace, honor, a good conscience...."

The front-door knocker clanked. Farquar answered it. A skinny old man with a radiation scar twisting across his temple handed him a tiny cylinder. "Radiogram for you, Willard." He grinned across the hall at Opperly. "When are you going to get a phone put in, Mr. Opperly?"

The physicist waved to him. "Next year, perhaps, Mr. Berry."

The old man snorted with good-humored incredulity and trudged off.

"What did I tell you about the Thinkers making overtures?" Farquar chortled suddenly. "It's come sooner than I expected. Look at this."

He held out the radiogram, but the older man didn't take it. Instead he asked, "Who's it from? Tregarron?"

"No, from Helmuth. There's a lot of sugar corn about man's future in deep space, but the real reason is clear. They know that they're going to have to produce an actual nuclear rocket pretty soon, and for that they'll need our help."

"An invitation?"

Farquar nodded. "For this afternoon." He noticed Opperly's anxious though distant frown. "What's the matter?" he asked. "Are you bothered about my going? Are you thinking it might be a trap-that after the Maelzel question they may figure I'm better rubbed out?"

The older man shook his head. "I'm not afraid for your life, Willard. That's yours to risk as you choose. No, I'm worried about other things they might do to you."

"What do you mean?" Farquar asked.

Opperly looked at him with a gentle appraisal. "You're a strong and vital man, Willard, with a strong man's prides and desires." His voice trailed off for a bit. Then, "Excuse me, Willard, but wasn't there a girl once? A Miss Arkady?"

Farquar's ungainly figure froze. He nodded curtly, face averted.

"And didn't she go off with a Thinker?"

"If girls find me ugly, that's their business," Farquar said harshly, still not looking at Opperly. "What's that got to do with this invitation?"

Opperly didn't answer the question. His eyes got more distant. Finally he said, "In my day we had it a lot easier. A scientist was an academician, cushioned by tradition."

Willard snorted. "Science had already entered the era of the police inspectors, with laboratory directors and political appointees stifling enterprise."

"Perhaps," Opperly agreed. "Still, the scientist lived the safe, restricted, highly respectable life of a university man. He wasn't exposed to the temptations of the world."

Farquar turned on him. "Are you implying that the Thinkers will somehow be able to buy me off?"

"Not exactly."

"You think I'll be persuaded to change my aims?" Farquar demanded angrily.

Opperly shrugged his helplessness. "No, I don't think you'll change your aims."

Clouds encroaching from the west blotted the parallelogram of sunlight between the two men.

As the slideway whisked him gently along the corridor toward his apartment, Jorj was thinking of his spaceship. For a moment the silver-winged vision crowded everything else out of his mind.

Just think, a spaceship with sails! He smiled a bit, marveling at the paradox.

Direct atomic power. Direct utilization of the force of the flying neutrons. No more ridiculous business of using a reactor to drive a steam engine, or boil off something for a jet exhaust-processes that were as primitive and wasteful as burning gunpowder to keep yourself warm.

Chemical jets would carry his spaceship above the atmosphere. Then would come the thrilling order, "Set sail for Mars!" The vast umbrella would unfold and open out around the stern, its rear or Earthward side a gleaming expanse of radioactive ribbon perhaps only an atom thick and backed with a material that would reflect neutrons. Atoms in the ribbon would split, blasting neutrons astern at fantastic velocities. Reaction would send the spaceship hurtling forward.

In airless space, the expanse of sails would naturally not retard the ship. More radioactive ribbon, manufactured as needed in the ship itself, would feed out onto the sail as that already there became exhausted.

A spaceship with direct nuclear drive-and he, a Thinker, had conceived it completely except for the technical details! Having strengthened his mind by hard years of somno-learning, mind-casting, memory-straightening, and sensory training, he had assured himself of the executive power to control the technicians and direct their specialized abilities. Together they would build the true Mars rocket.

But that would only be a beginning. They would build the true Mind Bomb. They would build the true Selective Microbe Slayer. They would discover the true laws of ESP and the inner life. They would even-his imagination hesitated a moment, then strode boldly forward-build the true Maizie!

And then ... then the Thinkers would be on even terms with the scientists. Rather, they'd be far ahead. No more deception.

He was so exalted by this thought that he almost let the slideway carry him past his door. He stepped inside and called, "Caddy!" He waited a moment, then walked through the apartment, but she wasn't there.

Confound the girl, he couldn't help thinking. This morning, when she should have made herself scarce, she'd sprawled about sleeping. Now, when he felt like seeing her, when her presence would have added a pleasant final touch to his glowing mood, she chose to be absent. He really should use his hypnotic control on her, he decided, and again there sprang into his mind the word —a pet form of her name-that would send her into obedient trance.

114

No, he told himself again, that was to be reserved for some moment of crisis or desperate danger, when he would need someone to strike suddenly and unquestioningly for himself and mankind. Caddy was merely a wilful and rather silly girl, incapable at present of understanding the tremendous tensions under which he operated. When he had time for it, he would train her up to be a fitting companion without hypnosis.

Yet the fact of her absence had a subtly disquieting effect. It shook his perfect self-confidence just a fraction. He asked himself if he'd been wise in summoning the rocket physicists without consulting Tregarron.

But this mood, too, he conquered quickly. Tregarron wasn't his boss, but just the Thinker's most clever salesman, an expert in the mumbo-jumbo so necessary for social control in this chaotic era. He himself, Jorj Helmuth, was the real leader in theoretics and all-over strategy, the mind behind the mind behind Maizie.

He stretched himself on the bed, almost instantly achieved maximum relaxation, turned on the somno-learner, and began the two hour rest he knew would be desirable before the big conference.

Jan Tregarron had supplemented his shorts with pink coveralls, but he was still drinking beer. He emptied his glass and lifted it a lazy inch. The beautiful girl beside him refilled it without a word and went on stroking his forehead.

"Caddy," he said reflectively, without looking at her, "there's a little job I want you to do. You're the only one with the proper background. The point is: it will take you away from Jorj for some time."

"I'd welcome it," she said with decision. "I'm getting pretty sick of watching his push-ups and all his other mind and muscle stunts. And that damn somno-learner of his keeps me awake."

Tregarron smiled. "I'm afraid Thinkers make pretty sad sweethearts."

"Not all of them," she told him, returning his smile tenderly.

He chuckled. "It's about one of those rocket physicists in the list you brought me. A fellow named Willard Farquar."

Caddy didn't say anything, but she stopped stroking his forehead.

"What's the matter?" he asked. "You knew him once, didn't you?"

"Yes," she replied and then added, with surprising feeling, "The big, ugly ape!"

"Well, he's an ape whose services we happen to need. I want you to be our contact girl with him."

She took her hands away from his forehead. "Look, Jan," she said, "I wouldn't like this job."

"I thought he was very sweet on you once."

"Yes, as he never grew tired of trying to demonstrate to me. The clumsy, overgrown, bumbling baby! The man's disgusting, Jan. His approach to a woman is a child wanting candy and enraged because Mama won't produce it on the instant. I don't mind Jorj-he's just a pipsqueak and it amuses me to see how he frustrates himself. But Willard is...."

"...a bit frightening?" Tregarron finished for her.

"No!"

"Of course you're not afraid," Tregarron purred. "You're our beautiful, clever Caddy, who can do anything she wants with any man, and without whose...."

"Look, Jan, this is different —" she began agitatedly.

"...and without whose services we'd have got exactly nowhere. Clever, subtle Caddy, whose most charming attainment in the ever-appreciative eyes of Papa Jan is her ability to handle every man in the neatest way imaginable and without a trace of real feeling. Kitty Kaddy, who...."

"Very well," she said with a sigh. "I'll do it."

"Of course you will," Jan said, drawing her hands back to his forehead. "And you'll begin right away by getting into your nicest sugar-and-cream war clothes. You and I are going to be the welcoming committee when that ape arrives this afternoon."

"But what about Jorj? He'll want to see Willard."

"That'll be taken care of," Jan assured her.

"And what about the other dozen rocket physicists Jorj asked to come?"

"Don't worry about them."

The President looked inquiringly at his secretary across his littered desk in his homey study at White House, Jr. "So Opperly didn't have any idea how that odd question about Maizie turned up in Section Five?"

His secretary settled his paunch and shook his head. "Or claimed not to. Perhaps he's just the absent-minded prof, perhaps something else. The old feud of the physicists against the Thinkers may be getting hot again. There'll be further investigation."

The President nodded. He obviously had something uncomfortable on his mind. He said uneasily, "Do you think there's any possibility of it being true?"

"What?" asked the secretary guardedly.

"That peculiar hint about Maizie."

The secretary said nothing.

"Mind you, I don't think there is," the President went on hurriedly, his face assuming a sorrowful scowl. "I owe a lot to the Thinkers, both as a private person and as a public figure. Lord, a man has to lean on *something* these days. But just supposing it were true —" he hesitated, as before uttering blasphemy —"that there was a man inside Maizie, what could we do?"

The secretary said stolidly, "The Thinkers won our last election. They chased the Commies out of Iran. We brought them into the Inner Cabinet. We've showered them with public funds." He paused. "We couldn't do a damn thing."

The President nodded with equal conviction, and, not very happily, summed up: "So if anyone should go up against the Thinkers-and I'm afraid I wouldn't want to see that happen, whatever's true-it would have to be a scientist."

Willard Farquar felt his weight change the steps under his feet into an escalator. He cursed under his breath, but let them carry him, a defiant hulk, up to the tall and mystic blue portals, which silently parted when he was five meters away. The escalator changed to a slideway and carried him into a softly gleaming, high-domed room rather like the antechamber of a temple.

"Martian peace to you, Willard Farquar," an invisible voice intoned. "You have entered the Thinkers' Foundation. Please remain on the slideway."

"I want to see Jorj Helmuth," Willard growled loudly.

The slideway carried him into the mouth of a corridor and paused. A dark opening dilated on the wall. "May we take your hat and coat?" a voice asked politely. After a moment the request was repeated, with the addition of, "Just pass them through."

Willard scowled, then fought his way out of his shapeless coat and passed it and his hat through in a lump. Instantly the opening contracted, imprisoning his wrists, and he felt his hands being washed on the other side of the wall.

He gave a great jerk which failed to free his hands from the snugly padded gyves. "Do not be alarmed," the voice advised him. "It is only an esthetic measure. As your hands are laved, invisible radiations are slaughtering all the germs in your body, while more delicate emanations are producing a benign rearrangement of your emotions."

The rather amateurish curses Willard was gritting between his teeth became more sulfurous. His sensations told him that a towel of some sort was being applied to his hands. He wondered if he would be subjected to a face-washing and even greater indignities. Then, just before his wrists were released, he felt-for a moment only, but unmistakably-the soft touch of a girl's hand.

116

That touch, like the mysterious sweet chink of a bell in darkness, brought him a sudden feeling of excitement, wonder.

Yet the feeling was as fleeting as that caused by a lurid advertisement, for as the slideway began to move again, carrying him past a series of depth-pictures and inscriptions celebrating the Thinkers' achievements, his mood of bitter exasperation returned doubled. This place, he told himself, was a plague spot of the disease of magic in an enfeebled and easily infected world. He reminded himself that he was not without resources-the Thinkers must fear or need him, whether because of the Maelzel question or the necessity of producing a nuclear power spaceship. He felt his determination to smash them reaffirmed.

The slideway, having twice turned into an escalator, veered toward an opalescent door, which opened as silently as the one below. The slideway stopped at the threshold. Momentum carried him a couple of steps into the room. He stopped and looked around.

The place was a sybarite's modernistic dream. Sponge-carpeting thick as a mattress and topped with down. Hassocks and couches that looked butter-soft. A domed ceiling of deep glossy blue mimicking the night sky, with the constellations tooled in silver. A wall of niches crammed with statuettes of languorous men, women, beasts. A self-service bar with a score of golden spigots. A depth-TV-screen simulating a great crystal ball. Here and there barbaric studs of hammered gold that might have been push-buttons. A low table set for three with exquisite ware of crystal and gold. An ever-changing scent of resins and flowers.

A smiling fat man clad in pearl gray sports clothes came through one of the curtained archways. Willard recognized Jan Tregarron from his pictures, but did not at once offer to speak to him. Instead he let his gaze wander with an ostentatious contempt around the crammed walls, take in the bar and the set table with its many wine glasses, and finally return to his host.

"And where," he asked with harsh irony, "are the dancing girls?"

The fat man's eyebrows rose. "In there," he said innocently, indicating the second archway. The curtains parted.

"Oh, I *am* sorry," the fat man apologized. "There seems to be only one on duty. I hope that isn't too much at variance with your tastes."

She stood in the archway, demure and lovely in an off-the-bosom frock of pale blue skylon edged in mutated mink. She was smiling the first smile that Willard had ever had from her lips.

"Mr. Willard Farquar," the fat man murmured, "Miss Arkady Simms."

Jorj Helmuth turned from the conference table with its dozen empty chairs to the two mousily pretty secretaries.

"No word from the door yet, Master," one of them ventured to say.

Jorj twisted in his chair, though hardly uncomfortably, since it was a beautiful pneumatic job. His nervousness at having to face the twelve rocket physicists —a feeling which, he had to admit, had been unexpectedly great-was giving way to impatience.

"What's Willard Farquar's phone?" he asked sharply.

One of the secretaries ran through a clutch of desk tapes, then spent some seconds whispering into her throat-mike and listening to answers from the soft-speaker.

"He lives with Morton Opperly, who doesn't have one," she finally told Jorj in scandalized tones.

"Let me see the list," Jorj said. Then, after a bit, "Try Dr. Welcome's place."

This time there were results. Within a quarter of a minute he was handed a phone which he hung expertly on his shoulder.

"This is Dr. Asa Welcome," a reedy voice told him.

"This is Helmuth of the Thinkers' Foundation," Jorj said icily. "Did you get my communication?"

The reedy voice became anxious and placating. "Why, yes, Mr. Helmuth, I did. Very glad to get it too. Sounded most interesting. Very eager to come. But...."

"Yes?"

"Well, I was just about to hop in my 'copter-my son's 'copter-when the other note came."

"What other note?"

"Why, the note calling the meeting off."

"I sent no other note!"

The other voice became acutely embarrassed. "But I considered it to be from you ... or just about the same thing. I really think I had the right to assume that."

"How was it signed?" Jorj rapped.

"Mr. Jan Tregarron."

Jorj broke the connection. He didn't move until a low sound shattered his abstraction and he realized that one of the girls was whispering a call to the door. He handed back the phone and dismissed them. They went in a rustle of jackets and skirtlets, hesitating at the doorway but not quite daring to look back.

He sat motionless a minute longer. Then his hand crept fretfully onto the table and pushed a button. The room darkened and a long section of wall became transparent, revealing a dozen silvery models of spaceships, beautifully executed. He quickly touched another; the models faded and the opposite wall bloomed with an animated cartoon that portrayed with charming humor and detail the designing and construction of a neutron-drive spaceship. A third button, and a depth-picture of deep star-speckled space opened behind the cartoon, showing a section of Earth's surface and in the far distance the tiny ruddy globe of Mars. Slowly a tiny rocket rose from the section of Earth and spread its silvery sails.

He switched off the pictures, keeping the room dark. By a faint table light he dejectedly examined his organizational charts for the neutron-drive project, the long list of books he had boned up on by somno-learning, the concealed table of physical constants and all sorts of other crucial details about rocket physics —a cleverly condensed encyclopedic "pony" to help out his memory on technical points that might have arisen in his discussion with the experts.

He switched out all the lights and slumped forward, blinking his eyes and trying to swallow the lump in his throat. In the dark his memory went seeping back, back, to the day when his math teacher had told him, very superciliously, that the marvelous fantasies he loved to read and hoarded by his bed weren't real science at all, but just a kind of lurid pretense. He had so wanted to be a scientist, and the teacher's contempt had cast a damper on his ambition.

And now that the conference was canceled, would he ever know that it wouldn't have turned out the same way today? That his somno-learning hadn't taken? That his "pony" wasn't good enough? That his ability to handle people extended only to credulous farmer Presidents and mousy girls in skirtlets? Only the test of meeting the experts would have answered those questions.

Tregarron was the one to blame! Tregarron with his sly tyrannical ways, Tregarron with his fear of losing the future to men who really understood theoretics and could handle experts. Tregarron, so used to working by deception that he couldn't see when it became a fault and a crime. Tregarron, who must now be shown the light ... or, failing that, against whom certain steps must be taken.

For perhaps half an hour Jorj sat very still, thinking. Then he turned to the phone and, after some delay, got his party.

"What is it now, Jorj?" Caddy asked impatiently. "Please don't bother me with any of your moods, because I'm tired and my nerves are on edge."

He took a breath. When steps may have to be taken, he thought, one must hold an agent in readiness. "Caddums," he intoned hypnotically, vibrantly. "Caddums...."

The voice at the other end had instantly changed, become submissive, sleepy, suppliant. "Yes, Master?"

Morton Opperly looked up from the sheet of neatly penned equations at Willard Farquar, who had somehow acquired a measure of poise. He neither lumbered restlessly nor grimaced. He removed his coat with a certain dignity and stood solidly before his mentor. He smiled. Granting that he was a bear, one might guess he had just been fed.

"You see?" he said. "They didn't hurt me."

"They didn't hurt you?" Opperly asked softly.

Willard slowly shook his head. His smile broadened.

Opperly put down his pen, folded his hands. "And you're as determined as ever to expose and smash the Thinkers?"

"Of course!" The menacing growl came back into the bear's voice, except that it was touched with a certain pleased luxuriousness. "Only from now on I won't be teasing the zoo animals, and I won't embarrass you by asking any more Maelzel questions. I have reached the objective at which those tactics were aimed. After this I shall bore from within."

"Bore from within," Opperly repeated, frowning. "Now where have I heard that phrase before?" His brow cleared. "Oh, yes," he said listlessly. "Do I understand that you are becoming a Thinker, Willard?"

The other gave him a faintly pitying smile and stretched himself on the couch, gazed at the ceiling. All his movements were deliberate, easy.

"Certainly. That's the only realistic way to smash them. Rise high in their councils. Out-trick all their trickeries. Organize a fifth column. Then *strike!*"

"The end justifying the means, of course," Opperly said.

"Of course. As surely as the desire to stand up justifies your disturbing the air over your head. All action in this world is nothing but means."

Opperly nodded abstractedly. "I wonder if anyone else ever became a Thinker for those same reasons. I wonder if being a Thinker doesn't simply mean that you've decided you have to use lies and tricks as your chief method."

Willard shrugged. "Could be." There was no longer any doubt about the pitying quality of his smile.

Opperly stood up, squaring together his papers. "So you'll be working with Helmuth?"

"Not Helmuth. Tregarron." The bear's smile became cruel. "I'm afraid that Helmuth's career as a Thinker is going to have quite a setback."

"Helmuth," Opperly mused. "Morgenschein once told me a bit about him. A man of some idealism, despite his affiliations. Best of a bad lot. Incidentally, is he the one with whom...."

"...Miss Arkady Simms ran off?" Willard finished without any embarrassment. "Yes, that was Helmuth. But that's all going to be changed now."

Opperly nodded. "Good-by, Willard," he said.

Willard quickly heaved himself up on an elbow. Opperly looked at him for about five seconds, then, without a word, walked out of the room.

The only obvious furnishings in Jan Tregarron's office were a flat-topped desk and a few chairs. Tregarron sat behind the desk, the top of which was completely bare. He looked almost bored, except that his little eyes were smiling. Jorj Helmuth sat across the desk from him, a few feet back, erect and grim-faced, while shadowy in the muted light, Caddy stood against the wall behind Tregarron. She still wore the fur-trimmed skylon frock she'd put on that afternoon. She took no part in the conversation, seemed almost unaware of it.

"So you just went ahead and canceled the conference without consulting me?" Jorj was saying.

"You called it without consulting me." Tregarron playfully wagged a finger. "Shouldn't do that sort of thing, Jorj."

"But I tell you I was completely prepared. I was absolutely sure of my ground."

"I know, I know," Tregarron said lightly. "But it's not the right time for it. I'm the best judge of that."

"When will be the right time?"

Tregarron shrugged. "Look here, Jorj," he said, "every man should stick to his trade, to his forte. Technology isn't ours."

Jorj's lips thinned. "But you know as well as I do that we are going to have to have a nuclear spaceship and actually go to Mars someday."

Tregarron lifted his eyebrows. "Are we?"

"Yes! Just as we're going to have to build a real Maizie. Everything we've done until now have been emergency measures."

"Really?"

Jorj stared at him. "Look here, Jan," he said, gripping his knees with his hands, "you and I are going to have to talk things through."

"Are you quite sure of that?" Jan's voice was very cool. "I have a feeling that it might be best if you said nothing and accepted things as they are."

"No!"

"Very well." Tregarron settled himself in his chair.

"I helped you organize the Thinkers," Jorj said, and waited. "At least, I was your first partner."

Tregarron barely nodded.

"Our basic idea was that the time had come to apply science to the life of man on a large scale, to live rationally and realistically. The only things holding the world back from this all-important step were the ignorance, superstition, and inertia of the average man, and the stuffiness and lack of enterprise of the academic scientists-their worship of facts, even when facts were clearly dangerous.

"Yet we knew that in their deepest hearts the average man and the professionals were both on our side. They wanted the new world visualized by science. They wanted the simplifications and conveniences, the glorious adventures of the human mind and body. They wanted the trips to Mars and into the depths of the human psyche, they wanted the robots and the thinking machines. All they lacked was the nerve to take the first big step-and that was what we supplied.

"It was no time for half measures, for slow and sober plodding. The world was racked by wars and neurosis, in danger of falling into the foulest hands. What was needed was a tremendous and thrilling appeal to the human imagination, an Earth-shaking affirmation of the power of science for good.

"But the men who provided that appeal and affirmation couldn't afford to be cautious. They wouldn't check and double check. They couldn't wait for the grudging and jealous approval of the professionals. They had to use stunts, tricks, fakes —*anything to get over the big point*. Once that had been done, once mankind was headed down the new road, it would be easy enough to give the average man the necessary degree of insight to heal the breach with the professionals, to make good in actuality what had been made good only in pretense.

"Have I stated our position fairly?"

Tregarron's eyes were hooded. "You're the one who's telling it."

"On those general assumptions we established our hold on susceptible leaders and the mob," Jorj went on. "We built Maizie and the Mars rocket and the Mind Bomb. We discovered the wisdom of the Martians. We *sold* the people on the science that the professionals had been too high-toned to advertise or bring into the market place.

"But now that we've succeeded, now that we've made the big point, now that Maizie and Mars and science do rule the average human imagination, the time has come to take the second big step, to let accomplishment catch up with imagination, to implement fantasy with fact.

"Do you suppose I'd ever have gone into this with you, if it hadn't been for the thought of that second big step? Why, I'd have felt dirty and cheap, a mere charlatan-except for the sure conviction that someday everything would be set right. I've devoted my whole life to that conviction, Jan. I've studied and disciplined myself, using every scientific means at my disposal, so that I wouldn't be found lacking when the day came to heal the breach between the Thinkers and the professionals. I've trained myself to be the perfect liaison man for the job.

"Jan, the day's come and I'm the man. I know you've been concentrating on other aspects of our work; you haven't had time to keep up with my side of it. But I'm sure that as soon as you see how carefully I've prepared myself, how completely practical the neutron-drive rocket project is, you'll beg me to go ahead!"

Tregarron smiled at the ceiling for a moment. "Your general idea isn't so bad, Jorj, but your time scale is out of whack and your judgment is a joke. Oh, yes. Every revolutionary wants to see the big change take place in his lifetime. Tcha! It's as if he were watching evolutionary vaudeville and wanted the Ape-to-Man Act over in twenty minutes.

"Time for the second big step? Jorj, the average man's exactly what he was ten years ago, except that he's got a new god. More than ever he thinks of Mars as a Hollywood paradise, with wise men and yummy princesses. Maizie is Mama magnified a million times. As for professional scientists, they're more jealous and stuffy than ever. All they'd like to do is turn the clock back to a genteel dream world of quiet quadrangles and caps and gowns, where every commoner bows to the passing scholar.

"Maybe in ten thousand years we'll be ready for the second big step. Maybe. Meanwhile, as should be, the clever will rule the stupid for their own good. The realists will rule the dreamers. Those with free hands will rule those who have deliberately handcuffed themselves with taboos.

"Secondly, your judgment. Did you actually think you could have bossed those professionals, kept your mental footing in the intellectual melee? You a nuclear physicist? A rocket scientist? Why, it's —Take it easy now, boy, and listen to me. They'd have torn you to pieces in twenty minutes and glad of the chance! You baffle me, Jorj. You know that Maizie and the Mars rocket and all that are fakes, yet you believe in your somno-learning and consciousness-expansion and optimism-pumping like the veriest yokel. I wouldn't be surprised to hear you'd taken up ESP and hypnotism. I think you should take stock of yourself and get a new slant. It's overdue."

He leaned back. Jorj's face had become a mask. His eyes did not flicker from Tregarron's, yet there was a subtle change in his expression. Behind Tregarron, Caddy swayed as if in a sudden gust of intangible wind and took a silent step forward from the wall.

"That's your honest opinion?" Jorj asked, very quietly.

"It's more than that," Tregarron told him, just as unmelodramatically. "It's orders."

Jorj stood up purposefully. "Very well," he said. "In that case I have to tell you that —"

Casually, but with no wasted motion, Tregarron slipped an ultrasonic pistol from under the desk and laid it on the empty top.

"No," he said, "let me tell you something. I was afraid this would happen and I made preparations. If you've studied your Nazi, Fascist and Soviet history, you know what happens to old revolutionaries who don't move with the times. But I'm not going to be too harsh. I have a couple of the boys waiting outside. They'll take you by 'copter to the field, then by jet to New Mex. Bright and early tomorrow morning, Jorj, you're leaving on a trip to Mars."

Jorj hardly reacted to the words. Caddy was two steps nearer Tregarron.

"I decided Mars would be the best place for you," the fat man continued. "The robot controls will be arranged so that your 'visit' to Mars lasts two years. Perhaps in that time you will have learned wisdom, such as realizing that the big liar must never fall for his own big lie.

"Meanwhile, there will have to be a replacement for you. I have in mind a person who may prove peculiarly worthy to occupy your position, with all its perquisites. A person who seems to understand that force and desire are the motive powers of life, and that anyone who believes the big lie proves himself strictly a jerk."

Caddy was standing behind Tregarron now, her half-closed, sleepy eyes fixed on Jorj's.

"His name is Willard Farquar. You see, I too believe in cooperating with the scientists, Jorj, but by subversion rather than conference. My idea is to offer the hand of friendship to a selected few of them-the hand of friendship with a nice big bribe in it." He smiled. "You were a good man, Jorj, for the early days, when we needed a publicist with catchy ideas about Mind Bombs, ray guns, plastic helmets, fancy sweaters, space brassieres, and all that other corn. Now we can afford a soldier."

Jorj moistened his lips.

"We'll have a neat explanation of what's happened to you. Callers will be informed that you've gone on an extended visit to imbibe the wisdom of the Martians."

Jorj whispered, "Caddums."

Caddy leaned forward. Her arms snaked down Tregarron's, as if to imprison his wrists. But instead she reached out and took the ultrasonic pistol and put it in Tregarron's right hand. Then she looked up at Jorj with eyes that were very bright.

She said very sweetly and sympathetically, "Poor Superman."

Coming Attraction

Women will always go on trying to attract men...
even when the future seems to have no future!

The coupe with the fishhooks welded to the fender shouldered up over the curb like the nose of a nightmare. The girl in its path stood frozen, her face probably stiff with fright under her mask. For once my reflexes weren't shy. I took a fast step toward her, grabbed her elbow, yanked her back. Her black skirt swirled out.

The big coupe shot by, its turbine humming. I glimpsed three faces. Something ripped. I felt the hot exhaust on my ankles as the big coupe swerved back into the street. A thick cloud like a black flower blossomed from its jouncing rear end, while from the fishhooks flew a black shimmering rag.

"Did they get you?" I asked the girl.

She had twisted around to look where the side of her skirt was torn away. She was wearing nylon tights.

"The hooks didn't touch me," she said shakily. "I guess I'm lucky."

I heard voices around us:

"Those kids! What'll they think up next?"

"They're a menace. They ought to be arrested."

Sirens screamed at a rising pitch as two motor-police, their rocket-assist jets full on, came whizzing toward us after the coupe. But the black flower had become a thick fog obscuring the whole street. The motor-police switched from rocket assists to rocket brakes and swerved to a stop near the smoke cloud.

"Are you English?" the girl asked me. "You have an English accent."

Her voice came shudderingly from behind the sleek black satin mask. I fancied her teeth must be chattering. Eyes that were perhaps blue searched my face from behind the black gauze covering the eyeholes of the mask. I told her she'd guessed right. She stood close to me. "Will you come to my place tonight?" she asked rapidly. "I can't thank you now. And there's something you can help me about."

My arm, still lightly circling her waist, felt her body trembling. I was answering the plea in that as much as in her voice when I said, "Certainly." She gave me an address south of Inferno, an apartment number and a time. She asked me my name and I told her.

"Hey, you!"

I turned obediently to the policeman's shout. He shooed away the small clucking crowd of masked women and barefaced men. Coughing from the smoke that the black coupe had thrown out, he asked for my papers. I handed him the essential ones.

He looked at them and then at me. "British Barter? How long will you be in New York?"

Suppressing the urge to say, "For as short a time as possible," I told him I'd be here for a week or so.

"May need you as a witness," he explained. "Those kids can't use smoke on us. When they do that, we pull them in."

He seemed to think the smoke was the bad thing. "They tried to kill the lady," I pointed out.

He shook his head wisely. "They always pretend they're going to, but actually they just want to snag skirts. I've picked up rippers with as many as fifty skirt-snags tacked up in their rooms. Of course, sometimes they come a little too close."

I explained that if I hadn't yanked her out of the way, she'd have been hit by more than hooks. But he interrupted, "If she'd thought it was a real murder attempt, she'd have stayed here."

I looked around. It was true. She was gone.

"She was fearfully frightened," I told him.

"Who wouldn't be? Those kids would have scared old Stalin himself."

"I mean frightened of more than 'kids.' They didn't look like 'kids.'"

"What did they look like?"

I tried without much success to describe the three faces. A vague impression of viciousness and effeminacy doesn't mean much.

"Well, I could be wrong," he said finally. "Do you know the girl? Where she lives?"

"No," I half lied.

The other policeman hung up his radiophone and ambled toward us, kicking at the tendrils of dissipating smoke. The black cloud no longer hid the dingy facades with their five-year-old radiation flash-burns, and I could begin to make out the distant stump of the Empire State Building, thrusting up out of Inferno like a mangled finger.

"They haven't been picked up so far," the approaching policeman grumbled. "Left smoke for five blocks, from what Ryan says."

The first policeman shook his head. "That's bad," he observed solemnly.

I was feeling a bit uneasy and ashamed. An Englishman shouldn't lie, at least not on impulse.

"They sound like nasty customers," the first policeman continued in the same grim tone. "We'll need witnesses. Looks as if you may have to stay in New York longer than you expect."

I got the point. I said, "I forgot to show you all my papers," and handed him a few others, making sure there was a five dollar bill in among them.

When he handed them back a bit later, his voice was no longer ominous. My feelings of guilt vanished. To cement our relationship, I chatted with the two of them about their job.

"I suppose the masks give you some trouble," I observed. "Over in England we've been reading about your new crop of masked female bandits."

"Those things get exaggerated," the first policeman assured me. "It's the men masking as women that really mix us up. But, brother, when we nab them, we jump on them with both feet."

"And you get so you can spot women almost as well as if they had naked faces," the second policeman volunteered. "You know, hands and all that."

"Especially all that," the first agreed with a chuckle. "Say, is it true that some girls don't mask over in England?"

"A number of them have picked up the fashion," I told him. "Only a few, though-the ones who always adopt the latest style, however extreme."

"They're usually masked in the British newscasts."

"I imagine it's arranged that way out of deference to American taste," I confessed. "Actually, not very many do mask."

The second policeman considered that. "Girls going down the street bare from the neck up." It was not clear whether he viewed the prospect with relish or moral distaste. Likely both.

"A few members keep trying to persuade Parliament to enact a law forbidding all masking," I continued, talking perhaps a bit too much.

The second policeman shook his head. "What an idea. You know, masks are a pretty good thing, brother. Couple of years more and I'm going to make my wife wear hers around the house."

The first policeman shrugged. "If women were to stop wearing masks, in six weeks you wouldn't know the difference. You get used to anything, if enough people do or don't do it."

I agreed, rather regretfully, and left them. I turned north on Broadway (old Tenth Avenue, I believe) and walked rapidly until I was beyond Inferno. Passing such an area of undecontaminated radioactivity always makes a person queasy. I thanked God there weren't any such in England, as yet.

The street was almost empty, though I was accosted by a couple of beggars with faces tunneled by H-bomb scars, whether real or of makeup putty, I couldn't tell. A fat woman held out a baby with webbed fingers and toes. I told myself it would have been deformed anyway and that she was only capitalizing on our fear of bomb-induced mutations. Still, I gave her a seven-and-a-half-cent piece. Her mask made me feel I was paying tribute to an African fetish.

"May all your children be blessed with one head and two eyes, sir."

"Thanks," I said, shuddering, and hurried past her.

"...There's only trash behind the mask, so turn your head, stick to your task: Stay away, stay away-from-the-girls!"

This last was the end of an anti-sex song being sung by some religionists half a block from the circle-and-cross insignia of a femalist temple. They reminded me only faintly of our small tribe of British monastics. Above their heads was a jumble of billboards advertising predigested foods, wrestling instruction, radio handies and the like.

I stared at the hysterical slogans with disagreeable fascination. Since the female face and form have been banned on American signs, the very letters of the advertiser's alphabet have begun to crawl with sex-the fat-bellied, big-breasted capital B, the lascivious double O. However, I reminded myself, it is chiefly the mask that so strangely accents sex in America.

A British anthropologist has pointed out, that, while it took more than 5,000 years to shift the chief point of sexual interest from the hips to the breasts, the next transition to the face has taken less than 50 years. Comparing the American style with Moslem tradition is not valid; Moslem women are compelled to wear veils, the purpose of which is concealment, while American women have only the compulsion of fashion and use masks to create mystery.

Theory aside, the actual origins of the trend are to be found in the anti-radiation clothing of World War III, which led to masked wrestling, now a fantastically popular sport, and that in turn led to the current female fashion. Only a wild style at first, masks quickly became as necessary as brassieres and lipsticks had been earlier in the century.

I finally realized that I was not speculating about masks in general, but about what lay behind one in particular. That's the devil of the things; you're never sure whether a girl is heightening loveliness or hiding ugliness. I pictured a cool, pretty face in which fear showed only in widened eyes. Then I remembered her blonde hair, rich against the blackness of the satin mask. She'd told me to come at the twenty-second hour-ten p.m.

I climbed to my apartment near the British Consulate; the elevator shaft had been shoved out of plumb by an old blast, a nuisance in these tall New York buildings. Before it occurred to me that I would be going out again, I automatically tore a tab from the film strip under my shirt. I developed it just to be sure. It showed that the total radiation I'd taken that day was still within the safety limit. I'm not phobic about it, as so many people are these days, but there's no point in taking chances.

I flopped down on the day bed and stared at the silent speaker and the dark screen of the video set. As always, they made me think, somewhat bitterly, of the two great nations of the world. Mutilated by each other, yet still strong, they were crippled giants poisoning the planet with their dreams of an impossible equality and an impossible success.

I fretfully switched on the speaker. By luck, the newscaster was talking excitedly of the prospects of a bumper wheat crop, sown by planes across a dust bowl moistened by seeded rains. I listened carefully to the rest of the program (it was remarkably clear of Russian telejamming) but there was no further news of interest to me. And, of course, no mention of the Moon, though everyone knows that America and Russia are racing to develop their primary bases into fortresses capable of mutual assault and the launching of alphabet-bombs toward Earth. I myself knew perfectly well that the British electronic equipment I was helping trade for American wheat was destined for use in spaceships.

I switched off the newscast. It was growing dark and once again I pictured a tender, frightened face behind a mask. I hadn't had a date since England. It's exceedingly difficult to become acquainted with a girl in America, where as little as a smile, often, can set one of them yelping for the police-to say nothing of the increasing puritanical morality and the roving gangs that keep most women indoors after dark. And naturally, the masks which are definitely not, as the Soviets claim, a last invention of capitalist degeneracy, but a sign of great psychological insecurity. The Russians have no masks, but they have their own signs of stress.

I went to the window and impatiently watched the darkness gather. I was getting very restless. After a while a ghostly violet cloud appeared to the south. My hair rose. Then I laughed. I had momentarily fancied it a radiation from the crater of the Hell-bomb, though I should instantly have known it was only the radio-induced glow in the sky over the amusement and residential area south of Inferno.

Promptly at twenty-two hours I stood before the door of my unknown girl friend's apartment. The electronic say-who-please said just that. I answered clearly, "Wysten Turner," wondering if she'd given my name to the mechanism. She evidently had, for the door opened. I walked into a small empty living room, my heart pounding a bit.

The room was expensively furnished with the latest pneumatic hassocks and sprawlers. There were some midgie books on the table. The one I picked up was the standard hard-boiled detective story in which two female murderers go gunning for each other.

The television was on. A masked girl in green was crooning a love song. Her right hand held something that blurred off into the foreground. I saw the set had a handie, which we haven't in England as yet, and curiously thrust my hand into the handie orifice beside the screen. Contrary to my expectations, it was not like slipping into a pulsing rubber glove, but rather as if the girl on the screen actually held my hand.

A door opened behind me. I jerked out my hand with as guilty a reaction as if I'd been caught peering through a keyhole.

She stood in the bedroom doorway. I think she was trembling. She was wearing a gray fur coat, white-speckled, and a gray velvet evening mask with shirred gray lace around the eyes and mouth. Her fingernails twinkled like silver.

It hadn't occurred to me that she'd expect us to go out.

"I should have told you," she said softly. Her mask veered nervously toward the books and the screen and the room's dark corners. "But I can't possibly talk to you here."

I said doubtfully, "There's a place near the Consulate...."

"I know where we can be together and talk," she said rapidly. "If you don't mind."

As we entered the elevator I said, "I'm afraid I dismissed the cab."

But the cab driver hadn't gone for some reason of his own. He jumped out and smirkingly held the front door open for us. I told him we preferred to sit in back. He sulkily opened the rear door, slammed it after us, jumped in front and slammed the door behind him.

My companion leaned forward. "Heaven," she said.

The driver switched on the turbine and televisor.

"Why did you ask if I were a British subject?" I said, to start the conversation.

She leaned away from me, tilting her mask close to the window. "See the Moon," she said in a quick, dreamy voice.

"But why, really?" I pressed, conscious of an irritation that had nothing to do with her.

"It's edging up into the purple of the sky."

"And what's your name?"

"The purple makes it look yellower."

Just then I became aware of the source of my irritation. It lay in the square of writhing light in the front of the cab beside the driver.

I don't object to ordinary wrestling matches, though they bore me, but I simply detest watching a man wrestle a woman. The fact that the bouts are generally "on the level," with the man greatly outclassed in weight and reach and the masked females young and personable, only makes them seem worse to me.

"Please turn off the screen," I requested the driver.

He shook his head without looking around. "Uh-uh, man," he said. "They've been grooming that babe for weeks for this bout with Little Zirk."

Infuriated, I reached forward, but my companion caught my arm. "Please," she whispered frightenedly, shaking her head.

I settled back, frustrated. She was closer to me now, but silent and for a few moments I watched the heaves and contortions of the powerful masked girl and her wiry masked opponent on the screen. His frantic scrambling at her reminded me of a male spider.

I jerked around, facing my companion. "Why did those three men want to kill you?" I asked sharply.

The eyeholes of her mask faced the screen. "Because they're jealous of me," she whispered.

"Why are they jealous?"

She still didn't look at me. "Because of him."

"Who?"

She didn't answer.

I put my arm around her shoulders. "Are you afraid to tell me?" I asked. "What *is* the matter?"

She still didn't look my way. She smelled nice.

"See here," I said laughingly, changing my tactics, "you really should tell me something about yourself. I don't even know what you look like."

I half playfully lifted my hand to the band of her neck. She gave it an astonishingly swift slap. I pulled it away in sudden pain. There were four tiny indentations on the back. From one of them a tiny bead of blood welled out as I watched. I looked at her silver fingernails and saw they were actually delicate and pointed metal caps.

"I'm dreadfully sorry," I heard her say, "but you frightened me. I thought for a moment you were going to...."

At last she turned to me. Her coat had fallen open. Her evening dress was Cretan Revival, a bodice of lace beneath and supporting the breasts without covering them.

"Don't be angry," she said, putting her arms around my neck. "You were wonderful this afternoon."

The soft gray velvet of her mask, molding itself to her cheek, pressed mine. Through the mask's lace the wet warm tip of her tongue touched my chin.

"I'm not angry," I said. "Just puzzled and anxious to help."

The cab stopped. To either side were black windows bordered by spears of broken glass. The sickly purple light showed a few ragged figures slowly moving toward us.

The driver muttered, "It's the turbine, man. We're grounded." He sat there hunched and motionless. "Wish it had happened somewhere else."

My companion whispered, "Five dollars is the usual amount."

She looked out so shudderingly at the congregating figures that I suppressed my indignation and did as she suggested. The driver took the bill without a word. As he started up, he put his hand out the window and I heard a few coins clink on the pavement.

My companion came back into my arms, but her mask faced the television screen, where the tall girl had just pinned the convulsively kicking Little Zirk.

"I'm so frightened," she breathed.

Heaven turned out to be an equally ruinous neighborhood, but it had a club with an awning and a huge doorman uniformed like a spaceman, but in gaudy colors. In my sensuous daze I rather liked it all. We stepped out of the cab just as a drunken old woman came down the sidewalk, her mask awry. A couple ahead of us turned their heads from the half revealed face, as if from an ugly body at the beach. As we followed them in I heard the doorman say, "Get along, grandma, and watch yourself."

Inside, everything was dimness and blue glows. She had said we could talk here, but I didn't see how. Besides the inevitable chorus of sneezes and coughs (they say America is fifty per cent allergic these days), there was a band going full blast in the latest robop style, in which an electronic composing machine selects an arbitrary sequence of tones into which the musicians weave their raucous little individualities.

Most of the people were in booths. The band was behind the bar. On a small platform beside them, a girl was dancing, stripped to her mask. The little cluster of men at the shadowy far end of the bar weren't looking at her.

We inspected the menu in gold script on the wall and pushed the buttons for breast of chicken, fried shrimps and two scotches. Moments later, the serving bell tinkled. I opened the gleaming panel and took out our drinks.

The cluster of men at the bar filed off toward the door, but first they stared around the room. My companion had just thrown back her coat. Their look lingered on our booth. I noticed that there were three of them.

The band chased off the dancing girl with growls. I handed my companion a straw and we sipped our drinks.

"You wanted me to help you about something," I said. "Incidentally, I think you're lovely."

She nodded quick thanks, looked around, leaned forward. "Would it be hard for me to get to England?"

"No," I replied, a bit taken aback. "Provided you have an American passport."

"Are they difficult to get?"

"Rather," I said, surprised at her lack of information. "Your country doesn't like its nationals to travel, though it isn't quite as stringent as Russia."

"Could the British Consulate help me get a passport?"

"It's hardly their...."

"Could you?"

I realized we were being inspected. A man and two girls had paused opposite our table. The girls were tall and wolfish-looking, with spangled masks. The man stood jauntily between them like a fox on its hind legs.

My companion didn't glance at them, but she sat back. I noticed that one of the girls had a big yellow bruise on her forearm. After a moment they walked to a booth in the deep shadows.

"Know them?" I asked. She didn't reply. I finished my drink. "I'm not sure you'd like England," I said. "The austerity's altogether different from your American brand of misery."

She leaned forward again. "But I must get away," she whispered.

"Why?" I was getting impatient.

"Because I'm so frightened."

There were chimes. I opened the panel and handed her the fried shrimps. The sauce on my breast of chicken was a delicious steaming compound of almonds, soy and ginger. But something must have been wrong with the radionic oven that had thawed and heated it, for at the first bite I crunched a kernel of ice in the meat. These delicate mechanisms need constant repair and there aren't enough mechanics.

I put down my fork. "What are you really scared of?" I asked her.

For once her mask didn't waver away from my face. As I waited I could feel the fears gathering without her naming them, tiny dark shapes swarming through the curved night outside, converging on the radioactive pest spot of New York, dipping into the margins of the purple. I felt a sudden rush of sympathy, a desire to protect the girl opposite me. The warm feeling added itself to the infatuation engendered in the cab.

"Everything," she said finally.

I nodded and touched her hand.

"I'm afraid of the Moon," she began, her voice going dreamy and brittle as it had in the cab. "You can't look at it and not think of guided bombs."

"It's the same Moon over England," I reminded her.

"But it's not England's Moon any more. It's ours and Russia's. You're not responsible."

I pressed her hand.

"Oh, and then," she said with a tilt of her mask, "I'm afraid of the cars and the gangs and the loneliness and Inferno. I'm afraid of the lust that undresses your face. And —" her voice hushed —"I'm afraid of the wrestlers."

"Yes?" I prompted softly after a moment.

Her mask came forward. "Do you know something about the wrestlers?" she asked rapidly. "The ones that wrestle women, I mean. They often lose, you know. And then they have to have a girl to take their frustration out on. A girl who's soft and weak and terribly frightened. They need that, to keep them men. Other men don't want them to have a girl. Other men want them just to fight women and be heroes. But they must have a girl. It's horrible for her."

I squeezed her fingers tighter, as if courage could be transmitted-granting I had any. "I think I can get you to England," I said.

Shadows crawled onto the table and stayed there. I looked up at the three men who had been at the end of the bar. They were the men I had seen in the big coupe. They wore black sweaters and close-fitting black trousers. Their faces were as expressionless as dopers. Two of them stood above me. The other loomed over the girl.

"Drift off, man," I was told. I heard the other inform the girl: "We'll wrestle a fall, sister. What shall it be? Judo, slapsie or kill-who-can?"

I stood up. There are times when an Englishman simply must be mal-treated. But just then the foxlike man came gliding in like the star of a ballet. The reaction of the other three startled me. They were acutely embarrassed.

He smiled at them thinly. "You won't win my favor by tricks like this," he said.

"Don't get the wrong idea, Zirk," one of them pleaded.

"I will if it's right," he said. "She told me what you tried to do this afternoon. That won't endear you to me, either. Drift."

They backed off awkwardly. "Let's get out of here," one of them said loudly, as they turned. "I know a place where they fight naked with knives."

Little Zirk laughed musically and slipped into the seat beside my companion. She shrank from him, just a little. I pushed my feet back, leaned forward.

"Who's your friend, baby?" he asked, not looking at her.

She passed the question to me with a little gesture. I told him.

"British," he observed. "She's been asking you about getting out of the country? About passports?" He smiled pleasantly. "She likes to start running away. Don't you, baby?" His small hand began to stroke her wrist, the fingers bent a little, the tendons ridged, as if he were about to grab and twist.

"Look here," I said sharply. "I have to be grateful to you for ordering off those bullies, but —"

"Think nothing of it," he told me. "They're no harm except when they're behind steering wheels. A well-trained fourteen-year-old girl could cripple any one of them. Why, even Theda here, if she went in for that sort of thing...." He turned to her, shifting his hand from her wrist to her hair. He stroked it, letting the strands slip slowly through his fingers. "You know I lost tonight, baby, don't you?" he said softly.

I stood up. "Come along," I said to her. "Let's leave."

She just sat there. I couldn't even tell if she was trembling. I tried to read a message in her eyes through the mask.

"I'll take you away," I said to her. "I can do it. I really will."

He smiled at me. "She'd like to go with you," he said. "Wouldn't you, baby?"

"Will you or won't you?" I said to her. She still just sat there.

He slowly knotted his fingers in her hair.

"Listen, you little vermin," I snapped at him, "Take your hands off her."

He came up from the seat like a snake. I'm no fighter. I just know that the more scared I am, the harder and straighter I hit. This time I was lucky. But as he crumpled back, I felt a slap and four stabs of pain in my cheek. I clapped my hand to it. I could feel the four gashes made by her dagger finger caps, and the warm blood oozing out from them.

She didn't look at me. She was bending over little Zirk and cuddling her mask to his cheek and crooning: "There, there, don't feel bad, you'll be able to hurt me afterward."

There were sounds around us, but they didn't come close. I leaned forward and ripped the mask from her face.

I really don't know why I should have expected her face to be anything else. It was very pale, of course, and there weren't any cosmetics. I suppose there's no point in wearing any under a mask. The eye-brows were untidy and the lips chapped. But as for the general expression, as for the feelings crawling and wriggling across it —

Have you ever lifted a rock from damp soil? Have you ever watched the slimy white grubs?

I looked down at her, she up at me. "Yes, you're so frightened, aren't you?" I said sarcastically. "You dread this little nightly drama, don't you? You're scared to death."

And I walked right out into the purple night, still holding my hand to my bleeding cheek. No one stopped me, not even the girl wrestlers. I wished I could tear a tab from under my shirt, and test it then and there, and find I'd taken too much radiation, and so be able to ask to cross the Hudson and go down New Jersey, past the lingering radiance of the Narrows Bomb, and so on to Sandy Hook to wait for the rusty ship that would take me back over the seas to England.